NEIGHBORS WITH THE SINGLE DAD

SINGLE DADS OF SEATTLE, BOOK 8

WHITLEY COX

For Tricia.
My old neighbor who I miss every day.
Sorry we moved.

1

RAIN POURED and wind pounded the city of Seattle on a cold and miserable March night. Luckily, for all the patrons inside the very happening Ludo Lounge, where ladies drank for half price until eleven, it could be a zombie apocalypse or the rapture and nobody would be the wiser.

The outside world ceased to exist.

Over the last hour, the music in the lounge had picked up, going from smooth, club jazz to full-on dance music with a bass that Scott Dixon could feel in the very deepest parts of his chest. It was no longer cocktail hour—it was time to dance.

Which, for many, also meant it was time to start looking for a hookup.

Not Scott though. He wasn't there for that, at least not tonight.

He hardly ever saw Donovan Smythe anymore, now that Scott had switched companies. But a couple of weeks ago, Donovan called, excited about his wedding and insisting that Scott come to his bachelor party. Scott, people-pleasing middle child that he was, agreed.

Now he was regretting it.

There was a reason he and Donovan weren't that close anymore.

Donovan was a bit of a tool, and so were his friends. The group had been obnoxious assholes, hitting on and offending waitresses and talking about heading to a strip club to go and throw quarters at the entertainers.

Scott ordered himself a drink at the bar, turned and leaned back against it, watching the embarrassing theatrics back at the bachelor party table. He cringed inwardly when one of the guys let out a thunderous belch and the rest cheered.

The bartender could take his sweet time making Scott's drink. He had no intention of heading back to those buffoons anytime soon.

"Drink's up, man," the bartender said behind him, only when Scott went to turn back around, a freight train, or something very akin to such, slammed into his side.

"Hey, watch—" His gripe died on his lips as he watched the woman who'd crashed into him teetering on high heels as she hooked it around the corner toward the bathrooms.

"Sorry," she called back, waving a hand, her long red hair flipping behind her as she disappeared.

He thanked the bartender for his drink but didn't budge. The bachelor partiers had ordered Donovan a muff diver, and the man of the hour's face had just been shoved into a heaping pile of whipped cream.

Philistines.

Scott took a sip of his whiskey and leaned his elbow on the bar. There was also another reason why he hadn't moved yet. He wanted to catch another glimpse of the whirling dervish with hair of fire before he rejoined his group.

It didn't take long—maybe thirty seconds—before the redhead in the heels returned, her face scrunched up in what looked like pain, her green eyes darting frantically around the bar.

He approached her. "Is everything okay?"

Her eyes stilled, pinning on him. Her lips dipped into a deep frown as she shook her head. "I have to pee and the line for the women's bathroom is ten miles long. I'll never make it."

Scott placed a hand on her shoulder and gently moved her out of the way, glancing down the corridor for the bathrooms with its black painted walls. Sure enough, the line for the women's bathroom stretched at least fifteen women deep. The men's room, on the other hand, had no line at all.

He grabbed her hand. "Follow me." At a quick clip, he hauled her down the hallway and turned in to the men's room, heaving the heavy door open with one hand while encouraging her to step inside with the other.

Her emerald eyes went wide. "This is the men's room!" Her voice was low, almost a hiss.

Scott shrugged. "So?"

But her desperation won out, and with a quick eye shift down the hall toward the long line of women doing the bathroom dance, she nodded, then stepped inside.

"Hello?" Scott called out into the bathroom. "Anybody in here?"

Luckily, there was no answer.

His beautiful companion let out a sigh of relief, her slender shoulders slumping just a touch as she pushed past him.

"You go do what you need to do, and I'll stand watch outside, give you some privacy." Before she could come up with any more ridiculous protestations, he headed back out.

He still had his drink, so with one hand in his pocket, his shoulder against the doorjamb, he sipped his whiskey and waited for her to emerge.

Not four minutes later, a throat clearing behind him and a gentle tap on his shoulder let him know she was finished. He unblocked the door and held his hand out for her to go ahead of him, not just because he was a gentleman, but also because he wanted to check out her ass.

This woman was hot!

Tall and slim with nice curves, long legs and ... yes! A rocking ass. And it was only played up by the sexy black pants she wore and those gold, strappy fuck-me heels. He gained ground, so he was right behind her. Not to be weird or anything—he just wanted to double-check if she was taller than him in those heels.

Phew.

Not quite.

Scott was a nice six-foot-two, and this beautiful creature didn't quite come up to his forehead. Not that he was an anti-heightest (was that a thing?). He just *preferred* to be taller than the women he dated.

Whoa, now you're dating her? You don't even know her name. Slow down there, Sparky. Just because you haven't gotten laid in ... a while, let's just leave it at that. Doesn't mean you need to start picking out china patterns with the first pretty face to cross your path.

He shook himself mentally and stepped back, letting the woman get ahead of him a bit. They exited the corridor, reemerging into the lounge. In those few minutes they'd been gone, the place had filled up. It was wall-to-wall people, loud voices, laughing and some kind of hip-hop music. He couldn't make heads or tails of the lyrics.

Man, he felt old.

He could still hear his party over in the corner booth laughing it up like obnoxious drunkards though. They were hard to miss.

He was busy glancing in the direction of his party when

he was once again slammed, only this time it was in his chest, and it wasn't by a freight train but a voluptuous, green-eyed wall of beauty.

"Thank you," she said, tucking a strand of hair behind her ear. "You're a lifesaver."

He grinned at her. "All in a day's work. Glad you're okay."

She thrust her hand out. "Eva."

He wrapped his fingers around hers, loving the way her hand felt in his. "Scott." Her shake was firm but her hand soft and feminine. Her nails were painted in a subtle French manicure, and she wore no wedding ring.

"Can I buy you a drink for your gallantry, Scott?" She released his hand and pulled her clutch purse out from beneath her arm, her eyes twinkling as her mouth slid up into a mischievous smile. "It's the least I can do." Her eyes drifted to the right, and she cringed when a group of women decked out in pink sashes and horrendous wigs let out a loud, shrill cheer. "I'm also not eager to rejoin the bachelorette party I'm here with, so any opportunity to stay away, I'm all for."

Without waiting for him to respond, she pushed her way through the crowd hovering in front of the bar, rested her breasts on the bar and leaned forward.

Like a dog with a bone, the muscly bartender lasered in on her in seconds, ignoring patrons who had been waiting far longer. "What can I getcha?" he asked, leaning onto the bar, his gaze drifting down from Eva's face to where her gold heart pendant was wedged between the swells of her breast.

Scott would have done the exact same thing if he'd been that bartender—it would have been impossible not to.

Did she know what she was doing?

She had to. She didn't strike him as a bimbo, just a woman who knew how to get what she wanted, how to work it.

And there was nothing wrong with working what the good lord gave you. Scott worked his megawatt smile more times than he could count, to charm a waitress or barista into giving him extra fries with his burger or an extra shot of espresso in his coffee.

"I'll have a tequila, please. Añjeo or extra añjeo on the rocks, if you have it." The bartender nodded. Scott had quietly followed her to the bar and was now beside her. "What are you drinking?" she asked.

"Whiskey."

She nodded. "And a whiskey for my hero, here." She glanced back at Scott, her smile wide, sexy and her eyes teasing.

What was she up to?

Moments later they had their drinks, and with Eva leading Scott like another dog with a bone, they managed to find a small section on a cushioned bench away from the crowd.

"You didn't have to buy me a drink," he said, taking a sip of his new whiskey.

She sipped her tequila and shrugged. "Like I said, I'm avoiding going back to those drunk-ass, marriage-loving women and their stupid crowns, leis and sashes." She rolled her eyes. "Thank God I'm not in the wedding party."

"How do you know the bride?"

She shrugged again. "Friend since beauty school."

"Beauty school?"

She nodded. "Yeah, I'm a hairdresser and aesthetician."

Well, that explained why she was walking, talking perfection. The woman knew how to take care of herself. Though Scott would put money on her looking gorgeous without an ounce of makeup on too.

"What do you do?"

"I'm in advertising."

She nodded again, then began to bob her head in time with the beat of the music.

Then the conversation ended.

The air between them began to grow awkward.

He didn't know this woman enough to *like* her, but he certainly found her hot, and what he'd met so far, he liked. Now he just had to figure out a way to charm her into wanting to ditch her party completely and maybe go grab a slice of pizza with him down the block or something. His stomach rumbled at the thought of Guy's Pies. Best pizza by the slice in the entire city.

He took another sip of his drink and cleared his throat. "So uh ... what do you think of my hair? You being a hairdresser and all. Am I an abomination?" He cringed.

Seriously? Wasn't that like asking a stranger who'd just revealed they were a doctor to take a look at a mysterious mole on your back? He even had doctor friends, and he never asked them for medical advice. He asked his brother for legal advice, but when there's a lawyer in the family, why wouldn't you milk that cow?

Her smile was slow but sexy as hell. She lifted her hand from her lap and ran her fingers through his hair over and over again until he closed his eyes from just how good it felt.

If she brought out those nails and scraped his scalp, he was not to blame if his leg started to kick and shake uncontrollably.

"You have great hair," she finally said, causing him to open his eyes again. Her gaze was soft and appraising, her smile sweet. "It's nice and thick, soft. You've got a great hairline too." She tugged at the sides.

"Yeah? What would you do to it if I gave you carte blanche?"

Her eyebrows twitched up a bit. "Carte blanche?"

He nodded. "Yeah."

She raked her top teeth over her bottom lip, continuing to run her fingers through his hair. She set her drink down and added the fingers from her other hand, turning her body so they were now face-to-face. She tilted his head down so he was forced to stare directly down her blouse into her cleavage. He knew he should shut his eyes, but he just couldn't. It was like staring at an eclipse—so damn beautiful, but it might very well get him in some major trouble too.

"Honestly, I don't think I'd do much," she said. "Maybe go a bit shorter on the sides, tidy up the back of your neck a little, but whoever you see does a pretty good job."

"I see an eighty-three-year old barber down by Beechers Cheese. The guy takes nearly an hour to cut my hair, but he does a good job."

She chuckled, and oh, what a laugh. It was deep and throaty and sexy as fuck. She still hadn't stopped running her fingers through his hair. "A bit of silver on the sides here, huh?"

He nodded. "Yeah, starting to get some."

Her touch was strong but gentle. Confident but curious. "But not too much. I'm guessing the men in your family all have their hair, but they went gray early?"

His head bobbed again, in awe of this woman and the pure magic her hands wielded. He was putty. She could pet him like that all night long and he'd lay like a chocolate lab at her feet. "Uh, yeah. My dad started going gray by the time he was forty, my grandpa too. My dad's more salt than pepper now, but both gramps are combing tinsel."

She chuckled that raspy laugh again. "I like that term. You're cute." She still hadn't released his hair.

He hoped she never did.

"You're beautiful."

Eventually, unfortunately, she pulled her hands from his hair and batted long, dark lashes at him as she ducked her head, her smile coy and slightly hidden. "Thank you." She lifted her head again, her gaze settling on him. "Full disclosure?"

You're a hooker and this is all an elaborate ruse?

"Sure."

She took a deep breath, which only amplified her killer rack. The buttons on her emerald-green silk sleeveless blouse strained against her inhale. Scott did everything in his power not to stare.

He was weak. It was impossible.

"It's my first night away from my kids in ... " She shook her head and blew out a breath in exasperation. "God, I don't know how long. So it's been a while. I just signed the papers last month finalizing a very ugly, very messy, very painful divorce, and my kids are with my sister and her fourteen-year-old daughter. It's the first night where my children have been okay being away from me overnight. We've tried a few times, but my little guy—Kellen, he's five—gets upset when I leave. But I needed a night out ... desperately. We're moving out of my sister's place in a few weeks, as I finally bought my own house now that the divorce has gone through." Her eyes turned sad. "It's been tough on my boys." A wary glint invaded the sadness in the dark flecks of yellow around her irises as she waited for Scott to reply.

All he did was nod, and hope that his small smile and eyes conveyed his understanding and sympathy. She had no reason to be wary of him or his reaction to her honesty, to her plight. He'd been there himself and knew how hard a divorce could be on everyone involved—especially the kids. He took a leap of faith and rested his hand on her arm. "Been through a messy divorce myself. I have a son, and I totally get where you're coming from right now. It's hard on the kids. It's hard on everyone."

If she thought that her declaration was going to turn him

off, she couldn't be further from wrong. If anything, her honesty, her openness just made her more intriguing. She had wounds and scars just like him. She was human.

Heat flared in her eyes, and she shifted closer to him and brought her voice down. "I have a room at the hotel next door," she said, the first sign of real, genuine nervousness entering her eyes. Her voice quavered slightly, and her throat bobbed in trepidation. "Would you ... like to join me there?"

EVA HADN'T PLANNED on inviting anybody up to her hotel room. She simply wanted a night away to herself. A night alone. A night to not have a furnace of a child in nothing but Marvel underpants crawling into bed beside her at two in the morning, and then another one crawling into her bed an hour later.

She wanted one night in a bed all by herself where she didn't have to share the pillows, the duvet or the mattress. She wanted one night to not be *mom, mama or mommy* and instead just be Eva Fletcher—no, wait, scratch that, Eva *Marchand*. No way was she hanging on to that asshole's last name, even if it was still attached to her sons. She would spend the rest of her life making sure her sons turned out nothing like their father.

Nothing.

Kellen and Lucas Fletcher would be nothing but respectful, kind and sensitive men who treated women like equals and didn't emotionally or psychologically abuse or manipulate them. Kellen and Lucas would grow up to be good men.

But for one night she wanted her sister, Celeste, to be with those future good men. She didn't want to have to worry about anybody's needs, worries or wants but her own.

For. Just. One. Night.

From the moment she met up with the bachelorette party in the party room of the hotel, she began to plot her exit. Began to plot her escape to the luxury of her terrycloth robe and room service.

The party had been fun at first, with the rep from Curiously Kinky at-home romance parties doing sex toy demos and playing "guess that lube flavor," but after a while, once the champagne and Jell-O shots had started to get passed around, all the women began to get annoying. They went from respectable women in their thirties and forties, mothers, wives and entrepreneurs, to squealing sorority divas. Or *woo girls.*

No thanks.

She needed to ditch the squealy, giggly bachelorette party ASAP.

But the best-laid plans somehow had a way of changing—and not always for the worse. Now she didn't want to be in her room alone. Not *so* alone, at least.

This Scott guy was hot. Like *really* hot. Tall, dark and drop-dead sexy. That beard—yum. Thick, dark and short. Not to mention the soulful dark brown eyes, long lashes and a slightly crooked nose that somehow made him all the more handsome. Because it meant he wasn't perfect. Eva was nowhere near perfect, so the last thing she needed was to be with a man who was. Not that this would be anything more than one night, but still, it was nice to know the man had flaws. Imperfections. That made him the perfect companion to chase away the post-divorce blues. To end her dry spell and give her vibrator a much-needed break.

"Eva ... " he breathed out slowly, having taken a moment to simply stare at her, which only made her panties grow increasingly damp. "I would love to. But I don't want to take advantage—"

"Oh, you wouldn't be. If anybody's going to be taking

advantage of anybody tonight, it would be *me* taking advantage of *you*. *I* will be using *you*."

His expressive eyes went wide. His brows flew up his forehead. "Is that so?"

She bit her lip and nodded. "It is. Give me fifteen minutes to go *freshen* up, and then meet me next door in room 301." She bobbed her eyebrows. "There's a liquor store across the street ... maybe some wine?"

His eager, boyish grin and nod made her laugh. She liked this guy. He was sexy, funny and seemed kind. A breath of fresh air. And after the claustrophobia and suffocation she'd experienced in the last few years of her marriage, she was in desperate need of some fresh air.

She'd also made herself a promise that she would stop forsaking herself for a man. Todd had all but destroyed her confidence and self-esteem, and it had taken a lot of therapy and support from her sister and parents to begin to rebuild that confidence.

For the first time in her life, she was going to take. And what she wanted was to take Scott up to her hotel room and have her way with him.

"You're sure?" he asked, his honest eyes turning tender as he squeezed her arm, a small wrinkle of concern appearing between his brows. "I do want to spend more time with you, but I kind of thought we could just go grab pizza."

Ohhh, pizza.

She liked the sound of that.

"Twenty minutes. Go grab pizza too. Wine and pizza."

The corners of his eyes crinkled. "I like you, Eva. You say exactly what you want. No guessing games. Okay, then. I'll meet you upstairs, room 301, in twenty minutes, and I'll bring pizza and wine."

"Zinfandel," she stated.

His smile turned devilish. "Zinfandel. Your wish is my

2

THE WIND and sideways rain hammered the windows of her hotel suite as Eva washed her hands in the bathroom, staring at the woman in the mirror in front of her. She barely recognized herself.

Gone were the dark bags beneath her eyes—and not just because she was great at applying her own makeup—and her cheeks had filled out again since she started eating full meals after the divorce had been finalized. Once she was finally granted her freedom.

She'd withered away to barely one hundred pounds by the time she worked up the courage to file for separation.

God, that had been a terrifying moment in her life. Absolutely terrifying.

She and Todd had been together for nearly ten years. They had two children together, an enormous home in a swanky part of town, were members of a country club. Their kids went to a charter school. From the outside looking in, their life was idyllic.

But from the inside looking out, Eva felt like she was in prison.

Todd had been the main breadwinner in their family. Everything was in his name. He took care of the finances. And as things in their marriage began to turn south over the years, he made sure to throw all of that in her face time and time again. He also threatened to take the boys from her, claiming that she'd never see them again if she ever tried to leave him.

Which was why it had taken her nearly three years to work up the courage to finally do it. She'd wasted away to practically a skeleton until that time, became a mouse, a recluse, ashamed of what their friends would say to her about how her appearance had changed. But she was too emotionally sick to eat. The way Todd belittled her, patronized her, bullied her, it made her ill. She had no appetite. Not when her guts were twisted in such tight knots of fear. Fear of his wrath, his emotional and psychological torment. She worried herself to near death.

He never beat her, but the scars from his words, from his manipulation would most likely be everlasting.

A little over a year ago, shortly before the kids' spring break, which also encompassed the Easter long weekend, she packed up her and the kids while Todd was away for business and moved in with her sister, Celeste, and Celeste's daughter, Sabrina. Then she filed a restraining order against her husband and also served him with separation papers.

Todd had been livid.

Restraining order be damned, when he received the separation papers he'd driven over to Celeste's house and banged on the door, hollering and demanding Eva give him his children. Celeste and a few of the neighbors called the cops, and Todd had been escorted out of the neighborhood by three police cars.

And that's when things in Eva's life really turned ugly.

The year waiting for her divorce to be finalized had been pure torture.

She only let the kids see their father because the court ordered her to, even though Kellen and Lucas begged not to go with him when he came to pick them up. They said he ignored him when he had them. But whenever she brought it up to Todd, he said that if he didn't get his kids, he'd *take* them from her and she'd never see them again. She fretted herself to the point of needing hospitalization, she'd lost so much weight. The assurances of the court were a cold comfort when her kids were out of her care.

That year had been absolute anguish. Besides threatening to take their children away from her, Todd dragged her through the mud until it was in her ears, eyes and up her nose. He used her weight loss against her, painting her as mentally unstable and a drunk. That the reason she didn't eat was because she drank all her calories. But her lawyer, Richelle LaRue, had been outstanding and never let Todd get away with a damn thing.

Eva now had full custody of Kellen and Luke, with the boys spending the majority of their time with her—not that Todd really had anything to do with them when he was around—and Todd paying not only alimony but child support as well.

With her divorce settlement, she was able to buy a small, modest house in a nice part of town, one that had a fully finished basement where she planned to set up her hair and aesthetics studio.

Before all the separation and divorce chaos, she'd worked two days a week at a salon near the boys' school, mostly taking care of the updos for wealthy older women who came in once a week to get their hair done.

But now, she planned to build herself a mini empire. The space in the basement was perfect. Lots of natural light, a sink, bathroom, plenty of space for not only a stylist's chair, hair dryer and waxing table, but also the perfect place where she could set up her foot spa for pedicures.

She planned to open Eva's Hair and Esthetics within a couple of weeks of moving into the new house. But she needed to get a handle on advertising. Word-of-mouth was only so useful. She needed to get her business onto social media, flyers, bus benches, billboards. She needed it all.

She blotted at her face with a piece of tissue and let out a shaky breath. "You can do this," she whispered. "You can do this."

A knock on the door made her jump nearly clear out of her skin.

You can't do this.

What had she been thinking? Inviting a total stranger up to her hotel room for sex.

She'd been with all of four men in her whole life. The guy who took her virginity the summer she turned seventeen; Gary, her boyfriend senior year of high school; Rick, her boyfriend after Gary moved to Boston for college; and then finally Todd. And she and Todd hadn't had sex in almost five years.

Now she planned to break that dry spell with who?

A seriously gorgeous man with a super sexy crooked nose and beard you want to rub all over your—

"Eva?"

Shit! Right. He was still standing on the other side of the hotel door.

She was busy daydreaming her nightmare of the past, and Scott, one of the most handsome men she'd met in a very long time, was patiently waiting for her to welcome him inside.

She blew out a breath, took one last look at herself in the vanity mirror and then went to open the door.

And of course, he was leaning against the doorjamb all casual-like, somehow balancing a wine bottle, coat and pizza box, all while hooking his thumb in his belt loop, which meant that his black button-down shirt pulled tight across his chest, showing off well-defined muscles and a breadth that took her own breath away.

She'd been aware of his height and size back at the bar, but there she'd been fueled by pheromones, tequila and confidence. Now, standing there in front of him, she felt like the mouse she'd fought so hard to no longer be.

"Thought you might have fallen asleep," he said lazily, hitting her with the full megawatt smile, enhanced by a single dimple on his left side, nice lips, that sexy, slightly crooked nose, and of course that beard. Oh lord, the beard.

She swallowed and pushed the door open more, allowing him to enter. "No, not asleep, just, uh … " She didn't bother finishing that sentence because the scent of pizza made every thought in her brain disappear.

"I wasn't sure what to get," he said, wandering into the hotel room and over to the table and chairs next to the window. "Whether you're a traditionalist, like a margherita pizza girl, or you like to walk on the wild side, like smoked salmon, capers and cream cheese."

Eva must have made a face because he started to laugh. "Not a fan of the wild side?"

She shook her head. "Not on my pizza. I'm all for some chicken and artichokes, but keep the cream cheese and fish on my bagel. Some things are not meant to be fusionized." She wrinkled her nose. "Is that a word?"

He opened up the pizza box. "It is now. I grabbed us a half-and-half. Half margherita, half pepperoni with sausage, bacon and mushrooms."

Her mouth began to water. "Now that's my kind of pizza."

"I grabbed a zinfandel with a twist-off lid, as I wasn't sure you'd have a corkscrew," he said, grabbing two mugs from next to the coffee maker and pouring them both a healthy splash of wine.

Eva hadn't been aware of just how hungry she was until he'd walked into the hotel room and she'd been smacked upside the head with the scent of all things heavenly. Oregano. Garlic. Tomato sauce. Cheese. Basil. Pepperoni. Was there anything in the world that smelled better?

"Here you go." He handed her the mug of wine, and that's when she caught Scott's scent. Masculine, powerful, fresh, and just a touch citrusy.

Okay, well, maybe pizza was the *second*-best scent in the world, because the man in front of her smelled pretty damn delicious too.

She took the mug and thanked him.

He lifted his just a touch higher in the air. "To ... " His crooked nose wrinkled, and he glanced up into the corner of the room. "To ... "

She smiled. He was cute when he was confused. "To heroes *not* in capes. You saved me from ... "

Peeing my pants.

"A very embarrassing fate," she finished, clinking her mug against his.

"To heroes not in capes," he repeated, taking a sip of his wine while eyeing her over the rim of his mug. The twinkle in the lighter brown flecks of his eyes spoke of mischief. Sure, Scott was a nice guy, but she could tell just by the way he smiled so confidently, held himself with such carefree ease and squinted just slightly when he stared at her, this man had a wicked side. And not necessarily the *bad* kind of wicked.

"So, shall we start?" he asked, setting his mug down on the table.

Well, that was blunt.

No foreplay, no seduction, nothing. Just right to the point. In and out. Wham, bam, thank you, ma'am.

She choked on the wine in her throat and began coughing, her eyes widening as the thought of dying in a hotel room with a sexy stranger began to edge its way to the forefront of her mind. "Excuse me?" she gasped.

Scott pounded on her back. "I asked if you wanted to start."

She took another sip of her wine and glanced up at him, her eyes watering. "Um ... I've never ... this is, uh ... "

"I mean the pizza," he said, his warm chuckle sweeping over her like a velvet throw. He shook his head. "I'm not a complete asshole. Remember that *this* was all your idea. I just wanted to go for pizza. If you want to sit on your bed and watch movies, drink wine and eat pizza all night, I am A-OK with that." He grabbed a napkin from the side of the pizza box, then reached for a slice of pepperoni pizza, handing the napkin and pizza to her. "My mama raised a gentleman. No means no. You, beautiful Eva, hold *all* the power here."

You, beautiful Eva, hold all the power.

Had she ever heard any sexier words uttered?

Nope, she certainly hadn't.

She'd never held any kind of power ever either.

And yet, Scott just handed it all to her on a silver platter.

She swayed where she stood and reached out, gripping the back of the chair to stabilize herself. Was she already drunk on power? Did it happen that fast?

He stepped into her space and tilted her chin up with his knuckle. Her lips parted. "I really just want to get to know you, Eva. Any part of you."

Scott couldn't say he'd ever had a woman *literally* throw

herself at him. Sure, women had done so figuratively, but Eva actually launched herself into his arms, crushing her mouth against his and shoving her tongue down his throat.

Whoa!

He could not get a read on this woman. One minute she was all smooth and seductive, oozing sexy confidence and inviting him back to her hotel suite, saying she'd be the one taking advantage. The next minute she was nervous and choking on her wine. Only to turn around and leap into his arms and kiss him.

She confused the hell out of him but also intrigued him to no end.

He liked that.

He liked her.

Wrapping his arms around her back, he parted his lips and took control of their kiss, sweeping his tongue into her hot, wet mouth and tasting everything she had to offer. The sweet zinfandel tasted even better on her tongue.

A small, feminine moan slid up her throat, and she pressed her tits against his chest, his leg wedged between hers to keep them vertical.

Without breaking them apart, she set her mug down and somehow her pizza too and began to back up toward the bed, her hands free to roam across his chest, and began to unbutton his shirt.

But something tickled at the back of his neck—a warning? Red flags? Alarm bells? He broke the kiss, much to the protestations from his *other* head.

"Let's eat first. Have some wine and maybe talk a bit," he said gently, easing her down to the bed, then retreating to the table to grab her wine and pizza. "You're sending off some real conflicting signals, and I just want to make sure you know what you want."

Big, gorgeous green eyes looked up at him with total

confusion, and her puffy lips opened to form the perfect little *O*. He had to stop himself from groaning at how utterly fuckable she looked at that moment. How he wanted to do nothing more than grab all that hair into a tight ponytail at the base of her head and ease that little *O* over his now throbbing erection.

But his mama had raised a gentleman. He had a little sister, and even if he didn't, he could see that Eva wasn't entirely sure of what she'd proposed to him downstairs half hour ago. He needed to give her a bit more time to think things through. He also just wanted to get to know her better. Even though he had no problem with a one-night stand with no strings, no expectations and sometimes even no names, the tickle at the base of his skull told him Eva was not one of those women.

"A-are you having second thoughts?" she asked, accepting her wine and pizza. "D-did I do something wrong?" The slight shake in her voice made him want to scoop her up into his arms and hold her, take away whatever insecurities or pain she was clearly harboring.

But instead, he kicked off his shoes, grabbed his own slice of pizza and his mug of wine, then sat down at the head of the bed, propping himself up on the pillow. "You did absolutely nothing wrong, beautiful Eva. I just want us to get to know each other a bit first. Have a drink. Have a meal. Have a conversation."

The sexy line of her long throat lifted and dropped as she swallowed, still sitting on the edge of the bed, staring beneath the table. "Didn't we already do that downstairs? The drink and the conversation?" She blinked slowly, then pivoted her head to look at him. "What is it you want from me?"

Scott was midway through a bite of pizza, but he dropped the slice to the napkin, put it aside and leapt up to his knees, taking her mug of wine from her and setting it on the nightstand. Then he took her hand in his. "Eva, I don't want *anything* from you. Except to know that you're not going to regret something tomorrow. I hardly know you, but what I do know I like. But I've also had enough one-night stands to know that the women aren't usually as conflicted as you seem. I want to get to know you, that's all." He tugged on her hand. "Come sit. Eat, and let's talk. My son is with his mother tonight, and tomorrow is Sunday, so I have no curfew." He winked, hoping to settle some of her nerves.

She seemed to relax a bit and nodded, ditching her own shoes and climbing onto the bed beside him with her pizza. He handed her the mug of wine, and she took a sip.

Before reaching for his own wine, he grabbed the television remote and flicked the TV on, surfing until he found a rerun of *The Office*. Glancing over at her with raised eyebrows, he waited for the yay or nay.

She nodded, offering him a small smile.

He set the remote down and reached for his wine, taking a sip and then diving back into his pizza. "So, tell me what it is that makes Eva ... "

"Just Eva," she said through chewing.

He nodded, the corner of his mouth twitching. "Tell me what it is that makes *just* Eva tick."

3

GRATEFUL FOR NOT ONLY something in her stomach but the company as well, Eva was now far more relaxed than she had been an hour ago. Scott was sweet, kind, interesting, and absolutely hilarious. The man had her in stitches nearly the entire time they vegged on the bed gorging themselves on pizza and watching back-to-back episodes of *The Office*. By the time she stood up with jelly legs from the wine, she had tears in her eyes, she'd been laughing so hard.

Todd had never made her laugh like that. He'd made her shed tears a lot but never from laughter.

It was refreshingly wonderful, and she didn't want it to end.

"What's your ex like?" Scott asked as she climbed back onto the bed with a glass of water. She handed him one as well.

"A total narcissist," she said blandly. "A controlling, manipulative, emotional and psychological abuser. A pathological liar. A cheater." She glanced at him as she sipped her wine. "Pick one. My therapist never met him, so she can't actually diagnose him, but she said that based on everything

I've told her about the man, she can almost say for certain that Todd is a psychopath." The lights on the nightstands flickered. Too bad Todd wasn't dead and that was just his ghost haunting her. Next birthday wish, perhaps?

His mouth flattened into a thin line. "I'm sorry. That had to have been really difficult. Tough to finally get out of, I'm sure."

He didn't know the half of it. All she did was nod.

"And your ex?"

He exhaled and tucked his hands behind his head before he sank down into the pillows so he was lying down on the bed. "A narcissist too, not a psychopath though. Just selfish. But I think what bothered me about her the most, what ended our marriage, was just how damn inconsiderate she was. How disrespectful she was toward me. Treated me like her lapdog." He shook his head. "I know I'm a nice guy. I know that, and when it came to Katrin, nice guys really did finish last. She made plans on nights I had plans and would just expect me to cancel mine, even though I'd have made my plans eons ago and put it in our shared calendar. I mean one time—and this was when we were still dating and she lived for six months down in San Francisco for an apprenticeship —I took time off from my own job, flew down there, expecting to spend the weekend with her like we'd planned, only to turn up on her doorstep and find out from her room-mate that Katrin had taken off to Napa with some friends for the weekend."

Eva's bottom lip dropped open. "Are you kidding me?"

He shook his head. "I should have ended the relationship then and there, truthfully. And her excuse is always something super lame, like *That's just my truth, Scott. That's just my psychology. I'm not a very organized person, but it doesn't mean I'm a bad person. If you can't accept me for who I am, then that's your problem, not mine.*"

"I'm sorry, but what the fuck? If you can't accept her constant disrespect, then that's your problem, not hers?" She blinked a bunch of times. "You picked a real winner there, Scottie."

He made a noise of reluctant agreement in his throat. "Don't I know it. I mean, she couldn't send me a text the night before I flew all the way to San Francisco? Hell, an hour before I got on a fucking flight and been like *hey babe, I would really like to do a girls' weekend to Napa. Do you mind if we reschedule? Sorry for the last-minute change of plans.* Or something like that. Like at least fake your fucking remorse."

"But then you wouldn't have your son," she said quietly, feeling the exact same way about Todd and her own children. An enormous part of her wished she'd never given Todd her phone number that night at the Seahawks game after-party. Then the last ten years and the nightmare would never have happened. Her feelings of failure, of becoming invisible, a shell of who she once was, never would have happened. Who knows what she could have accomplished if she hadn't met Todd? Maybe she'd have her own spa by now. Her own spa chain. A franchise. Eva's Hair and Esthetics in every major city in Washington state.

An ache began to build in her chest at the thought of a life without having ever met Todd. How could she even imagine such a thing?

Because as much as Todd had hurt her, as much as he had destroyed who she was and who she had the potential to be, without him there would be no Kellen or Lucas. And the world without her children just didn't make a lick of sense.

Everything happens for a reason.

Her mother's vague, sunshiny, unicorns-shitting-rainbows mantra came back to her.

Yeah, maybe everything did happen for a reason, but not all reasons made sense. Not all reasons were good.

But Kellen and Lucas are good. Kellan and Lucas are perfect.

She squeezed her eyes shut as the regret from even wishing for a moment that she hadn't met Todd consumed her. She would walk through hell for her children. She would kill for her children. She'd endure all the years of manipulation, abuse and bullying from Todd all over again if it meant she had her children.

"You okay, there?" Scott's deep voice drew her out of the thick quicksand she'd been sinking into, and she opened her eyes.

"Yeah," she said on an exhale that strained her chest.

"You're absolutely right, you know," he said, eyeing her warily. "Without Katrin, I wouldn't have my son. So as much as she hurt me, made me feel like an afterthought, I'm grateful to her for our son. A world without Freddie just wouldn't make sense."

Finally, someone who understood her struggle. Her mental anguish over wishing you'd never met someone but knowing that without them, you wouldn't have the amazing things you did.

"Did you file for divorce or did your ex?" she asked, sinking down into the pillows and turning to face him, propping her head in her hand. She wanted to get off the topic of herself and focus on him. She was boring. Scott seemed far more interesting, far more worldly and experienced.

"I did," he replied. "I suggested counseling and tried telling her how disrespected I felt, but it all fell on deaf ears. We tried counseling for a while, but even the counselor said it wasn't sinking in with Katrin. So in the end, I couldn't do it anymore. I couldn't be treated like a second-class citizen in my own marriage. When my opinion stopped mattering, that was the end of it."

"And your son? How did he take it all?"

"Freddie?" Scott let out a deep breath and shut his eyes.

"He was a trooper through all of it. We split when he was three, and he's six now, so I don't think he really remembers much." He shook his head but didn't open his eyes. "She's still inconsiderate, selfish and disrespectful to me, my time and plans, but at least I'm no longer married to her and having to put up with it on a daily basis. I get my kid on set days of the week, and we sit down every two months and go over any changes. If she needs to make a last-minute change, I have the right to decline her—and just to prove a point, I have."

Eva smiled. "Good."

He opened his eyes. "What about your ex. Does he see your kids much?"

She snorted, then scoffed. "No. His children are a burden. An inconvenience. He used them as pawns in the divorce, but otherwise he has very little to do with them, which is fine by them, because they want nothing to do with him."

"So you don't get much free time then?"

She shook her head. "Nope. But my boys are good kids, and even though I certainly feel drained or tapped out some days, I wouldn't trade them for the world."

He rolled over on his side like she was and propped his head in his hand. "I wouldn't trade Freddie for anything either."

Sexy, kind and an attentive father. This guy certainly seemed like the whole damn package.

But there had to be a catch.

Todd had seemed like a great guy at first too. Then his manipulative monster came out of hiding after they said their vows—after it was too late.

Did Scott have a monster lurking somewhere deep? Did all men?

"What is it you would like, Eva?" he asked, drawing her from her roaming appraisal of him, her eyes having drifted over his face, down the length of his body and ultimately lingering on the V of his dark-wash jeans just a fraction longer than was seemly.

She blinked a couple of times, not understanding the question. "What do you mean?"

He lifted an eyebrow almost impatiently, as if her not understanding the question was taxing on him. "What is it you *want*, Eva? You invited me up to your hotel room saying that you'd be the one taking advantage, and I'd like for you to explain that to me. What kind of advantage had you planned on taking?"

Heat raced into her cheeks and wormed its way down her chest. Even if Scott hadn't said a single word to her, the way he was looking at her, so earnestly, so seriously and focused, she would have probably swallowed her own tongue. But the fact that he actually asked her what she wanted, asked what her plan was, made it all the more exciting.

"Hmm?" He reached out and tucked a strand of hair behind her ear. "What is it that *Eva* wants? Is it still the same thing as down in the bar? Or have your intentions changed?"

She swallowed and dragged her bottom lip between her teeth. "I ... I haven't been with anybody in quite a while, and the last person I was with was—"

"Your manipulative jerk of a husband," he said, finishing her sentence for her perfectly.

With a sigh, she nodded. "Exactly."

"And he was controlling," he asked.

"Very much so."

"In all things?"

"Yes."

"Including the bedroom."

"Especially there." Which ordinarily she had no problem with. She was actually quite submissive in bed, preferring to just go with the flow and ride it out. But Todd had taken things to a whole new level. His level of control had stopped being sexy years ago. After a while, sex was only when he wanted it, how he wanted it, and if she was lucky enough to have an orgasm, she should consider herself grateful. The man never really put any energy into *her* pleasure. It was very much a *wham, bam, thank you, ma'am* kind of thing. By the end, she loathed even the thought of him touching her and would lie and say she had a really heavy period or a migraine and then go sleep in the spare bedroom.

Just as well. Turned out Todd was sleeping with his massage therapist anyway, so it's not like he missed the sex. And after she snuck and stole his phone one time to see if her suspicions of his affair were true, she realized just *how* horrible a person Todd really was.

Not only was he sleeping with his massage therapist, but he was also one of those horrid cyberbullies. You know, the keyboard warrior guys. The middle-aged white men who bully and haunt women, threatening to rape and kill them if they don't appreciate the unsolicited dick pics. Yeah, Todd was *that* kind of guy.

For the most part, Todd ignored her when they were in the house together, and when she started sleeping in the guest room every night, he stopped making a stink when he started sleeping with his massage therapist. Except for that one night ...

"Earth to Eva," Scott said with a chuckle, lightly running his hand over her arm. "You okay? Not too much wine?"

She shook her head to dislodge the thoughts of Todd and send them flying out of the room. She hoped they landed in the toilet where they belonged. "I'm okay," she replied. "Just remembering how controlling he really was." She shuddered. "Glad that chapter of my life is over."

"You wanna burn the whole book? Start a whole new story? I can get my hands on some lighter fluid. I'm pretty sure we can figure out a way to get up to the roof of this place and torch some shit in a trash can."

The idea of setting fire to every memory she had of Todd held appeal. "That doesn't sound like a half-bad idea, actually."

His smile got real again, and his eyes gleamed. "Back to my original question, though. What do you want, Eva?"

The way he said her name was intoxicating. Her name on his lips held promises of what he could and would do to her. The subtle scrape of his top teeth over his bottom lip as he enunciated the *V* in her name. It was erotic and sexy, and with that deep, masculine rumble, she felt a quake way down in her core each and every time he said it.

"I want to be in control," she whispered. "I don't normally take control in bed, and generally I prefer not to. But my ex was *very* controlling ... very selfish."

"And you want a night all about you?"

She shook her head and pushed up to the sitting position, happy that she hadn't had any more wine and had all of her wits. Boldly she shoved him to his back and swung her leg over his torso so that she was straddling him. "I want a night I will never forget," she whispered. Her fingers went to task on the buttons of his shirt. "I want a night with a stranger where there is no manipulation, no head games or expectations, no pre-conceived ideas. Just ... " She leaned down and drew one of his exposed nipples in between her teeth, tugging until he hissed out in either pleasure or pain, she didn't know—or care—which. "Two people enjoying each other. Give and take. I want you to show me what I've been missing these past few lonely, celibate years. And I want to remember what it's like to be with a real man."

With adrenaline and arousal now fueling her every move, she sprinkled gentle kisses across his hard, muscular chest over to his other nipple, scissoring her teeth across the tight bud.

"Eva"—his hands in her hair stopped her effort—"you're sure?"

With one hand still propping herself up, she moved the other one down between them to his now very noticeable, very hard, very impressive erection. She unsnapped his jeans, slid down the zipper and slipped her hand inside, taking him in her palm. "I'm very sure," she whispered, stroking him as much as she could, given their awkward position. "I need this, Scott." She lifted her head and pressed her lips to his, just enough to touch, not enough to kiss. "I need you."

FUCK, she was something else. Sweet and sexy and so goddamn gorgeous, Scott lay there in awe of his luck as Eva continued to undress him, taking her time and making sure those nails of hers drove him to the very edge of insanity.

After unfastening each and every black button of his dress shirt, she took her sweet time kissing and swirling that slippery little tongue over his chest and abs, raking her nails along his ribcage and down his sides. When she reached the waist of his pants with her lips, her fingers walked their way up his torso, and she took each of his nipples between her thumbs and forefingers, twisting until he gasped from the pain.

"Eva," he growled in warning, resting his hand on her head.

She released his nipples, then ran her nails back down to his waistband. He lifted his hips to help her remove his jeans. She did so quickly, chucking them to the floor and leaving him lying there with a tent pitched in his gray boxer shorts. He glanced down his body to where she hovered above him, her eyes hooded, her pink tongue sliding across her lips, licking her chops.

A small, damp, heart-shaped patch of fabric over the head of his cock said he was leaking precum. Well, of course he was. He'd been hard for a long fucking time lying there next to Eva and those tits of hers. Listening to her speak with that sexy, throaty voice. Like she was on the business end of one of those 1-900 sex chat lines. Did they still have those?

He was old.

But how could he not be hard, lying in a bed, staring at Eva? Talking to Eva, listening to Eva. The woman was what wet dreams were made of, and Jesus Christ, he was only human. He also hadn't gotten laid since New Year's Eve, so his *other* head was doing a whole hell of a lot of its own thinking these days.

"Baby," he said hoarsely, "you don't have to." He threaded his fingers into her hair, the silky red tendrils slipping through. Like magic strands of fire splayed across his stomach.

She shook her head and relieved him of his boxers. He lifted his hips once again, and she slid them down and over his legs. "I'm not," she said, tossing his boxers into the pile with his jeans.

Huh.

She slipped off the bed, her eyes never leaving his as she began to unbutton her blouse, taking her sweet time, just like she had with him.

"Touch yourself," she demanded, her eyes flicking from his face down to his shaft. "I want to watch you. I want to see what you do when you're alone."

She didn't have to ask him twice.

Scott was not shy. Never had been, and even though he certainly didn't go around touching himself in public, he also had zero qualms taking himself into his palm and showing her just how he liked to get down to business.

He gripped his cock in his right hand and squeezed his fist up and around the head until it turned a dark purple, then he stroked back down to the base and up again.

Heat flared in the yellow-green of her eyes, and her tongue once again darted out and slid across her lips.

"You going to just take in the show, or do I get a show of my own?" he asked, tightening his grip around the head, a bead of precum emerging onto his crown.

"That depends," she whispered, letting her green blouse slip off her shoulders, revealing a cream-colored lace bra with absolutely zero padding. Her hard nipples pointed at him, called to him, demanded he take them in his mouth and ease their ache.

"Depends on what?" he asked, still stroking himself.

"Depends on what you plan to do with *that*." She tilted her head, and her gaze lasered in on the now even bigger bead of precum on his crown.

With his thumb, he wiped it off. "Your mouth or mine?"

She took the couple of steps toward the bed and leaned over, giving him the perfect few of the best fucking cleavage he'd ever seen. Fuckable cleavage. A valley built for a cock. "Mine," she murmured. Then she showed him exactly how well she could suck. That tongue of hers swirled around the pad of his thumb like it was the head of his cock, and her eyes fluttered closed, a soft hum rumbling up from the depths of her throat.

When she pulled away and her eyes opened, she smiled. "Yum."

"Holy fuck," he breathed.

Her grin grew. She stood up and took a few steps away from him again. "Get back to work," she said playfully, pointing to his paused hand. He hadn't even realized he'd quit. He was just too caught up in her mouth around his thumb to concentrate on two things at once. After all, there wasn't much blood heading to his brain at the moment.

With his free hand, he saluted her. "Yes, ma'am." Then he went back to work, showing her just how he liked to get the job done. Now, when he took himself in the shower, he'd be envisioning Eva sucking his thumb with her hot little mouth, her perfect tits right there just begging for his cum.

Her fingers hooked into the belt loops at her waist, and she shimmied her tight black pants down over her shapely legs, revealing a matching thong to her bra. She was perfect. Curvy but fit. With hips he could hold on to, a slim waist, and thighs that he couldn't wait to have squeezing the side of his head. The best fucking earmuffs he could ever imagine.

"Wanna fuck your tits, baby," he said, his hips jerking off the bed voluntarily. "You have the best fucking tits I've ever seen."

Her smile was warm and bright. "The best *fucking* tits, or the best *fuckable* tits?"

He grinned. "Both."

"Never had my tits fucked before."

He groaned. "Oh, Eva ... let me be your first."

"But then ..."

"Let's fuck with a condom, and I'll get you off as many times as we can. Then we'll rip the condom off, and I'll fuck your tits."

"Won't it be messy?"

Hell, yes, it would be. That was half the fun of it.

"Then we'll have a shower."

She dragged her teeth over her lip but didn't reply.

Was that a maybe?

"Let's start here and see where the night goes." She reached around behind her back and unclasped her bra, letting those luscious mounds tumble out, taunting him.

Then she slipped out of her thong, revealing a perfectly waxed pussy with just a thin strip of hair over her mound. His ex had gotten waxed as well. She said she used to get the "two postage stamp" package. It looked like Eva went with a "three postage stamp" package, and she pulled it off flawlessly. He really didn't care either way though. One postage stamp, two, three, none, or the whole damn envelope—who the fuck cared? What mattered was how she responded when he was inside her, when his tongue was on her clit and his fingers on her G-spot. He couldn't give a damn how much hair she had between her thighs as long as he got to eventually use those thighs as earmuffs.

"You're fucking perfection," he murmured.

"Fucking perfection or *fuckable* perfection?"

His chuckle was strained as his need to come began to inch forward. "Both."

She swayed her hips toward him. "Before we do any *tit*-fucking or any kind of fucking, I'd like to see how skilled you are with that tongue of yours. I know you can talk. I know you can joke, but frankly, I'm a little tired of listening to you."

He snorted. This confident side of her was sexy as fuck.

The sparkle in her eye and the tug at the corner of her mouth said she was joking, but joking or not, he loved how relaxed she finally was. How cool she was in her own skin, now that they knew each other a bit more and it wasn't just a nameless fuck to scratch an itch. Even if they never saw each other again, he didn't want Eva to regret tonight or feel ashamed of herself in any way.

And the woman certainly had nothing to be ashamed about.

He inched over into the center of the bed and watched as she climbed up and straddled his face, her cleft hovering just inches over his mouth. A drip landed on his lips, and he swept it off with his tongue.

Just like he thought—sweet as could fucking be.

"Show me how a real man eats pussy, Scott. Show me what I've been missing." Then she lowered her slit down to his mouth, and he showed her *exactly* what she'd been missing—and then some.

4

HOLY.

Fucking.

God.

Eva's eyes threatened to roll into the back of her head for what felt like the millionth time as she gyrated her hips, swirling her slick, swollen cleft around Scott's oh-so-talented, oh-so-diabolical tongue. The man was definitely showing her what she'd been missing those ten years with Todd, and then all those other years with all those other severely lacking boyfriends.

The man beneath her was a master at seduction, a master at making a woman feel comfortable and relaxed, and a master at eating pussy like it was his favorite meal in the world—maybe it was?

She held on to the headboard and let her head fall forward between her arms, her breasts feeling extra heavy as the orgasm drew near.

She'd never had more than one orgasm during sex—if she even got that. But something told her that with Scott working his magic, she'd be able to have multiples. Hell, she was willing to give it a shot at least. It wasn't every day you met a man as handsome, charming and kind as the man she was currently trying to suffocate. At least he *seemed* kind. He didn't pressure her into sex—unlike Todd, who ...

She couldn't think about that right now. If she thought about Todd, about *that*, she'd never find an orgasm.

Scott was not Todd.

One of his fingers dipped into her sopping cleft, and then he drew it up between her cheeks, caressing her tight hole but not breaching it. She puckered against his finger as his pressure grew a bit more intense. She'd never ... but that wasn't to say she hadn't thought about it. But tonight was not that night. No matter how patient, how skilled, how incredible Scott was, she'd have to scratch that inquisitive itch another time with another man.

Because Scott was just a one-time, one-night thing.

Up and down, back and forth through her crease he drew his finger, never pushing for more, taking her pinched hole as a cue not to go any farther.

She ground down on his tongue as he began doing harder, quicker flicks over her clit. She was close again. The thought of letting Scott take her in a place no man had ever gone was enough to get her back to that sweet point of pure bliss.

She rotated her hips in a circular fashion and tilted her pelvis down so he could take more of her clit into his mouth. He did just that—the smart man. He sucked like his life depended on it, like a fucking Hoover, and she exploded.

Eva's whole body convulsed and spasmed as the orgasm shot up from between her legs, where Scott worked his nose to the clit-stone, and then spread down to her toes and up to the top of her head and out to each fingertip. Her nipples tingled, her chest heaved, and her thighs shook. She squeezed her eyes closed tight, allowing the sensations to consume her. Bright lights flashed behind her closed lids, and her fingers began to cramp.

As the climax languidly began to dissipate, pulling itself back in toward her center like a flower closing up for the night, she opened her eyes and released her death grip on the headboard.

A gentle tap on her thigh and a muffled sound from below reminded her that her pleasure was not from her own making—as it had been for years—but actually due to the overwhelming generosity and sexy seduction of the man whose wide brown eyes looked a touch panicky.

He tapped her thigh a bit more frantically, and she lifted up more onto her knees.

Scott inhaled, and his chest heaved. "Sorry. I couldn't breathe." He took another deep breath, then released it. "You just kept grinding down more and more. I knew you were close, so I didn't want to stop you. But ... " His grin was devilishly handsome. "Not a bad way to die if that's what it'd come to, though."

She rolled her eyes and climbed off him, sitting up on her knees on the bed, nibbling on her lips as she watched him lick his and wipe his fingers over his face before he licked those too. Dewy beads of her arousal clung like diamonds to the wiry hair of his beard, glistening in the muted light of the nightstand lamp.

He caught her watching him and grinned again. "Can't waste a drop."

Every cell in her body began to recharge.

"Now, about those gorgeous tits of yours," he said, his deep and low voice sending a sizzle through her veins as he flipped over to his belly and up onto all fours. "You still gonna let me fuck 'em?"

She'd let him do anything to her at this point. She was mush for brains and a slave to his passion. If he was half as good at everything else in bed as he was with his tongue between her legs, she would leave here tomorrow morning with a smile on her face and a spring in her step, no doubt about it.

Eva was finally getting her groove back.

———————

SHE HADN'T REPLIED yet to his probe about fucking her tits. But the glimmer in those gorgeous green eyes of hers said she'd already thought it over, she was just embarrassed to admit she wanted to.

He prowled across the bed on all fours toward her, starting at the foot of the bed and making his way north, never once taking his eyes off her.

He loved how each inch he moved forward, her cheeks grew an even darker shade of red. Her throat bobbed a little harder, and her nostrils flared a little wider. Her tongue darted out and slid across her lips, lips he couldn't wait to feel wrapped around his shaft as he stroked her hair, cupped her cheek and felt himself slide to the back of her throat and then out again. Felt her teeth scrape against his length as he knocked her tonsils and she swallowed everything he gave her.

With a swipe of his hand, he grabbed her feet and tugged them out from beneath her, pulling her down the bed until she was flat on her back. She let out a squeal of surprise but didn't struggle. Her sigh of contentment and her arms looping around his neck as he climbed up her body said she was anything but afraid.

His iron-bar cock rested against her belly. "What do you say, sweet Eva?"

She dragged her teeth over her lip and nodded. "Yes, but first, fuck me ... please."

Anything for you, angel.

He grinned as he lowered his mouth to hers. "With pleasure." He didn't take her mouth but just continued to hover. "Taste yourself," he ordered. "Taste your sweetness on my lips." Her eyes gleamed with intrigue and perhaps even slight hesitation, but she did as she was told, slipping her tongue across his top, then his bottom lip. "Best damn thing I've tasted in a while," he said before he finally crushed his lips to hers, took control of the kiss, and showed her once again just how talented he was with his tongue. She opened for him without reservation and lifted her hips so he was now notched—unsheathed—at her core. The wet, warm heat of her pussy against the head of his cock caused a deep, primitive growl to bubble up from the back of his throat uncontrollably.

Reluctantly, he broke the kiss and shifted. "Precum, baby. We can't be too careful." He sat up on the bed and reached for his pants off the floor, retrieving the sleeve of condoms. He'd bought a box but ditched the box the moment he left the drugstore, preferring to just shove the packets straight into his pocket.

Swallowing, she licked her lips and nodded. "Right, sorry. It just felt ... *feels* so good."

It most certainly fucking did, and he'd give his left nut to raw-dog it with this gorgeous creature, but not tonight. Maybe if he got her phone number, they could meet up again and see where things went.

He ripped open the foil packet and rolled the condom on over his shaft, making sure it was secure at the base before he turned back to face her and crawled up the length of her body. "I am clean," he said. "Got checked last month after ... " He let the rest hang in the air. The last thing he needed to do was regale her with his past conquests. Total mood killer.

She nodded. "I'm clean too. But I'm not on any birth

control right now, so ... condoms are a must." Her nails raked down his back, chasing a shiver. "But nothing feels as good as the real thing."

He lunged forward and nipped her bottom lip. "You got that right." Then he eased himself inside her, slowly, allowing her body to acclimatize to his girth.

She squeezed her eyes shut and tilted her chin to the sky, her lips parting just enough for little puffs of warm air to hit his cheek.

"Holy fuck, you're tight," he ground out, feeling her squeeze around him as she adjusted herself beneath his weight, her muscles relaxing with each inch.

"Yeah," she breathed out.

"Like crazy fucking tight."

Eva shoved her nipple into his face. "Suck it," she panted.

Yes, ma'am. He ducked his head and drew her tight bud into his mouth, laving at it, raking his teeth over it, tugging it until she sucked in air and squirmed beneath him.

Normally, Scott took control in the bedroom. He preferred it. But Eva's little demands and zest for control turned him on like crazy.

"I want to be on top," she whimpered, lifting her hips up to meet him, which allowed her to take him deeper.

Fuck, he wanted that too.

"Hell, yes," he grunted, wrapping his arm under and around her back, intertwining their legs and then rocking them side to side across the bed so that she was now on top, but they never disconnected. "Sit up and let me watch those fuckable tits bounce," he encouraged, reaching behind him to better prop the pillows behind his head.

Grinning, she acquiesced to his request and perched atop his waist. He slid deeper into her tight, slick channel. She squeezed around him, and he had to chomp down hard on the inside of his cheek not to come.

With her hands on his chest for stability, she began to bob up and down, taking him all the way to the base, then back out to the tip, giving a little hip swirl and a squeeze when there was nothing but his pulsing crown left inside her. Was she trying to kill him? Because he was definitely seeing a bright light and hearing some angels sing.

He reached up and tugged on her nipples, pinching them both and twisting, which caused her green eyes to flare. Then her lids dropped back down to half-mast. A gush of warm liquid poured over his balls.

"Touch yourself," he ordered, throwing her own earlier demands back at her. "Let's get you there together."

Heat and need flickered in her eyes as she nodded, letting her hand drift down her torso and between her legs.

"You're so fucking wet, babe. Pouring that honey all over my balls."

Her cheeks pinked up in a seriously sexy way just as two of her fingers began rubbing rough circles over her clit.

"Nothing to be ashamed of, Eva. The wetter the woman, the better. Means I'm doing my job right." He tugged again on her nipples, and her mouth opened, her chin tilted toward the ceiling, and she began to lift and drop her hips faster and harder. "That's right, baby. So fucking beautiful. God, Eva, you're the sexiest thing I've ever seen."

"Oh God," she whispered, her fingers working double-time now, her tits jiggling in his palms with each hard thud of her hips. "So fucking close."

"Yeah, you are." He reared up and latched onto one of her hard peaks, sucking until he felt her still, gasp, and then begin to shudder. His teeth scraped across her chest to the other breast as she continued to come, her pants and whimpers only seeming to grow rather than ebb. Her hand between them was still going berserk.

Was this just one long orgasm, or was she having multiples and they were just rolling into each other?

He released one of her breasts and reached behind her, dipping his finger enough to gather some of her wetness, then he trailed that slippery finger up her crease, pausing over her tight rosette. It puckered beneath his touch, so he didn't push, but the way her cries of delight increased told him she wasn't hating where he was right now.

Slowly, her body grew lax against his, and her breathing became less ragged. Her whimpers were more like kittenish mewls, and her skin held a mist of perspiration.

"Wow!" she whispered, glancing down at him with glassy —almost mystified—eyes.

He reclined back into the pillows. "Yeah?"

She nodded. "Yeah. That was like four back to back to back to back. I wasn't sure they'd ever end."

"We make a good team."

Red now replaced the pink in her cheeks. "We do."

"I think there's a puddle beneath my ass," he joked. "And my balls are soaked."

Her mouth opened, but before she could say anything, he took that as an invitation and grabbed her by the nipples and pulled her down to him, once again taking her mouth like he owned it. Because tonight, he kind of did.

After a few minutes of sucking on her tongue, he broke the kiss, cupping her cheek. "You can say no, and we can just finish this way if you'd prefer."

Her round mounds pressed into his chest, and when he glanced down between them, the sight of her cleavage made his cock jerk inside her.

Any part of her she allowed him, he'd take as a gift, but God how he hoped she'd let him fuck her tits.

He'd always been a tit man. Would always be a tit man.

And this woman had tits for days. Probably the best rack he'd ever seen, ever tasted, ever ... everything.

With the grace of a gazelle, she swung her leg over his waist until she was perched on her knees on the bed next to him, then she made to remove the condom.

Fuck, yes!

He helped her relieve him of the latex cock sock, then reached for a tissue from the box on the nightstand.

"I ... I've never done this before," she said, grabbing both breasts in her palms and mashing them together. "Do you lie down or do I lie down?"

He twisted his lips in thought for a moment. It'd been so long since he'd tit-fucked anybody, what was the best way to do it?

He tapped his chin, then pulled at his still-damp beard. "Let's have me stay like this, and you sort of hover over me from the side there, smoosh your tits together just like that and then slide my dick between them."

"Lube?" she asked, getting into position.

He nodded. "You've got plenty." Then he dipped his fingers behind her and drew out her wetness, slathering it over his raging hard cock and then some between her breasts.

Licking her lips, she hunkered down and did as he'd described, sliding his dick between the ripe melons of perfection, her nipples once again diamond-hard, the areolas dark and dusky and beautifully puckered. He groaned before he could stop himself, and his hips lurched up off the bed.

"Fuck, yeah." He gritted his teeth, determined not to blow his load too soon. "Oh, God, baby, yeah, just like that."

Up and down she worked her compressed breasts, taking his full length. Her tits were so big that at one point, his cock was completely hidden, only for the shiny crown to emerge out the top, and then the naked vixen dipped her head and fucking lapped up the precum from the tip.

He was so fucking close.

Her ass was up in the air now, her body hunched over his waist, her stomach muscles tight as she used both her hands to keep her breasts pressed together. He had the absolute perfect view of her plump, glistening pussy lips and tight, hairless rosette.

With his fingers, he gathered her wetness and slipped back into her channel, fucking her with two fingers while pressing against her anus with his thumb. She churned and moaned as he felt her quiver around him.

"Fuck, Eva, you have no idea how amazing this feels."

Between the image of his dick sliding between her tits, his fingers disappearing into her cleft and her anus loosening and tightening with each press of his thumb, he was going to shoot his load like a fucking rocket any second.

"A bit faster, baby," he murmured, curling his fingers inside her pussy. She squeezed around him.

She picked up speed, fucking him quicker with her tits, the soft, cushiony velvet of them surrounding his cock feeling amazing. He fucked her pussy harder and faster with his fingers, mimicking her speed.

"Oh God, Scott ... " She moaned, her cadence faltering just a bit.

"Gonna come, Eva," he grunted, the need to shut his eyes and let the sensations take over at an all-out war with his desire to watch himself come all over her chest.

"Me too," she mewled.

He pressed a bit harder against her asshole with his thumb and on her G-spot with his fingers, and the woman detonated around him, her body shaking from the release as she continued to fuck him with her tits.

The squeezing of her walls around his fingers, the pouring of her sweet honey over his palm and the fact that when she came, she loosened enough for him to slip his thumb inside sent him over the edge.

And just like a rocket, he blasted off all over Eva's chest. His body stilled as the orgasm ripped through him from the center outward. Every thick, ropy spurt that landed across her bodacious mounds made him come just all the harder. She was on the way down from her own orgasm and hovered there in awe, her mouth open, eyes wide, watching as he covered her chest and neck in his hot, white seed.

But she didn't look the least bit disgusted.

In fact, she looked the opposite. Intrigued. Turned on. Excited.

Scott had never believed in love at first sight. That shit was garbage. But after the way Eva had just let him fuck her tits, and based on the way she was looking at him now, he was beginning to think that love at first tit-fuck was actually plausible.

5

Six weeks later ...

THE MOST OBNOXIOUS sound of vehicles beeping and backing up, men hollering and large truck doors slamming interrupted and then subsequently drowned out the pleasant chirp and warble of the robin just outside Scott's bedroom window.

What the fuck?

It was goddamn Sunday morning. Who the fuck was waking up the birds, let alone the neighbors?

Rubbing the sleep out of his eyes, he swung his legs over the side of the bed and shoved his feet into his black, thick-soled slippers.

Yeah, men could wear slippers and still be manly. The hardwood and tile in his house hurt his back otherwise. He was old, but he was still manly.

Scratching his balls and wrinkling his nose at his deflating half-chub, he wandered over to his bedroom window and opened the blinds.

The new neighbor next door was finally moving in and

appeared to be a hoarder, based on how much shit was being carted out of the massive moving truck.

Big, burly men with hams for arms and pot roasts for legs stalked up and down the ramp, in and out of the truck, unloading box after box. It seemed to be endless. His boredom won out first, and he let the drapes slide closed again as he scratched his ass and headed for the shower.

It'd been a particularly late poker night at his brother Liam's last night, and Scott had enjoyed himself a fair few whiskeys. Now his frontal lobe was paying for it, reminding him that he was not in fact a twenty-something bar stud who could down a forty and not feel it the next day but instead was a thirty-nine-year-old man with gray in his hair, his beard, his pubes, with a bad back and a preference for going to bed at a reasonable hour.

What was wrong with lights out at ten thirty? A perfectly respectable time to call it a night while getting a solid eight hours and waking up in time to enjoy the best part of the morning.

He opened the sliding glass door to the shower and turned on the water, leaving his hand beneath the spray until it turned warm, then he stepped inside.

He scrubbed his hand down his face and tilted his chin up so the water pelted him directly between the eyes. His head continued to throb.

But, like it did nearly every fucking time he took a shower now, his cock rose to attention and demanded action.

After that one night with Eva over six weeks ago, he hadn't been able to stop thinking about her. Particularly when he was in the shower. After she'd let him come all over her chest, the two of them had enjoyed a long, sexy, mind-blowing shower of their own, where she showed him just how talented, how perfect her mouth was, and he in return gave her more orgasms than she could count.

They'd fallen into bed laughing, both of them passing out, exhausted from all the endorphins and orgasms, only for Scott to wake up the next morning to an empty bed, an empty hotel room and not a phone number or note in sight.

Thankfully, she also hadn't robbed him. He still had his phone, wallet and keys. That was always the worry though, wasn't it? You think you can read people, only to be blindsided by beauty and tit-fucking and then wind up naked, gagged and without your money or your clothes as you writhe and scream on the bed because you're tied to the headboard.

It never happened to him, but it did happen to a friend—and Scott had been the one to find him. That image of his college roommate Steve still haunted him, particularly whenever he saw his buddy eat a plum or cherry tomato. *Shudder.*

But not Eva. She'd been perfect. And if it hadn't been for the emptiness he felt in his balls the next morning, he would have started to think she was all a glorious dream.

He'd gone so far as to ask the front desk for her phone number, email address or even a last name, but apparently, they had either been given explicit instructions not to give out her information or they were just assholes doing their jobs. Either way, he'd returned home with zilch.

Well, not zilch. He had his memories. And they were what fueled his fantasies. Eva's mouth, her tight pussy, her rocking tits, they were what he thought of, what he shut his eyes and envisioned as he gripped his fist around his cock and brought himself that small bit of relief.

Up and down he rubbed until a bead of precum emerged on the tip, only to get washed away by the pummeling water. His fist sped up as he remembered the pillowy softness of her breasts and the way they hugged his cock just right. And that tight little slit of hers. Jesus, fuck. He'd never have guessed in a million years that she'd had kids, she was so damn tight. Like a born-again virgin or some shit. He felt it all. Every pulse, every single contraction of her orgasm rippled around his cock, around his fingers as she came, spilling her sweet nectar over his tongue.

"Fuck," he ground out, squeezing his cock at the head only to drag his fist back down to the base. He was so fucking close. Squeezing his eyes shut tighter, he brought back the memory of Eva on her knees in the shower, dipping her head to take one of his balls in her mouth, sucking on it, licking it. She hadn't balked at a damn thing. She'd been eager and willing to explore and give just as much as he had. Then, rather than catching his cum, she'd pulled his cock out of her mouth and encouraged him to explode across her face—like a goddamn porno!

She'd lapped at the sensitive head of his cock as hot, ropy cum spurt from his crown and into her open mouth. She wore a big, beautiful smile on her face as she blinked through the water and stared up at him.

Yeah, that fucking did it.

Just like he had that night, Scott came hard. Only this time, instead of watching his cum decorate Eva, he watched it land on the shower floor and disappear down the drain. Far less appealing, not at all hot, but he worked with what he had, and that was the memory of Eva and her beautiful face covered in his cum.

Another five minutes, and he was scrubbed clean, turning off the shower and grabbing a dark gray towel from the rack.

More racket from outside and next door drew his attention to the window in the bathroom, and he peered out.

Well, hello!

That was not the ass of one of the moving men, no, it certainly was not.

She was bent over with her cheeks in the air, round and

full and perky, tucked up in a pair of dark green yoga pants, swiveling back and forth as if caught in the wind.

Jesus, fuck. His cock twitched beneath the towel.

Maybe he should take a wander over next door and go meet his new neighbor. Take her a plate of cookies or a casserole or something.

Who the fuck was he kidding? He'd never made a casserole in his goddamn life. Burgers? Yes, he was a pro. Steak? Nobody barbecued a better one. Ribs? You bet your ass his could win a blue ribbon. Even his mac and cheese was Michelin-star-worthy. But casserole? Fuck no.

A call from in the house caused the woman attached to the rocking ass to stand straight up. He couldn't tell what color her hair was. She had a baseball cap on, and her hair appeared to be in two braids over her shoulders. The glare of the sun made it impossible to see anything but sexy shadows. But what he could tell was that she also had a fucking awesome figure.

Curvy but fit, with a nice waist and hips he could really hold on to.

Was she going to turn around?

Voices from inside the house grew louder, and his new neighbor headed inside, showing him just how well she moved in those yoga pants.

Ah, fuck. Now he had another boner.

He needed to figure out how to make a casserole and go over and introduce himself, otherwise, he was going to be stuck inside all afternoon with his fist, lube and a box of tissues staring out the window—and that was just creepy.

AFTER ANOTHER QUICK round of self-abuse---not staring out the window—followed by coffee and a breakfast smoothie to

help combat the hangover, Scott was pulling on his own baseball cap and heading out the door to go and meet the new
neighbor. Of course, it would be just his luck that Ms. Green
Yoga Pants had a hunky mountain of muscle living with her
who got to peel her out of those tight yoga pants every night.

Either way, he needed to find out for himself. Maybe Mr.
and Mrs. Green Yoga Pants had kids Freddie's age, and they
could all play together. Lord knew the neighborhood needed
more young blood in it. He seemed to be surrounded by blue-
hairs. Septuagenarians to the left of him, octogenarians to the
right, there he was, stuck in the middle with a loud kid who
liked to ride his bike up and down the sidewalk until
bedtime. All while making the absolute noisiest fire-engine
sound he could.

But the new neighbor was moving into where Mr. Octogenarian had once lived. Only Mr. Octogenarian had finally
given up the good fight and moved into an assisted living
facility with his lady friend, Mrs. Sexagenarian. A big neighborhood scandal indeed. She was a whopping fourteen years
younger than him, still had her original hips and was
divorced, not widowed—or at least so said Edith the Septuagenarian on Scott's left.

Yeah, they needed some young blood in the neighborhood for sure. Not that Scott didn't like his neighbors,
because they were all lovely, kind older people; they were
just big gossips. Whether he was out for a run, collecting
the mail, raking leaves or taking Freddie out with his bike,
he was stopped by a neighbor from somewhere down the
road and given the full update on *everyone* in all the other
houses.

He could just imagine the talk down at the duck pond
about this new neighbor moving in. Every blue-hair on the
street would probably be by within the week to say hello and
offer their own bit of suburbia intel.

And if you start banging your neighbor, you'll only become part of that gossip.

Motherfucker. He hadn't thought of that.

You're also getting ahead of yourself. She's probably married.

Probably.

He turned the corner around the eight-foot-high cedar hedge that separated his yard from the neighbor's. The big moving truck took up one side of the driveway, while a white Toyota Sienna took up the other.

Hmm. A minivan.

The wheels of the soccer mom.

He walked around the moving truck, past the dropped ramp and glanced inside. A bright red and blue wooden toy box with the initials K and L on the front of it surrounded by painted pictures of trains, boats and airplanes sat stacked beneath a bunch of cardboard boxes.

The boxes were labeled. "Master bedroom." "Kids' room." "Kitchen."

Okay, so there were definitely kids moving in.

That was a plus.

How old?

Boys?

Girls?

It didn't much matter. Freddie made friends with everyone. But it would be nice for his son to find children similar to his age to play with. Katrin lived in a condo now, and there were no kids there. By the time Freddie came to stay with Scott, he was champing at the bit to run around the backyard.

Scott shoved his hands in his pockets and shuffled his feet in the driveaway covered in boxes and totes. The garage door was up, the inside full of boxes too.

Had he had this much shit when he moved in? It didn't feel like it.

He glanced into the open hatch of the minivan, with

beach buckets and shovels in a mesh bag, what appeared to be two boyish-looking children's bikes (not that that meant anything) and ... a weird-shaped sink? Black with a bizarre dip on one side.

Voices from the house and the open door had him spinning on his heel, the feeling of being caught ratcheting up his spine. Not that he was really doing anything wrong—besides being a bit nosy.

Damn it, the neighborhood was wearing off on him.

A woman with red hair up in a bun, black yoga pants and a pink tank top emerged from the house, her green eyes narrowing the moment she spotted him.

This was not the woman from earlier—she was still hot though. And she looked a hell of a lot like Eva—or was he just obsessed now and thinking every woman looked like her?

Scott waved like an idiot. "Hi, I'm your new neighbor." He stuck out his hand. "Welcome to the neighborhood. I just live next door." Like an even bigger idiot, he hooked the thumb of his free hand over his shoulder, should she not know where next door was.

Idiot.

Her look remained wary, but she took his hand. "Celeste. And this isn't my house. I'm just helping my sister move."

Oh, sister. Interesting.

"Eves!" Celeste called into the house. "Come meet your new neighbor." With a sly grin, she released Scott's hand and continued on toward the big moving truck.

"Huh?" The woman in the ball cap, white tank top and dark green yoga pants popped her head around the corner, her eyes bright, smile stunning, and breasts ... holy fuck! It was her!

Scott's cock jerked, his heart lurched, and he nearly tripped where he stood.

Her recognition of him was nearly as instant, but she didn't appear to be having the same kind of reaction.

"Eva!" he blurted out, taking a couple of steps toward her.

She tucked a stray strand of hair behind her ear and glanced down at her black, slip-on tennis shoes. "Hi, Scott."

"You're my new neighbor?"

She still hadn't looked at him. She toed at a rock on the driveway. "Looks that way, huh?"

"You never thought you'd see me again." This was all too bizarre. He had to find out why she'd left him the way she had. Why she'd snuck out of her own hotel room without even a goodbye, let alone her number.

Then again, she had been rather clear about it just being one night. She hadn't even given him her last name. She wanted to remain *Just Eva*. Had that been her plan all along? Sleep with him and then scram before the continental breakfast started?

"I ... " She lifted her gaze to his. "I just wanted one night for myself."

Right. "And now ... "

She blinked and shook her head, a small, demure smile tugging at one corner of her lips. "And now you're my neighbor, and the thought of *popping over for a cup of sugar* takes on an entirely new connotation." That demure smile filled out and tilted the other corner of her lips. "It's good to see you, Scott."

He exhaled. Thank fuck. That could have gone in an entirely different direction, and he was so glad it didn't. "It's so good to see you, Eva."

She eyed him beneath her ball cap. "You busy?"

For sex? Uh, no, he wasn't busy. He had, however, just jerked off twice this morning to thoughts of her though. Once when he knew it was her, the second time to her ass when he didn't know it was her.

He gave a quick mental check to his dick, twitched it and thought about boobs. It moved. He was good to go.

Phew.

With a smile he knew made the ladies swoon, he stepped toward her and tucked his finger beneath her chin. "For you, never."

She bit her lip and tilted her head up, gazing at him with a look that had filled his dreams and fantasies for the past six weeks. She reached out and wrapped a hand around his bicep, squeezing. He flexed, and her green eyes flared. "Do you wanna ... "

Fuck, he was practically salivating now. Panting like a dog staring at a ribeye left on the counter to rest.

"Absolutely."

She squeezed his bicep again. "Awesome, thank you. We can really use the extra set of hands. Boxes are labeled, but anything that isn't labeled can just go in the garage." Then she released his arm and skipped—yes, *skipped*—off toward the moving truck.

Scott's mouth dropped open, and he whipped around to gape at her. "You played me!"

She spun around but continued to walk backward, an enormous, gorgeous grin on her face. "I have no idea *what* you're talking about." Then she ducked into the moving truck, leaving Scott standing there in the driveway with a big, stupid smile on his face and a feeling he hadn't felt in a very long time heating up in his heart.

HOW THE HELL was it even possible?

He was hotter than when she'd met him six weeks ago. Sexier. More doablse than ever. And boy, oh boy, did she want to do him—again.

And again, and again, and again.

Unable to put her finger on it—though she really wanted to—Eva stared at the sexy line of Scott's beard-covered throat as he tipped back his mug of wine and took a long sip, a half-eaten slice of pizza in his other hand, poised in midair.

Pizza and wine in mugs—it seemed to be a recurring thing between them, if you could call doing something twice recurring.

His bicep flexed as he lifted his arm to take a bite of his pizza, and she was forced to bear down hard and repress her sudden urge to moan.

Had he been beefing up at the gym over the last few weeks? Was that it? He seemed *bigger*. More toned and bulked. She'd certainly caught herself more than once gawking at his muscles as he unloaded boxes and furniture all afternoon. And then when he got to work assembling her sons' beds and the cords in his forearms stood out, she nearly had an orgasm on the spot.

Whatever it was, be it bigger muscles, a fuller beard, shinier hair or just the fact that she'd missed him these last six weeks, Scott was one fine-looking man.

The movers were long gone, and Celeste had gone home to check on her fourteen-year-old daughter Sabrina, who'd been watching Lucas and Kellen all day. But Scott had stuck around. Apparently, he didn't get his son until Monday evening, so he "had all the time in the world" to help Eva unpack and assemble furniture.

They were sitting on her couch in the living room, surrounded by boxes, with all the lights on, the radio playing and a bottle of wine and box of pizza between them. She had no clue where her wineglasses were, so after opening a box marked *kitchen* and finding two Christmas mugs, she opened the bottle of wine she'd received from a client for doing their wedding makeup and poured them each a mug.

"So," Scott started, checking her out over the rim of his mug, "you going to tell me why you did a *wham, bam, thank you, sir?* Was it not good and you couldn't bring yourself to face me in the morning?" A sexy smirk tugged at one corner of his mouth.

Oh, he knew damn well that it had been good. Fuck, it'd been ten million times better than *good*. It'd been riveting. Earth-shattering, soul-claiming. Sex with Scott in that one night surpassed any and every other sexual experience she'd ever had. He had literally ruined her for any and all other men, and she'd spent the last six weeks kicking herself profusely for bailing on him without getting his number—or at the very least his last name.

"Hmm, *Just* Eva. Was it not up to your expectations?"

She rolled her eyes. "I'm sorry, okay? I just ... like I said, I just wanted one night for myself, and I thought that maybe it would be awkward in the morning."

He pursed his lips in an attempt not to smirk. "Or it could have been an incredible morning. *Wink, wink.*" He smiled that sinfully sexy smile that had won her over, that had made her strip naked and let him come all over her chest—and face.

"And it probably would have been. I'm sorry if I made you feel used. If I made you feel like a piece of meat."

And she was sorry. Sorry that she'd tortured herself with the memories of his tongue, fingers and cock this past month and a half rather than have access to the real things. One of her kids usually ended up in her bed in the middle of the night, so she couldn't even take matters into her own hands to satisfy the craving. She was dying here staring at the real deal, knowing all he was capable of.

But he didn't seem too put out and shrugged. "As long as you haven't suddenly become a vegan, I don't mind being treated like a piece of meat." His dark brown gaze turned avid and his smile diabolical. "But I'm no flank steak. I'm a porter-house, woman. Prime cut. Top choice. Straight from the plains of Texas." Then he mooed low and long before snorting like a bull and stomping his foot on the hardwood.

She tossed her head back and laughed. Damn, he was funny. And sweet, and a gentleman, and so freaking sexy. Her memory drifted back to his cock sliding in between her breasts—he was also a dirty, kinky bugger. But that only made her like him all the more. A multifaceted man with endless sides.

So long as all those sides were likable (unlike Todd, a charmer one minute, a demon the next), she could really see herself falling for Scott.

"Well," she started, "I happen to make a mean beef stew with a flank steak. It's all in how you treat your meat. Cook it slow and low. Until it's so tender and juicy it melts in your mouth."

That diabolical grin grew wider and even more sinister, which made the wine-drunk butterflies (because butterflies were notorious lightweights) take haphazard flight in her belly.

"There were a lot of innuendos piled in there," he said, his voice deadpan.

She stopped, thought about what she'd just said. Her brows lifted on her forehead. He was right. *Slow and low. How you treat your meat. Melts in your mouth. Tender and juicy.* She'd just served him a whole lot of dirty right there, when she'd really just been talking about making a stew.

Speaking of, she needed to find her slow cooker. Kellen loved her beef stew.

The song on the radio changed, and Scott's brows danced on his forehead before he set his mug down on a cardboard box labeled *living room crap*, crammed the last bite of pizza into his mouth and stood up. "Come on, *Just* Eva, let's dance."

He grabbed her hand and hauled her to her feet before she could protest, taking her to a more cleared-out area in front of the hearth and wrapping his arms around her, setting them off to a fun sway in time with the beat.

Laughing, because what else could she do, she began to dance with him. "You're nuts, you know that?" Her hands fell to his broad shoulders at the same time his leg wedged between hers.

That panty-dropping smile of his was now just inches from her mouth. "Nuts, fun, a great dancer, I'll take whatever compliment you're willing to throw my way. I'm easy." He scrunched up his face, bobbed his head and sang along with the chorus. "Besides, when the song literally tells you to *dance in the living room*, you have to listen."

"You know this is the Jonas Brothers, right?"

"So?" He shrugged. "I'm secure enough in my masculinity to enjoy a good Jo-Bro song when it comes on the radio. I'd dance to 'N Sync too, if 'Bye Bye Bye' came on. My little sister *loved* them. Same with BSB. Say what you will, but their shit is catchy."

"You have a sister?"

Hmm, what had Scott been like as a big brother? A bully? Overprotective? A best friend?

He pulled her closer at the same time he nodded. "I do have a sister. Bianca is two years younger than me, and my brother Liam is two years older. I'm the handsome, people-pleasing, well-adjusted, funniest middle child."

That made her laugh. Scott made her laugh a lot. "Well, you seem awfully well-adjusted to me."

"And handsome and funniest. You forgot those qualities." His feigned expression of being offended dissolved as soon as she began to play with the hair at the nape of his neck. His eyes semi-closed, and his head lolled back. "Oh, baby, you know just how to make this bull moo."

She snorted. "You're ridiculous."

The song over the radio ended, and then the DJ began to blather on about some liquidation sale at a furniture store in Auburn. Scott didn't pull away from her though. Didn't let go. If anything, he pulled her tighter against him, his playful gaze taking a serious turn. "I love your smile," he whispered, his wine and pizza breath once again something she ordinarily wouldn't have liked on another man, but something she had no qualms with when it was coming from Scott.

They stopped moving altogether but remained connected, remained touching. She swallowed hard and lifted her gaze from his super-sexy beard to his super-sexy eyes. "Scott ... "

"I like you, Eva," he murmured, pressing his lips to her temple. "I can be a piece of meat if that's what you need. I can be good neighbor who loans you his leaf blower or a cup a sugar ... or ... " His lips skimmed down her jaw. "I can be more."

She squeezed her eyes shut and tilted her head toward the ceiling, allowing his mouth greater access to her neck. His teeth raked across her throat to the sensitive hollow, where he swirled his tongue and then traced it across her exposed clavicle.

It'd be so easy to just let him guide her back to the couch, tear his shorts and T-shirt off and have her way with him. Straddle his waist and sink down until he filled her. But she couldn't ...

Could she?

A groan she had zero control over bubbled up from deep inside her chest as his tongue wended its way back up the side of her neck to just below her ear.

"Eva ... "

"Scott ... " She gripped the ends of his hair and pulled until he lifted his head. The look of lust in his eyes was all she needed, was all that was required for her to crush her mouth to his, pry his lips apart and kiss him like he held all the solutions to the world's problems.

His hands wrapped firmer around her waist until their bodies were pressed together, his arousal tucked tight against her thigh. He returned her kisses with a fervor she felt right down to her toes, taking over the kiss, leading her lips, her tongue, molding her body just the right way so that everything felt a million times better. And all from just a simple kiss.

Her hands fell from the nape of his neck to his chest, and she made to push him to the couch, have her way with him, feel even better than she already felt. This house was meant to be a new beginning in every way—why not christen it with a man who knew how to make her body hum?

But he didn't budge like she thought he would and instead he broke the kiss, pulling away and running his fingers through his hair. "Thank you for the pizza and wine, Eva, but I should get home." He headed toward the sliding glass door that led out onto the sundeck. "Welcome to the neighborhood." Then, just like that, he was gone. Out into the brisk April night, his footsteps on the wooden stairs down to the backyard echoing through the house.

And Eva just stood there, her eyes fixed to the closed door, mouth open, nipples hard, pussy throbbing.

He just left?

How could he just ... leave?

She glanced at the bottle of wine on the counter in the kitchen and headed for it, her brain a cloud of fuzzy confusion. Did Scott just turn her down?

She unscrewed the wine bottle and tipped it up to her lips just as there was knock at the door, causing her to choke on the wine in her throat and cough most of it up onto her white tank top.

Was it Todd?

She glanced around her box-filled kitchen for a weapon of some kind. Didn't the man know she had a restraining order against him? He was supposed to stay a minimum of five hundred feet away from her at all times. Celeste handled the hand-offs of Kellen and Lucas so Eva didn't have to even see her ex.

But coming here, to her new house when she was all by herself, was totally his MO.

Opening up a cardboard box, she found a big, heavy kitchen knife and made her way to the front door to peer through the peephole.

It most definitely wasn't Todd.

Setting the knife down on the hutch she'd found at a flea market and had chalk-painted last week. "Did you forget something?" she asked, flinging open the door to reveal a sexy, smiling Scott.

He nodded and looped his arm around her waist, hauling her against him. "Yeah, this." He crushed his mouth to hers and kissed her even more wildly, more passionately than before, stealing the breath clean from her lungs and turning her legs to jelly.

When they finally came up for air, she was lightheaded and more turned on than ever.

"I'll be whatever you want me to be, Eva, but just know that if I had *my* way, I'd be *more*. I'm going to give you time to think. One night with no names, no expectations is one thing, but we're neighbors now. You need to really think about what it is you want." He swiped his thumb over her bottom lip. "Let me know if you need anything. I'm *right* next door." Then he kissed her again, once, closed-mouthed but no less fierce, only to release her—against her will—and head down the path to the driveway, disappearing into the night and around the hedge that separated their houses.

She was about to close the door when she heard a faint but very distinct *moo* from just beyond the hedge, followed by, "Goodnight, *Just* Eva."

Laughing and smiling a smile that hurt her face, she shut the door and leaned back against it, her heart thundering, her pulse racing and her hope for the future seeming brighter than it had in a very long while.

6

SCOTT TOSSED on his sunglasses as he locked the door to his red Toyota Tacoma and headed toward his office building. Dynamic Creative Marketing and Advertising was located in downtown Seattle, not three blocks from Pike Place Market, with its fish-tossing mongers and kitschy shops. He could walk to all the best food trucks and restaurants for lunch, as well as his buddy Mason's sports bar for an after-shift drink.

He'd been at Dynamic Creative for two months now and, so far, had loved every single minute of it. Even though he applied for the vacant COO position and was more than qualified for it, the man in charge of hiring—Remy Barker— didn't think Scott was right for that position and offered him the senior marketing consultant position instead.

Scott hadn't been pleased at first, since Remy was a good fifteen or so years younger than him and had clearly earned his position through nepotism, but Scott took the job anyway. Dynamic Creative was *the* leading advertising and marketing firm in the city—possibly the state—and he wanted his foot in the door no matter what.

So even though he wasn't one of the top dogs running

things, he was still in charge of a shitload. On day one, he was assigned his own team and given a snazzy corner office with a view of the Ferris wheel on the water. Not *too* shabby, but he'd have preferred the fancy letters behind his name too and the salary to go along with it.

He knew he had a bit of a strut when he entered the building, but so fucking what? He was happy. He had a sexy new neighbor, he'd rubbed one out that morning, and he was starting another great week at his awesome job.

What better way to start a Monday than that?

Tapping his fingers on Sondra's desk as he entered the office, he smiled at the grandmotherly receptionist and asked her about her weekend.

"It was great, hon, thanks. And yours?"

He couldn't keep the cocky grin from his face if he tried. "It was awesome, thanks."

"Your nine o'clock appointment is waiting for you in your office, Mr. Dixon," Sondra went on. "I grabbed him a coffee." She handed Scott his messages.

Right! Mr. Fletcher, the whale of a client that Remy wanted Scott to land. Finally, Mr. Fletcher had agreed to take Scott's call, and the two had spoken on the phone for only a brief five minutes, but those five minutes seemed to be enough, and the man agreed to come in and have a proper meeting with Scott. Hear his pitch and find out just what Scott and his team could really do for Fletcher Holdings.

And Fletcher Holdings held *a lot*. Nightclubs, strip clubs, lounges, vape shops, and a few casinos outside city limits. He seemed to have his hand in over a dozen pies, but the newest confection he'd gotten involved with was a distillery, and Dynamic Creative wanted a piece of that pie. They wanted to help Mr. Fletcher bring Fletcher Spirits to the masses.

Sondra wished him luck and handed him his mug of

coffee—just like she did every morning—and he headed toward his office, whistling.

Yes, today was a day to whistle.

He was about to land this VIP client with the pitch of a lifetime, and hopefully before the week was over, Eva would be coming over for a *cup of sugar*—or more.

"Mr. Fletcher," he started, stepping into his office, where a man in a dark suit with dark hair sat with his back to Scott. The man stood up and turned around. "I'm Scott Dixon. So nice to meet you. Thank you very much for coming in today." He offered his hand.

"Please, call me Todd." His smile encompassed his entire face, and his eyes became laser focused. He shook Scott's hand, his grip firm, almost too firm, as if he were trying to establish some kind of dominance. It sent a frisson of unease racing to the base of Scott's skull, but he chalked it up to the client simply trying to make sure Scott knew who was in charge. He braced himself for a bit of a pissing match. That always seemed to be the way when the whale was an alpha asshole who was used to bossing people around.

Well, so was Scott, and soon Mr. Todd Fletcher would realize just *who* was running this show. And it wasn't him.

Todd's smile was wily, almost too big to be real. "It was the least I could do after your quick phone pitch. I definitely want to hear more. Sounds like you and your team could make me a buttload of money."

Scott chuckled as he released Todd's hand and continued on into the office and around to his desk. "That's the plan. Making you a buttload of money makes us a buttload of money, so we're in for a win-win here."

They both took their seats, smiling. Todd sipped his coffee and inclined his head toward the photo of Freddie that sat on the windowsill. "That your boy?"

Scott took a sip of his own coffee. "Sure is. Freddie. Hell of a kid."

"Got two sons of my own, lights of my life."

"Kids are great, aren't they? Keep you feeling young. Until you wrestle with them, then the next morning as you struggle to get your ass out of bed and you feel twenty years older."

Todd's pale ice-blue eyes didn't crinkle at the sides or sparkle, but he laughed. "So true." He cleared his throat, his face turning serious, thick brows narrowing. "I'm a busy man, Scott, so let's get down to brass tacks. What can you and your team do for Fletcher Holdings that no other marketing team can?"

Scott planted both hands on his chrome desk and grinned. "Well, Todd, I'm glad you asked." Then he proceeded to wow the man with each and every one of his plans until Todd's socks were so far knocked off, they were clear across the room.

"READY TO GO, BUDDY?" Scott asked as he swung Freddie's Ironman backpack over his shoulder and helped his son into his sweater. "Did you have a good day?"

Freddie nodded as he took Scott's hand, and they headed out of the classroom where after-school care was held. He yawned wide, tilting his head back, which made his poker-straight strawberry-blond hair flop back. "Yeah, it was a good day, Dad, but I missed you."

"I missed you too, pal." They continued on out of the school and into the parking lot. "What did you and your mom get up to this weekend?"

Freddie's mouth dipped into a small pout. "She was busy with work, so I spent a lot of time with Grandma and Grandpa."

Irritation itched along Scott's arms. Not that Scott begrudged his son spending time with his maternal grandparents, but what bothered him was how often Katrin used her parents as a babysitting service when she had Freddie. Whether she left for a work thing or to go out on a date, Freddie was with his grandparents a lot. And all Freddie said he ever did with his grandparents when they had him was watch the news while he helped his grandfather roll cigarettes.

The first time Scott heard that, he'd nearly blown a gasket. He drove right over to the Davids' house and asked if they were smoking in the same space as his son. Both Dennis and Barb smoked like chimneys, so the house smelled like cigarettes—that was one thing—however, if they smoked around his son, Scott would make sure they never fucking saw him again.

Dennis and Barb swore up, down and sideways that they never smoked around Freddie, that Freddie just liked helping his grandfather roll his smokes. What else could he do besides put the fear of God into them and then make sure he and his son had an honest relationship and Freddie told him the truth about whether Dennis and Barb smoked around him? Oh, and bathe Freddie like he'd just wrestled a bunch of pigs after he came home smelling like an ashtray.

As he helped Freddie climb into the back seat of his truck, he bent down and sniffed his son's hair and clothes.

Fuck, he stunk. He was going to have to not only scrub every square inch of his kid in the bath tonight but also wash all his clothes, including his backpack and coat. You'd think his ex-wife would think to do that before she sent Freddie to school on Monday, but noooo. Not Katrin. How dare she consider anybody else—including her child—and how he might smell all day?

He made sure Freddie was all buckled in, double-checked

the seat belt and then pecked his son on the forehead. "I really did miss you, bud. House feels so empty and quiet without you."

Freddie grinned. "I missed you too, Dad. I'd rather just live with you all the days instead of spending some days with you and some days with Mom. We have more fun."

This was always the narrative when he picked Freddie up on Mondays and then when he dropped Freddie off at school Monday morning the following week, before his week with his mother started. He often cried when Scott dropped him off, clinging to his leg. It damn near ripped Scott's heart out each and every time.

The lawyers had advised him and Katrin to do a week on/week off custody arrangement, said it was easier on children with fewer transitions. And they had been right. When they divorced three years ago, Freddie got into the routine pretty quickly, and Scott's week with his son was awesome. Only now, since Freddie started kindergarten in September, he was showing signs of not wanting to be away from Scott for a full seven days, and his reluctance to go with his mother was becoming more vocal.

Liam, his brother and lawyer, had advised him to keep the arrangement as it was for now, until Freddie was bit older and the transition of starting school wore off. Most likely, Freddie was simply having a tough time adjusting to school and after-school care, and his angst was coming out in a resistance to being with Katrin. At least that's what Scott hoped was the case. He promised Liam he'd give Freddie a year to acclimatize to school, but if his kid was still resisting going to his mother's by the following September, Scott was going to revisit the custody agreement and see about getting Freddie full-time. No way should his kid be miserable if he didn't have to be.

"What's for dinner, Dad? I'm starving," Freddie asked as

Scott climbed in behind the steering wheel of his truck and turned on the engine.

"How does homemade mac and cheese sound with cut-up veggies on the side?" Freddie wasn't the most adventurous eater, but he also wasn't as picky as some kids. Like Scott, the kid enjoyed comfort food—meatloaf and mashed potatoes, mac and cheese, tomato soup and grilled cheese, beef stew, spaghetti. All the things that filled you up and made your mouth happy.

"Sounds good. With ranch dip for the veggies?" Freddie asked on another yawn.

"You know it, pal."

It was only a short drive from the school to Scott's house, and they were there in no time. Freddie hit the button to roll down his window. "Hey, looks like we have new neighbors."

Scott's head swung from the road to Eva's house, where sure enough, she and two little boys were hauling boxes from the back of her minivan to the front door. She looked like fucking perfection in brick-colored yoga pants, a dark gray hoodie and long red ponytail. Was there anything she didn't look like dynamite in?

"We do," he said, rolling his tongue back into his mouth. "I met the mom, and she seems very nice. Her sons are five and seven."

"That's older and younger than me," Freddie said with excitement. "Can we go over and meet them? Can we?" He was bouncing up and down in his booster seat, his tangible fatigue from a moment ago seeming to have vanished. "Maybe they can come over for dinner?"

"I don't know, buddy. They're probably still busy moving in." Scott turned in to his driveway and parked the truck. Freddie was out of his seat belt and opening the door before Scott even made it out of his own door.

"I'm going to say *hi*," Freddie said, leaping to the pavement and booking it down the driveaway and around the hedge. Thankfully there was about a six-foot span of grass between the hedge and the sidewalk, and then there was a bike lane between the sidewalk and the actual road, so Scott wasn't too worried about his kid getting hit by a car.

He was, however, worried about his kid just barging into somebody's house and making himself at home. Freddie was a very friendly kid by nature and had no qualms inviting himself somewhere if it was where he wanted to be.

"Freddie!" Scott called after his son, exhaling deep through his nose as he followed the path his son had taken down the driveaway and around the hedge.

He heard his son's chipper voice before he saw her face, a mask of amusement making her all the more beautiful. "Hi, I'm Freddie. A really old man used to live in this house before you. But don't worry, he didn't die in there. He just went to an *old forks* home."

Eva snorted before she smiled. "Well, it's *so* nice to meet you, Freddie. This is Kellen"—she rested her hand on the younger little boy's shoulder—"and this is Lucas."

All the boys waved at each other.

Her green eyes flicked up to Scott's, her grin as gorgeous as ever. "Good to know that nobody died in our house."

Scott shoved his hands in his pockets and rocked back on his heels. "I'm surprised you hadn't already been filled in about the previous owner from half the block. Are they leaving you alone?"

She scoffed. "Oh heck no. I had six women on my doorstep with cookies and gossip when I drove into the driveway after dropping the kids off at school. Then another three flitted in over the day as I was unpacking. I know *everything* about *everyone* now."

He bet she did. The whole street was already probably talking about Scott hanging out at Eva's last night. Old Ruthie across the street was a night owl and kept her drapes open twenty-four seven. She saw everything that happened around her and didn't go to sleep until well past midnight. As she was watching television, she probably saw Scott sneak back to his place.

Yeah, they were most likely the talk of the neighborhood now.

"You guys want to come over for dinner?" Freddie asked, eyeing the soccer ball under Lucas's arm. "We can play soccer in my backyard while my dad makes dinner. We're having mac and cheese." He glanced up at his dad but then back at the other little boys. "With *three* cheeses." He held his fingers up to show three. "Not just one. But *three*. Cheddar, havarti and ... " He scrunched up his nose in thought. "Dad, what's the other cheese?"

"Gouda, buddy."

Freddie nodded. "Right, gouda. It's gourmet."

Eva and Scott both hid their smiles by glancing away.

"Can we, Mom?" Kellen asked first. "I loooove mac and cheese. And you said that we were just going to have tuna on toast for dinner because you spent the whole day unpacking and haven't been shopping. Mac and cheese with *three* cheeses sounds way better."

"Yeah, I wasn't looking forward to tuna on toast," Lucas added. "I'd eat it, but I wasn't excited about it."

Heat blossomed in her cheeks as she lovingly gazed down at her children. "Guys, I promise to get some groceries tomorrow. Today just got away from me, what with all the unexpected guests. But we can't invite ourselves over for dinner ... "

"You're not," Freddie cut in. "I invited you." He glanced back up at Scott. "Right, Dad? They can come. You always make so much anyway."

Well, it was no cup of sugar, but it was something. With a

grin he knew would make her flush even redder, he rested his hand on his son's shoulder and fixed Eva with a smoldering look. "We'd love to have the new neighbors over for dinner. Welcome you to the neighborhood *properly*."

And oh, fuck, did he ever get what he wanted. Her complexion pinked up so nicely, and her lashes fluttered as she fought to hide her smile. Her sexy throat bobbed on a swallow before she lifted her gaze to his. "Well, thank you. We'd love to join you for dinner."

All three little boys cheered, disengaging themselves from their parents' grasps.

"Great!" Freddie cheered. "Come on. I'll show you my backyard. We have a soccer net. I can be goalie first if you guys want to take shots on me."

Kellen and Lucas nodded and took off after a running Freddie, down their driveway and around the hedge, the sound of their shoes slapping the concrete with each heavy step echoing from Scott's yard.

Then there they stood, in Eva's driveway, staring at each other.

"I'm, uh ... I'm just going to finish putting these boxes inside, and then I'll ... " She nibbled on her lip.

"Come over for dinner?" he said, finishing her sentence for her.

A lopsided smile curved her lips as she bent down to pick up a box that Kellen had left. "Yes. I'll come over to your house for dinner."

Fuck, he loved it when she got all flustered. "Great! Then I'll head home and get going on dinner. Just let yourself in when you've finished over here."

All she could do was nod, which only made him smile even wider.

He turned to go but then spun back around. "Oh, and Eva, just because it's meat-free Monday doesn't mean we've gone vegan." Then he mooed like he had last night and continued on up her driveway, wanting desperately to turn around and see her reaction but knowing that it probably made a better statement not to.

Damn, he forgot how much he liked the chase. Liked the flirting and wooing. How much it turned him on to win a woman over with his charm and his wit. He'd been out of the game for so long, he forgot how much he enjoyed it. And the way Eva reacted to him made it all the better. So responsive, so beautiful, and he was only just getting started.

7

EVA BLINKED HALF a dozen times and shook herself both physically and mentally as she stood in Scott's kitchen and cut up cucumbers and bell peppers on his bamboo cutting board. It was surreal. Completely and utterly surreal.

Six weeks ago, she'd been on her knees in the shower with Scott above her, his fist wrapped around her wet hair, his other hand cupping her cheek, and now, she was in his kitchen, cutting up vegetables for her sons and his son while he stood over the stove and stirred homemade three-cheese sauce into boiled penne.

It was domestic and wonderful with a man she hardly knew but found deliriously sexy, and it was throwing her for a serious loop.

She had no plans to start dating and certainly no plans to introduce any new man into the boys' lives, and yet there she was having a date or whatever this was with a new man who had already met her kids.

Even though nothing was going according to plan, she was really, really happy. And the view of Scott's back, his butt and his arms as he stood over the stove wasn't too bad either.

Was it really going to be this easy with him? With their kids? The first guy she met—the first guy she slept with after her divorce from Todd—turned out to be Mr. Right. And then he wasn't just Mr. Right, he was Mr. Right-Next-Door. And his kid got along with her kids—so far. Was it *really* that easy? Or was it a too good to be true kind of thing, and he had a sex-dungeon-style bunker hidden beneath the shed in his back-yard. Was she dropping her guard down too much? Or just enough?

She liked Scott, and even though things were complicated and messy in her world now, she somehow got the feeling that he didn't mind messy or complicated as long as he was considered and respected. And she felt the exact same way. Todd had never shown her the respect she deserved—not only as his wife, but as a woman, as a person. In the small amount of time she'd spent with Scott, he'd already shown her far more respect than Todd had in the ten years they were together.

Continuing to slice the cucumber, she let out a long, exhausted sigh.

Why did life have to be so damn confusing?

"Tired, Eva?" He swung her a glance over his shoulder, and the grin that accompanied the twinkle in his distract-ingly beauiful brown eyes made her insides liquefy and the knife on the cucumber slip and nearly take off her fingertip.

"Don't look at me like that," she scolded.

He managed to appear surprised. "Like what?"

"Like you've seen me naked. Don't let my kids catch you looking at me like that."

If it were possible, his smile grew even sexier beneath that irresistible beard. "But I *have* seen you naked. In fact, I can see you naked whenever I want."

Like his window looked into her window?

Creepy.

He turned around from the stove to face her, still smiling. "All I have to do is close my eyes." He shut his eyes. "I'm seeing you naked right now. In that position, you know the one, where your legs were thrown up over my shoulders and I was—"

"Hey!"

His eyes flashed open, the smile still devious, still enigmatic. Then he closed those baby browns again. "Oh, now you're naked, on your knees in the shower, and I'm just about to—"

"Scott!" Heat flooded her cheeks, but the pain that it took her to keep her smile at bay caused an ache to pulse in her jaw. Her lips twisted at the same time her stomach did a somersault.

He shrugged before turning back to the stove. "I'm just saying, I have a *great* memory and an even better imagination."

The man was incorrigible.

And funny.

And kind.

Don't forget sexy as hell and fan-fucking-tastic in bed.

She sighed again, rolled her eyes and continued cutting up the vegetables.

"So, when am I going to get to take you out on a proper date?" he asked, not bothering to turn back around. He stepped to the side and opening up a cupboard to grab some bowls. "I meant what I said before. If you want this to be casual and meaningless, I can do that. But something tells me you're not really into that." He tossed another look over his shoulder at her, pinning her with a heated gaze, and for some reason, the slight crook to his nose made him look dangerously handsome at the moment. "At least not for the long term," he finished. "You want more."

Gulp.

"And I would like to be more." He began scooping the mac and cheese into the bowls. "I would like to be a lot more. *Do* a lot more—with you." With two filled bowls, he turned around and made his way toward the kitchen table, but before he got there, he stopped just behind her. "Do you want *more*, Eva?" His warm breath against her neck had her fighting the urge to shiver. But she couldn't shiver. A reaction like that would only feed into his game. She wanted to make him work for it.

Whatever *it* was.

"Hmm, Eva. *Just* Eva. Do you want more?"

Hell, yes, she wanted more. She wanted all of it.

She gulped again.

"I want more, Scott," she whispered, not ready to turn around.

She didn't have to see him to know he was smiling. Warm lips landed on her neck, and she lost the battle with her urges and allowed her eyes to flutter shut.

"We'll start slow," he murmured, peppering more kisses along the back of her shoulders to the other side of her neck. "First, tell me your last name, your favorite color, and one secret about yourself hardly anyone else knows. Then we'll decide how much *more* we can handle."

"Marchand," she breathed. "Eva Danielle Marchand. I went back to my maiden name."

"Eva Marchand. Very French." His tongue danced just below her ear. "I like it."

"Green. Like the trees and the grass and all the plants. It's the color of Earth, of life, of all things new."

"And the color of your amazing eyes."

The warmth of him behind her had her entire body blushing. Need pooled in her belly, and a rush of wetness coated her panties. She was practically breathless, yet she hadn't moved an inch.

"When I was fourteen, I skipped school, caught the bus to Olympia and went to listen to Allison DeWitt speak at the library." She hadn't told a soul—besides Celeste—that she'd done that. Allison DeWitt was her all-time favorite author, and of course, she was speaking at a library on a school day and Eva's parents had to work, so how could she go?

Well, she made it happen. She even got Allison's autograph and, with her old Polaroid camera, a picture of her with the famous fantasy author. That picture still sat in her jewelry box—a reminder of when she had guts—when she went after what she wanted, no matter the cost.

Todd had eviscerated those guts, had destroyed her tenacity and drive.

But she was getting it all back. It wouldn't come overnight, but since leaving him, since filing for the restraining order, since filing for divorce and moving out on her own with the kids, she felt a million times stronger. She would be that school-skipping, tenacious woman again one day. She just had to give herself time.

"I love her books." Scott's voice was just a whisper against her heated skin. "Particularly the Sapphire Omen Series."

She spun around.

Scott backed up and lifted his hands in the air, the bowls of mac and cheese still in his grasp. His mouth opened in surprise, and his brows shot up into his hairline. "Whoa, whoa! Did I say something wrong?"

She glanced to where his eyes kept darting. She still had the big chopping knife in her hand.

Whoops!

Giggling awkwardly, she gently set it down on the counter, then faced him again. "Sorry. I was just so surprised to hear that someone else likes Allison DeWitt books."

He dropped his hands, and his face relaxed. Then he went about setting the bowls down on the table, only to return to the stove and begin dishing up more. "Are you kidding me? I'm a *huge* fan. Have been since I was a teenager. I live for her books. I can't believe you saw her speak. I tried to go see her last time she was in Seattle, but Katrin ... " He turned back around with two more steaming bowls. "Anyway, I *tried* to go see her, but apparently my wants aren't a real thing." His words were just as tight as his body language.

"I love that you love her books," Eva went on, piling all the chopped veggies onto a plate, then carrying them over to the table. "What's your favorite of hers?"

"Would have to be *Indigo Sacrifice* in the Sapphire Omen Series. Yours?"

She grinned. "Same."

"Well, then, we'll have *loads* to talk about on our date, won't we? Have you pre-ordered her new book?"

Biting her lip, she nodded. "I have."

He set the bowls on the table, then returned once more to the oven. "You still haven't answered my first question though."

"Which was?"

He approached her with the final bowl of heaping mac and cheese. "When are you going to let me take you out on a proper date?"

Butterflies took flight in her belly from the way he was looking at her—heated, dangerous, demanding. All things that normally would have been huge triggers for her, but from Scott, not so much. If anything, she was intrigued rather than ready to flee. Enticed, not turned off. Aroused not repulsed.

They were toe to toe now, the feel of his warm body invading her personal space enough to make her brain grow a little fuzzy. Reaching behind her, he placed the bowl on the table, but he didn't pull his hand away. He let it rest on her hip, and he tugged her into his body until there wasn't even room for air between them.

"Our brains are wired for connection," he said softly, bringing his other hand up next to her face and tucking a stray strand behind her ear. She closed her eyes at the welcome gentleness of his touch. "Our brains are wired for connection. As humans, we actively seek other humans. We seek intimacy and relationships. Partners." His large, warm palm cupped her cheek, and he tilted his head down until they were nose to nose. "But trauma rewires our brains for protection. We become guarded and wary, always fearful of more pain, more heartache."

Her chest lifted and fell at an alarming rate, and her eyes flew open, but what stared back at her didn't scare her an ounce. What gazed down at her, so close she was going cross-eyed, was an intense understanding. Patience and kindness. An ache formed inside her chest at the rush of emotions she felt for this man—a man she hardly knew.

"I know that it can be tough for wounded people to have healthy, meaningful relationships, but I want you to know, Eva, I have no intention of hurting you. We can take this as fast or as slow as you need to. You're setting the pace, not me."

A stuttered breath rattled past her parted lips, hitting his mouth. He breathed her in.

"How did you break your nose?" she whispered, needing to lighten the mood, take it down a couple of notches, slow things down. This was a pace she wasn't ready for. She was feeling things she shouldn't—not yet—and if she let her heart and libido drive the bus, she was going to end up in Scott's bed before the week was out.

No, she needed her brain to drive. Her brain knew the speed limit. Her brain knew when she should yield, accelerate or toss on the e-brake.

"Football," he murmured, not pulling away from her even an inch. "I was a running back in high school."

"Looks like you broke it more than once."

"Three times, actually. First time was in football. Other two times, my smart mouth got me into some trouble."

"All in high school?"

He grinned. "I've grown up a lot since then."

Yeah, he had. He was *all* man now.

The sound of boys chatting outside drew near, and within a couple of seconds, a door opened.

Scott pulled away from her but with obvious reluctance—she felt it too—and wandered back into the kitchen to begin pouring everyone water.

Moments later, three rosy-cheeked little boys entered the kitchen, all of them smiling, with windswept hair and dirt and grass stains on their clothes.

"I'm hungry," Freddie said. "Is dinner ready yet?"

"It is," Scott replied. "Can you three run and wash your hands, though, please?"

"I'll show you where the bathroom is," Freddie said, taking off at a run down the hallway. "We have a stool you can use, Kellen. You're short, like me. Lucas, you might not need one, as you're seven." Then, like sweaty little monsters with grumbling bellies, they disappeared around the corner.

Scott's gaze flew up to hers.

She shuffled where she stood and dipped her head, the power of his light brown eyes stripping her bare, until all that was left of her was the insatiable need to leap up into his arms and crush his mouth with hers.

"Let me know when you're free," he murmured, managing to carry all five drinking glasses over to the table at once. "I want to date you, Eva."

I want to date you, Eva.

Prickles ran laps along her arms. Fuck, she loved the way

he said her name. It shot fireworks through her and made goosebumps explode along her skin. The way he dragged his teeth over his bottom lip—was he doing it on purpose?

"Monday?"

His eyes lit up. "Next week?"

She nodded. "Didn't you know that Allison DeWitt is going to be in town for a signing?"

His bottom lip dropped open, and he shook his head. "How the fuck did I miss that?"

She lifted one shoulder. "I actually have an extra ticket to the event. I was going to see if Celeste wanted to go with me and Sabrina could babysit, but Celeste isn't really into her books—"

He grabbed the back of her head and captured her gasp with his lips. It was quick, it was chaste, but it was hot. "I'm going to fucking marry you, woman," he breathed, releasing her just in time before the boys came barreling back into the room.

She swallowed and blinked, watching him step away.

I'm going to fucking marry you, woman.

"And, yes, I would love to go to the book signing with you," he said, pulling out Freddie's chair for him. "It's a date," he mouthed.

It's a date.

8

"YOU'RE LATE," Liam murmured before he lifted his single-malt scotch to his lips and took a sip. "I don't like waiting."

Scott flipped his older brother the finger as he sat down between Adam and Atlas at the poker table, his cards face-down in front of him. "Sorry. Freddie couldn't find Mr. Timothy Goat."

"Who the fuck is Mr. Timothy Goat?" Aaron grunted, shifting in his seat. For once, the retired SEAL's dog tags were out of his tight green T-shirt, rather than tucked beneath them. Made him appear ten times more intimidating. Not that the redheaded, tattooed beast of a man wasn't already intimidating enough.

"He's Freddie's stuffed animal—a big fluffy orange goat. He can't sleep without him."

"Where was he?" Liam asked, already seeming to have lost his irritation and now appearing genuinely curious. Liam loved Freddie, and Freddie loved his Uncle Liam. Scott knew the moment he told his brother the reason for his tardiness was kid-related that Liam would shrug it off. Just like Scott, Liam lived for his child.

"Tangled up in his pajamas, from when he peeled them off this morning," Scott said, rolling his eyes.

His brother snorted, his dark brown eyes crinkling and laughing before his mouth split into a big grin. "Kids."

"We gonna fuckin' play or what?" Atlas grumbled, his blond head down, gray eyes serious. "Motherfuckers do nothing but gab."

Liam rolled his eyes. "Yes, we're going to play. Calm your fucking self. Nuts twisted or something? Jesus." He shot his fellow law partner a glare before facing the rest of the table, rubbing his hands together. "Let's play some poker."

Atlas turned over the first community card.

Scott scanned the table for tells.

Adam shifted in his seat like he usually did when he had a crappy hand.

Aaron scratched his nose, sniffed and then cracked his neck side to side three times, which meant his hand had potential.

Mason, Scott's good friend and single dad to baby Willow, yawned and squeezed his eyes shut. That usually meant he was packing pairs. The jackass.

Mark cleared his throat, Emmett sipped his beer twice without setting the bottle down, and Zak's dark red brows furrowed. They still needed more cards. His gaze shifted to his big brother. Liam was the wild card in the bunch. Even though Scott had known the man his entire life, shared a room with him for sixteen of those years and then saw his brother at least once a week for the past twenty-three years, Liam had an incredible poker face.

Maybe that was why he was a kickass attorney with an impeccable track record. Nobody could read him—therefore nobody knew whether he was bluffing or not. An essential tool when trying to leverage for your clients.

Liam swirled the scotch around in his glass, flicked his gaze to his cards, then the community card, then set his cards facedown on the table before he tossed two chips into the center. "I'm in."

Around the table, all the men placed their bets.

"Mom says you have new neighbors," Liam said. "More blue hairs?"

On Saturday nights, both Liam and Scott dropped their sons off for a sleepover with their parents. Jordie and Freddie were close in age and very close friends, in addition to being cousins. Liam and Scott's parents, Addie and Ralph Dixon, loved having the boys stay the night and usually spoiled them rotten.

"New neighbors?" Mason asked. "You didn't mention that last Friday when you were at the bar." On the weeks he didn't have Freddie, Scott spent Friday nights at Mason's sports bar, keeping his friend company, drinking free beer and watching the hockey game on the high-end big screen above the bar.

Scott lifted his shoulder. "Didn't have the neighbors then. They just moved in on Monday."

"Blue hairs?" Liam asked again. He often made fun of Scott and the neighborhood he lived in, with its geriatric population and all the gossip. Particularly since Liam lived on Lake Washington and rubbed proverbial shoulders with the upper echelon of Seattle's elite.

Scott shook his head. "Nope. Mom and two young boys, five and seven."

Eyes flared and brows rose around the table.

"Single mom?" Emmett asked. He'd landed his own single mom earlier that year, falling for the wonderful and beautiful Zara at a New Year's Eve party Scott had attended as well.

He nodded. "Yeah. "

Emmett's mouth formed an *O*, and he nodded.

"She hot?" Zak asked.

Fucking smokin'.

He nodded again. "Yeah."

Heads bobbed around their little trust circle, and the odd *nice* was murmured.

"Going out on Monday," he said with a mouth full of pretzels. "She scored tickets to the Allison DeWitt signing."

Everyone but Liam gave him a confused lip curl or brow raise.

"Well, now you *have* to marry this chick. If she's into that weirdo fantasy fiction like you, you can't fuck this up."

"This coming from the born-again bachelor, anti-love cynic?" Mason asked, his expression just as surprised as the rest of them as he lasered his focus in on Liam.

Liam lifted one shoulder. "I'm not saying their marriage will *last*. But Katrin thought those fantasy books were garbage —because they are—but if he can find someone who not only puts up with his geeky obsession but also takes part in it, well, then who am I to dismiss a temporary happily ever after?"

"You're a dick," Scott muttered to his older brother.

Liam shrugged again. "Perhaps, but I'm also rarely wrong. Marry her and have a blissful, geeky five to seven years. Then I'll represent you in the divorce and help you move out of that septuagenarian borough you and my nephew are living in."

"You're still a dick," Scott bit back, making sure his glare was extra fierce. Liam seemed neither fazed nor apologetic. In fact, he seemed a bit bored.

"Moving on," Atlas grunted. "Let's play some fucking poker. "

"Agreed." Mark nodded.

Adam fished his phone out of his back pocket, and his

thumb began to fly across the screen. "But first, *baby photos.*" He held up the screen of his phone, where a three-week-old baby Brielle was snoozing peacefully in her bassinet while Adam's daughter Mira and Mitch's daughter Jayda stood beside it with enormous grins.

"How are the girls handling having a new little sister slash cousin around?" Scott asked, grateful for the change of subject but also curious about how Mira, who spent half her time with Adam and Violet and the other half of her time with Mitch and Paige, was handling a new baby sister. Jayda was Brielle's cousin, so there probably wasn't as much jealousy involved—at least he assumed.

"They're handling it well," Adam said through a yawn. "Mira loves her sister. Almost a little *too* much. We keep having to say 'gentle with the baby,' otherwise we might have an *Of Mice and Men* situation on our hands."

"So no jealousy?" Atlas asked, his long fingers drumming nervously on the table.

Adam and Mitch shook their heads. "None so far," they both said.

Atlas hummed.

"Aria struggling with having Cecily in the house?" Scott asked Atlas.

One curt nod was all they got from the steely-eyed blond man.

"Fuck, that's hard," Zak muttered. His brows furrowed for a moment before he leaned his broad frame over and dug his phone out of his back pocket. "During the divorce, we sent Aiden to an art therapist here in the city. She worked miracles with him. Got him to really open up, express his feelings through art—kid still does it. When he's angry or hurt, he draws or paints, often spending hours in his room, forgetting to eat or sleep sometimes until his project is complete."

"Jesus," Aaron muttered. "That doesn't seem healthy."

"I thought so too at first, but once his project is done and he's let those feelings out in the most constructive way that works for him, he's back to his old self. I was skeptical of this woman at first, especially since I got a serious hippy-dippy vibe from her the first time I took Aiden, but she knows her shit and is fantastic with kids."

Atlas's phone next to his drinking glass vibrated. But he didn't even blink to acknowledge it.

Zak stowed his phone in his jeans once again. "There. I just texted you her information. Her name is Tessa Copland, and she—" He shook his head and smiled a smile of gratitude before running his big, meaty hand through his dark red hair. "She fucking saved my kid, is all I'm saying. You all saw how troubled Aiden was when everything with Loni went down. Tessa worked a goddamn miracle."

"Your kid was nine," Atlas said. "Aria is three."

"Doesn't matter. Tessa works with all ages. Just give her a call, or check out her website. It couldn't hurt."

Atlas grunted a response, which meant the conversation was over.

Nobody could really blame the man for his constant grumpiness. He was fucking exhausted. A widower of nearly two years, he was now raising his daughter Aria alone and had recently taken in his cousin's infant daughter, Cecily, after his cousin lost custody of her. Toss in the fact that Atlas was also a senior partner at Liam's law firm and apparently close to becoming a *name* partner, the man was stretched paper-thin. If they were all bigger assholes, they'd start placing bets on when his tether would finally snap.

But they weren't assholes, they were brothers, friends, family, and they did whatever they could do to help Atlas, which often meant taking Aria for a few hours so the man could take a deep breath without having to answer fifty million *why* questions. Scott did not miss those days.

When Freddie would ask *why* so many fucking times in a day, Scott felt like his head was going to explode. Only for the kid to ask the exact same fucking questions the next day. He got that it was appropriate age development and meant that his kid was eager to learn about the world and blah, blah, blah, but Jesus fucking Christ, "Why does a bird only have two legs but a zebra has four?" can only be asked so many times and be considered adorable only so many times before Scott was ready to rip himself bald or go insane.

"Meet her at the bar Monday for a drink so I can scope her out," Mason said with a sly grin, bringing the conversation back full circle to Scott's love life.

"I have a business meeting with a new client right before. He wants to meet for drinks, so maybe I'll suggest Prime and then just have Eva meet me there."

"Oooh, *Eva*," Zak said, making a dorky cooing noise. "How sexy."

Scott rolled his eyes, but the grin on his face began to hurt his jaw. Because as cheeseball as Zak was being, he wasn't wrong. Every damn thing about Eva oozed sexy. Her voice, her smile, her curves, her eyes, her wicked sense of humor, not to mention that brain of hers. She hadn't gone into much detail about her ex, but from the few things she'd said, Scott knew the woman had been through hell. And it took strength in spades to claw your way out of hell.

Eva was strong as fuck.

"Jesus fuck," Liam groaned. "My baby brother is a goner. Look at those dopey puppy-love eyes. Even just the mention of *Eva* and he's off in outer fucking space, mentally spanking the monkey to the soccer mom in her high-waisted mom jeans and messy bun."

"They're yoga pants and a baseball cap, thank you very

much," Scott snapped back. "But Eva would fucking rock high-waisted pants and a messy bun too."

He grimaced inwardly when his words came back to him. Damn it, he really did sound lovesick and obsessed. Fuck.

"Oh, bro." Zak laughed, leaning around Atlas and smacking Scott on the back. He shook his head before taking a sip of his beer. "You are fucking *gone!*"

9

EVA HADN'T BEEN on a date in ages—possibly longer. So even though she and Scott had seen each other naked, done despicably wonderful and wicked things to each other's bodies for hours, she toiled over what to wear on their date Monday night.

Thankfully, her baby sister came to the rescue, as Celeste often did—more than Eva would like to admit—and the two ran out shopping Monday morning after they dropped off their children at school.

What does one wear to drinks with a sinfully sexy man who she already had carnal knowledge of, but she still wanted to impress? Not to mention, have more carnal knowledge of, repeatedly, all over his house, her house and any flat surface they could find. She also wanted to remain casual and relaxed because after drinks, they were going to the Allison DeWitt book signing, and it just wouldn't do to show up to the bookstore in four-inch heels and a slinky gown with a thigh-high slit.

She needed to find a happy medium.

A sexy, flirty, casual happy medium.

Did such a thing exist?

Scott had texted her Sunday morning to let her know he had a work meeting right before their drinks but that he'd moved the meeting to the Prime Sports Bar and Grill, so she could just meet him there. Perfect! She loved that place and found it impossible to say no to one—but more often than not, *several*—of their blackberry mojitos.

While she and Celeste were out shopping, the man who always seemed to be on her mind these days texted her with a GIF of a cartoon man impatiently gnawing back and forth on his nails. He followed it up with a message that read, *Can't wait for tonight. I'm chewing my fingernails down to the quick in anticipation.*

Then another message popped up after. *I'm excited for our date too.* Winky face.

She'd literally laughed out loud in the change room, tossing her head back until hot tears pricked the corners of her eyes. She messaged him back. *You're a funny guy, Scott. A really FUNNY guy. Just remember who has the tickets.*

She thought for sure he was going to message back some smartass remark, because let's face it, the man was a total smartass. A hot, hilarious, sexy smartass, but a smartass no less.

But he didn't.

Her face fell as she stared at her phone for a few moments, waiting for his reply.

You wait for no man—ever!

Her sister's words rang in her mind.

Celeste was a warrior. Having married her high school sweetheart, only to lose him five years ago, the woman remained a pillar of strength for all of them. And when Eva was going through the worst of it all with Todd, Celeste kept repeating one thing over and over to her. *You wait for no man*

—*ever!* The good ones, the kind ones, the ones worth waiting for don't make you wait.

Then her sister's eyes would become damp and she would grow quiet for a couple of moments, her gaze wistful, caught up in a beautiful past with a man who should have been part of her present and future.

More times than she could count, Eva caught herself wishing it had been her husband who had fallen twelve stories onto exposed rebar and not Celeste's.

Sometimes the world was really fucking unfair.

With a final glance at her phone, she pouted, shrugged, then stowed it back in her purse and resumed trying on clothes. He was at work, so he probably just got a phone call or was pulled into a meeting. That was all it was, right? She hadn't pushed the envelope, had she?

Todd had zero sense of humor, so that message would have been interpreted as threatening and bitchy, and he would have told her just that. Along with a slew of other insults and put-downs until she felt no bigger than a cockroach trembling beneath her maniac of a husband's fancy, freshly polished, imported Italian loafer.

A nervous hollow began to grow in her stomach. Maybe the reason he wasn't messaging her back was because he was offended.

She pulled her phone back out and stared at it, as if the intense penetration of her eyes would will a message to pop up.

She was not only pathetic now, she was delusional.

Grumbling at how Todd had ruined her and any potential relationships with men she might have from here to eternity, she shoved her phone back into her purse, only for the sudden chirping ring of it to make her grab it again, fumbling to answer.

"Hello?"

"Even if you didn't have tickets to the book signing, I'd still be taking you out tonight. I can't get you out of my head, Eva." The deep rumble of his voice on the other end made her nipples grow diamond-hard. A gush of wetness soaked her panties.

No man had ever spurred such an instantaneous physiological response from her the way Scott did. Shallow puffs of air fled her thinly parted lips.

"And seeing you take the trash to the curb in those yoga pants today ... " He let out a whistle. "Damn, woman. You know the street is full of old-timers. Might give Harold across the way a jammer tucking your tush into those things and parading it around the neighborhood." The thick rattle of his chuckle only made the heat in her belly liquefy and ooze into her extremities.

"Scott." It was all she could say, and it came out as more of a shaky breath.

"You're under my skin, Eva."

And he was so deeply embedded under hers, she could hardly work, eat, sleep or breathe without his name or face commanding top billing in her mind.

"I ... " He'd rendered her speechless.

"I can't wait for tonight. I can't wait to see *you*."

She slid her tongue across her bottom lip, her cheeks flushed and eyes bright as she caught her reflection in the changing-room mirror. "Me either."

"Goodbye, Eva."

She swallowed. "Goodbye, Scott."

The butterflies in the melted goo that was her core fluttered their wings clean and began to flap around in a disorganized kaleidoscope. A man hadn't made her feel like this in a very long time—perhaps ever. Scott seemed like the real deal.

She only hoped he was the kind of deal that wasn't too good to be true.

AFTER SIX STORES that resulted in nothing but devastation and a sudden horrendous dislike for the new color of the season—blush pink, which totally washed her out, making her look like a freshly dead corpse—Eva and Celeste wandered down the sidewalk in the heart of Seattle, coffee cups in hand, the sun shining mockingly bright and warm overhead. It was springtime, and that usually meant the clouds were thick and filled with rain, drenching every last inch of the Emerald City. But today was a one-off.

You would think a one-off would also mean lucky and Eva would find the outfit of a lifetime that would not only knock Scott's socks off, but the rest of his clothes as well.

No such luck. The sun continued to mock her with its cheery glow and comforting warmth. She was not comforted. She had sweaty boobs and nothing to wear.

Fuck the sun.

As they were about ready to call it for the day and go find her car, Celeste's hand on her arm and sudden death grip halted them where they walked, causing grunts and grumbles from the people behind them. "Hold up," her sister said, hope in her tone. "Look!" She pointed with her coffee-cup hand to the mannequin that was being dressed in the window by a shopkeeper.

Eva's heart began to pound in her chest. It was perfect.

Celeste released her arm and yanked open the shop door. "Strip that mannequin!" she ordered.

Eva rolled her eyes as she followed her sister inside. Celeste always had a flair for the dramatic.

So after allowing her sister and the shopgirl to play Barbie with her, Eva handed over her credit card and walked out of the store with a whole new outfit that she was sure was going to make Scott's jaw drop (and maybe later that night, his pants too?).

But even after she tugged on the dark gray tapered pants that hugged her in all the right places and made her ass look like a million bucks, she couldn't hide the unease that trembled through her. The black belt cinched around the waist of her goldenrod silk sleeveless blouse never quelled the nerves either. Not even the Raspberry Rebel lip tint she slathered on in the hallway mirror helped with her confidence.

She was completely ill-equipped to go on a first date. Even if she'd already slept with the man, this was still their first date. It'd been over a decade since she'd been on a first date, and even then, she couldn't be sure she'd done very well.

"You've already established that you're sexually compatible and he has a kid who gets along with your kids," Celeste said, holding a glass of wine in her hand and leaning her slender frame against the wall as she watched a shaky-handed Eva slip into a pair of leopard print peep-toe pumps —a purchase that Celeste had insisted she make that morning. "I don't understand why you're so nervous. You've gotten through all the tough stuff. The rest is now gravy."

Gravy ...

Well, gravy or not, she was a sweaty, hot and frazzled mess by the time she got her butt into the cab and headed back downtown to meet Scott. There was no backing out now. He'd texted her when she was just a few blocks away saying he was still in his work meeting but hoped it wasn't going to run much longer. Then he'd followed that message up with a bunch of kissy-face emojis.

Was all this nervousness for naught?

He really was a sweet guy. Maybe she just needed to take a few deep, grounding breaths before she went in. She paid the cab driver and stepped out in front of the bar. The big, carved wooden sign to the new Seattle hotspot hung over the heavy double oak doors: PRIME SPORTS BAR AND GRILL. Not only did it have close to a dozen televisions hung throughout, broadcasting various sports games, but it was a popular place for business lunches, ladies' nights and everyone's favorite—music bingo.

The world of advertising didn't interest her at all, but her curiosity was no less piqued when Scott mentioned this *whale* of a client he had not only landed but was in charge of keeping happy. Who could be so important that they needed to have their ass kissed by someone like Scott? He seemed like the kind of guy who should be getting his ass kissed, not doing the lip service.

Scott's Tacoma was parked out front in one of the few, coveted street parking spots, which prompted her to wonder if they were going to stick around Prime for drinks or head somewhere quieter and more intimate, perhaps with a dark corner where the only light came from candles or dimly lit sconces.

She double-checked her lipstick in the tinted windows of Scott's vehicle, tucked her hair behind her ears and then glanced through the big window into the restaurant in search of her hot date.

She had no intention of disrupting his business meeting, but it would be cool to see if she recognized his important client. Maybe the guy's face was on a billboard or something. Perhaps a bus bench or a television commercial.

Ducking behind a column that held up a streetlight just outside, she scanned the interior of the restaurant, looking for a sexy man with dark hair and a slightly crooked nose.

She spotted him, and the smile that cracked on her face made the heat in her cheeks travel south.

Only she didn't just see Scott and his handsome smile or

the twinkle in his dark eyes. It was who he was sitting with, who he was laughing with.

The blood pumping through her veins slowly went from sizzling with desire and anticipation to ice-cold with fear.

She was frozen in place, with concrete in her feet, stone in her gut and a frigid fist violently squeezing her heart. She couldn't breathe. She. Could. Not. Breathe.

It was Todd.

Scott was smiling, Scott was laughing, Scott was joking with Todd.

With her ex.

The ex who had broken her down so much, she was still picking up the pieces of her soul. He had pulverized the entire entity of who she was into such minuscule fragments, there were small gaps and chips that would never be filled as she struggled each day to tape and glue the shards of herself back together. Todd had destroyed who she was as a person, a woman, a wife, a mother, and a friend. He'd alienated her from her family and friends. Now all she could do was hope that the pieces she did find, the pieces she managed to stick back together, would eventually be enough. Be whole enough to feel somewhat human, somewhat normal, somewhat like her old self.

He was demon in the flesh who haunted her day and night, and even though she had a restraining order against him, she knew that Todd didn't really give a flying fuck about that kind of thing. If he wanted to hurt her, he could, and he would. Todd was above the law. He always had been.

With the little bit of energy she had left, she spun herself around and out of sight of the window, plastering her back against the cool concrete column, her chest now heaving, struggling to draw in each much-needed breath as the fist around her heart and the anvil on her lungs began to squeeze and press down even harder.

Maybe her eyes were just playing tricks on her.

That couldn't be Todd.

Not with Scott. Not *her* Scott.

She knew if things between her and Scott progressed further that eventually one day he might meet her evil ex. She'd just hoped that she would have been able to control the environment in which they met. But like this ... no. Never.

Todd was Scott's client.

Todd was Scott's boss.

This couldn't be happening. She had to check again. Maybe she'd actually fallen while getting out of the cab, hit her head on the curb and was currently in a coma in the hospital, dreaming about her demonic ex laughing like old pals with her new boyfriend—or whatever Scott was.

Or maybe it was just a man who *looked* like Todd. He was, after all, tall, dark and handsome—but so were a lot of men. So was Scott. Only unlike Scott, who seemed to be kind and decent and handsome beneath the skin, Todd was nothing but pure garbage once you pulled back the gossamer-thin veil of humanity he presented to the world.

Hesitation filled her movements as she peered back around the column into the restaurant again.

Please don't let it be Todd. Anybody but Todd. Satan himself would be better than Todd.

Son of a bitch.

Her eyes weren't playing tricks on her. And she was almost certain she wasn't in a coma.

Nope.

That was Todd, the ice-blue eyed devil himself in a two-thousand-dollar suit.

With his smarmy smile, his dashing good looks and his psychopathic charm.

Was Scott falling for it?

He tossed his head back and laughed.

Shit. Not only was he falling for Todd's charm, he was eating it up out of the man's palm.

More ice dripped down her spine until she was once again frozen in place. Unable to move. So now all she could do was stare. Watch in horror as the two men, one she hated more than anything in the world, and one she could easily see herself one day loving, laughed and chatted, drank beer and ate pretzels like they were old college buddies.

Todd's eyes flashed up from his drink and swung in her direction. His steely gaze narrowed as if he recognized her or at the very least saw something behind her. But just as quick, his focus shifted back to Scott, who said something that made Todd laugh.

The wind was warm, but she nonetheless shivered where she stood, pulling her fitted black blazer tighter across her front.

She needed to get out of there. No way was she going into that bar now. No way was she going to run the risk of letting Todd see her, let alone realize that she was with Scott.

That had disaster written all over it.

With a still-heaving chest, foggy brain and trembling hands, she whipped her body back out of view and stood behind the column, her back once again up against the concrete.

Doubts crashed through her like the biggest of waves in a Pacific winter storm. White caps, squalls and all. She was drowning in doubt, in fear and confusion. Struggling to get her bearings and figure out which way was up. Her brain was hazy. She was losing oxygen. She couldn't see the surface.

Her fingers were glacier-cold as she fumbled for her phone from her purse and dialed her sister.

"Todd is in having a drink with Scott," she blurted out when Celeste's curious *hello* came across the line.

"What the hell? Why?"

"I think Todd's his client. I mean, it makes sense. Fletcher Holdings is huge."

"Has Todd seen you yet?"

She shook her head. "No. I'm still outside. I can't go inside. I can't let him see me. I ... I'm not even sure I can face Scott right now. I know he probably has no idea who Todd is to me, but knowing that the two of them have been so chummy for the last couple of hours makes me want to vomit."

"Understandable. The man is scum." Celeste brought her voice down to barely a whisper, which meant she was within earshot of small, nosy, curious ears.

"I'm going to call another cab and just come home."

"But what about the book signing?"

Allison DeWitt be damned. First date with Scott be damned. She was not mentally equipped to deal with any of this right now. She hadn't seen Todd in months, and things were finally getting better. She was sleeping better. She had cut her therapy sessions down from once a week to once a month. Her kids were sleeping in their own beds—most of the time. They were all settling in. Life was good.

But this—seeing him with Scott, she could already feel the setbacks happening.

"Come home," Celeste said sternly over the phone, interrupting Eva's thoughts. "I can practically hear you spiraling out of control over the phone. Get your ass home. Text Scott once you're in the cab. If he's a decent guy, he'll understand. Then maybe one day you can tell him the whole ugly story of terrible Todd."

Yeah, right.

"Get out of there," Celeste said. "If Todd leaves and catches you standing out there ... "

Shit. Right. That would not be good. The narcissist would probably think she was stalking him and interested in getting back together, while the only way she wanted Todd Fletcher was a minimum of five hundred feet away, though if she had her way, six feet under would do too.

With a final glance through the window, the phone and her sister still glued to her ear, she tucked her purse under her arm and headed down the sidewalk. Away from Prime Sports Bar and Grill, away from Todd, and regrettably away from Scott.

She only hoped that this wasn't her walking away from Scott forever.

He seemed like the kind of guy who was worth waiting for. Hopefully he would wait for her too.

10

A FLURRY of red out of the corner of Scott's eye drew his attention away from the narcissistic douche-canoe in front of him. God, how much longer was he going to have to laugh at this man's crude jokes?

Relishing anything that could distract his attention away from the pretentious fucker with the sparkly Rolex, he glanced out the window only to see a black coat and long, streaming red hair disappear down the sidewalk and out of view.

He hadn't known her long, but he'd watched her walk enough to know Eva's walk, even from the back. That was her.

But why was she leaving?

Where was she going?

His watch—which was not a sparkly-ass Rolex—said she should have been there by now. They would only have time to grab maybe one drink before they needed to head to the book signing. And even though he loved Prime and his buddy Mason, who was currently tending bar, this was not the place for an intimate and romantic first date.

Damn it, he needed to ditch Todd—and fast. But the

fucker would not shut up about himself or his success or how much he hated his ex-wife. Yeah, that had been a fun topic to get on—not. Scott made the mistake of mentioning his ex-wife in passing, and that Freddie was with her for the week, and apparently that was the only opening Todd needed to launch into a full-on ex-hating diatribe.

The man was convincing though. By the end of it, Scott wasn't a fan of the woman either. If she was half as terrible as Todd made her out to be, Scott hoped the woman got a hard-core reality check soon and did the right thing by her kids by seeking professional help.

Those poor kids.

A drunk mother who was also addicted to pills and had a penchant for stealing—jeez. And here he thought he'd had it rough with Katrin and her lack of consideration.

So as much as Todd appeared to be one of the world's biggest tools, at least his sons had him in their lives. A successful, healthy, stable parental figure.

He let out a slow breath.

At least Katrin wasn't an alcoholic, pill-popping klep-tomaniac.

Silver lining.

Todd finished his drink and exhaled, his eyes wandering over to the backside of the waitress who was currently bent slightly over a table to wipe it. "I'm going to hit the men's room, then head out."

Scott nodded then caught Mason's eye, nodding again. "I'll grab the bill."

And send Eva a text message to see where the heck she went.

"Thanks, man," Todd said, his eyes now lasered in on the waitress. The way he scanned her body as she stood up made Scott uncomfortable, but the waitress—who was most likely no older than twenty-five, if that—seemed to squirm beneath his gaze as well.

"Hazel!" Mason's voice bellowed across the bar, which caused the waitress to snap to attention. "Need you over here." Relief crossed the young woman's face as she high-tailed it across the busy bar toward the safe haven of her big, tattooed boss and the four-foot-wide solid wood bar that would now be between her and Todd.

Todd's nostrils flared as he watched Hazel cross the bar, his eyes turning a dark, stormy gray-blue that made the hair on the back of Scott's neck stand up.

Clearing his throat and knowing that he needed to go and say goodbye to Mason before he left to find Eva, he gave one final wave to Todd and headed toward the bar. Todd barely acknowledged him though. He was too busy scoping out another waitress across the room.

What a pig.

"I've got my eye on him," Mason said as Scott approached his good friend at the bar and dug out his credit card from his wallet. This was a business meeting, so the company was paying for it, but that didn't mean he couldn't collect his AirMiles while he was treating the douchebag client to some top-shelf scotch.

Todd still hadn't retreated to the bathroom like he said he was. His head was pointed at one of the televisions now, but his eyes were on the blonde waitress who was clearing a table to his right.

"Guy's a real pig," Mason said through gritted teeth.

"He hasn't even touched me, and yet I feel like I need a shower just after the way he was looking at me," Hazel said, grabbing Scott's credit card from him and ringing him up on the cash register.

"He's not a friend," Scott said, feeling the need to make that clear. "Business relationship only. But I need to keep the man happy if I want to keep my job. I'm sorry if—"

Hazel held up a hand and shook her head. "You did nothing wrong, Mr. Dixon."

"I keep telling you to call me Scott," he said with an eye roll.

"Where's your date?" Mason asked, plunking a full, frothy beer stein down on the bar next to a couple of lowballs filled with ice, clear liquid and limes on the rim.

Thanking Hazel for his receipt and credit card, Scott shoved both back into his wallet. "No clue. I thought for sure I saw her heading down the sidewalk away from the bar. Her hair is pretty unmistakable. I don't know why she was leaving though. I said to meet me here." He pulled out his phone and glanced at it. No messages.

"Maybe she misunderstood," Hazel offered, her eyes holding a sympathy usually reserved for those who had been rejected. Scott didn't know that look well, but he'd seen it given enough to his friends—particularly those guys at that bachelor party all those weeks ago—that he recognized it, and it felt weird being directed at him.

He shook his head. "No, she knew the plan." He punched in a quick *everything okay?* message to Eva and then waited. If she didn't respond, he'd call her. What if that wasn't her outside on the sidewalk and her cab was stuck in traffic? Or what if that *was* her on the sidewalk and she'd fallen and twisted her ankle?

He waited a few moments for a reply but got nothing.

"Gonna call her?" Mason asked.

He nodded and pulled up her number on his phone, hitting dial and then putting it to his ear.

It rang and rang and rang until the sweet and sultry sound of her voicemail came up. *Hello, you've reached Eva Marchand of Eva's Hair and Esthetics. If you'd like to make an appointment, please hit one to be directed to my business line. If you're calling with regards to a personal matter or something*

regarding the boys, please leave a message after the beep, and I will
return your call as soon as I can. Thank you and have a great day.
God, he could listen to that message and that sexy, gravelly voice of hers all day long.

He waited for the beep.

Beep.

"Eva, it's Scott. I'm at Prime and just finished up my work meeting. I'm sorry it ran late. The guy wouldn't stop talking about himself. Anyway, I thought I saw you heading down the sidewalk, but maybe that wasn't you. I hope everything is okay. Call me back. If you're still at home, I can come get you. We can grab drinks after the signing, or if we're too late for the signing, just go grab drinks and a bite. Please call me back and let me know you're okay. I can't wait to see you."

He hung up and let out a slow breath. That was a long message, and he fought back the feelings that he was coming on too strong and tried to convince himself that he was just showing her that he was interested. That he cared about her. Because he did. He was a nice guy, and even though Eva hadn't gone into explicit details about her ex, he knew that after what that guy had put her through, she deserved a nice guy to treat her like the goddess that she was.

Mason and Hazel were both standing behind the bar watching him, but then their eyes flicked up at the same time and followed something—or more likely *someone* —behind him.

A hard *thwack* landed on his shoulder. "Thanks for the drinks, buddy," Todd said, the scent of his musky cologne encircling Scott and overpowering his senses. It was probably embedding itself in his jacket too. He'd be smelling Todd for days now. "We'll chat later in the week, okay?"

Scott smacked on a big, fake smile. "You got it, Todd. Looking forward to working with you."

Todd's smile was big and grew even bigger when his

hawk-like stare shifted to Hazel behind the bar. He didn't say anything, but he didn't have to. The predator always remained quiet when stalking its prey. His smile was now toothy and sinister.

Hazel swallowed then smiled grimly. "See you next time."

The wooden doors banged shut a moment later, and all three of them watched as Todd sauntered down the sidewalk toward his waiting car and driver.

Hazel shuddered. "God, he's gross."

"Again, I'm not *thrilled* to be working with him. Food in my kid's belly and a roof over his head are what drive me to put up with tools like that."

"How is Freddie?" Mason asked.

"Doing great, thanks. So happy that Kellen and Lucas moved in next door. Our neighborhood needs some young blood in it. I think the boys will have a blast together this summer."

Mason nodded. "Good, good."

Scott checked his phone again. Still no call or text.

He was beginning to worry that something was wrong. Like maybe her cab driver had lost control behind the wheel, had a seizure or something and both he and Eva were upside down in a ditch on the I-5 while emergency vehicles blocked off traffic and the fire department prepared the jaws of life.

Or her phone died and she's just running late, you morbid freak.

"I'm going to run back to her place to see if everything is okay," he said, not really paying attention to Mason or Hazel behind the bar anymore. He was seriously starting to worry about Eva. He'd always had a bit of an overactive imagination, which was probably why he loved fantasy novels so much. They were gasoline for the bonfire of his creative thoughts.

"Let me know how it all goes," Mason called behind him

as he pushed the doors open and stepped out into the still warm April air. Spring was a funny season, particularly in the Pacific Northwest. One minute you could be washing your car in your driveaway in a T-shirt, working on your tan, then the next day you're digging your gloves and knit cap back out of the crawl space because a cold front had just blown in.

He reached his truck in no time and hit the fob, taking one last glance at his phone before he started the engine. They were most likely going to miss the book signing, and as much as that seriously sucked, he was more concerned about Eva and that she was all right.

Had that been her earlier walking past the bar?

Had something scared her off?

Had *he* scared her off?

Was she having second thoughts?

A million thoughts of his own paraded through his mind as he drove out of the downtown core and off into suburbia.

If she was having second thoughts about their relationship and the two of them dating, things were going to get mighty awkward if their boys all became friends.

Twenty minutes later he pulled into Eva's driveway, but he didn't even have to get out of his car to see that nobody was home. The lights were all out, and there was no vehicle in sight.

Wasn't Celeste supposed to be watching the boys at Eva's house?

Now things were really starting to freak him out.

But he had no idea where Celeste lived or what her number was. He was stuck.

He'd been not only stood up, but his date had vanished.

Even though he knew there would be no answer, he got out of his truck anyway and ran up to the front door. It was still early enough that he could ring the doorbell and not risk waking the kids.

He did that.

No answer.

Not that he really expected one.

Then he pounded on the door. "Eva!" he called out.

Still no answer.

Would it be too much for him to head around back to the sundeck doors and peer inside, make sure she was okay?

Yes, yes, it probably would be.

Damn it.

He didn't care that he was stood up. Well, yes, he did. It sucked major big time. But more, he cared that she was all right. Thoughts of her sadistic ex crawled back into his brain, and then he began to wonder if maybe the boy's father had shown up and kidnapped them all.

"She was here, but then they all left," came a grisly male voice to Scott's left. Ah, good old Mr. Gallagher, with his mile-long gray nose and ear hair and liver spots.

Scott approached the wooden fence that separated Eva's property from Mr. Gallagher's. "She was here? She was okay?"

Mr. Gallagher nodded, which caused his long, thick jowls to jiggle. "Yep. Cab dropped her off about thirty minutes ago, then she and the kids piled into the van and left. Her sister and niece followed."

Scott exhaled, and relief crashed into him like a runaway train. At least she was okay.

"Did she say anything to you?" he asked, hopeful but already knowing what Mr. Gallagher's answer would be.

Just as he suspected, the elderly man shook his head, the crease of his frown getting lost in the multitude of other lines on his face. "She didn't, I'm afraid. Looked mighty pretty though, all dressed up for a date or something."

Okay, so she *had* been planning to join him. Had something come up? An emergency with one of the kids?

"Did the kids seem okay?"

Again, Mr. Gallagher nodded, lifting his chin up and allowing his milky blue gaze to scan the tops of the tall evergreen trees in his backyard. "Kids seemed fine. No crying, if that's what you mean." He turned his attention back to Scott, and his overgrown brows, which met in the middle, furrowed deep. "You and the new neighbor courting or something?"

Or something.

At least he hoped it was something.

Mr. Gallagher was very kind, as was his wife, Mrs. Gallagher—but they were also two of the biggest gossips on the block. Particularly Mrs. Gallagher. She had half the neighborhood over for tea each week, and by Saturday she knew everything about everybody, and then she relayed it all to Scott as he stood in his driveaway and washed his truck.

If he gave Mr. Gallagher even a whiff of gossip, the entire street, hell, the entire subdivision would know by Friday. And if Eva was having second thoughts about their relationship, he didn't want to cause her or them any more strife or chaos than required.

So he shook his head. "No, sir. Not courting. Just getting to know the new neighbor. Her kids are Freddie's age, so we're becoming friends is all."

Mr. Gallagher's eyes developed a twinkle, and his mouth crooked up on one side. "I won't say a word of it to Mrs. Gallagher." He crossed his index finger over his chest. "Cross my heart."

Scott fought the urge to roll his eyes but instead simply thanked his neighbor and then headed back to his truck, pulled out of Eva's driveway and into his own.

He'd watch her yard like a hawk until daybreak if he had to, just to make sure she and the kids were okay. Then, and only then, when he saw her soccer-mom minivan in the driveway and it was a reasonable hour, would he head on over and ask to reschedule their date, because unless Eva was giving him the brush-off, he wasn't ready to let this woman go. She'd buried herself deep beneath his skin, her name was like a song he just couldn't stop singing, and her smile was something he would never grow tired of seeing.

He'd only known Eva Marchand for a short while, but what he did know, he liked. She was the real deal, and she was worth waiting for.

11

WITH THE BEST OF INTENTIONS, Scott stayed awake for as long as he could, one ear tuned to the house and driveway next door. But sleep was too enticing. Like a seductive vixen with red hair and green eyes, she lured him into her depths. He was snoring and drooling on his pillow when the sound of the recycling truck outside doing morning pickup abruptly woke him from his slumber. Literally peeling his face off his pillow, he sat up—still in his clothes—scratched his balls like he always did, then headed over to the window to see if Eva was home yet.

She wasn't.

No van. No kids. No recycling bins out.

Fear and unease tickled the back of his neck like an irritating wasp, and he swatted it away, hoping that Eva and the kids were sleeping at Celeste's for the night and they weren't all up at the hospital after having ingested rat poison disguised as Alphaghetti.

Freddie loved Alphaghetti.

So did Scott.

He needed a fucking shower, then coffee, and then he needed to get his ass to work. It was going to be a late fucking day too. Todd Fletcher liked Scott's pitch so much, he decided he not only wanted Dynamic Creative to take on his new distillery, but he wanted to turn over marketing the majority of his holdings to Scott and his team.

Cha-ching. But also, *fuck*.

This meant he would have to see more of Todd.

Didn't the man have a general manager or underling of some kind he could pawn all this shit off on? Scott would much rather work with the underling. With anybody else, really.

So the entire day was going to be spent poring over all the other companies that Todd owned—with his trusty marketing team, of course—and figuring out new and innovative ways to advertise. He was least looking forward to developing new marketing strategies for Todd's bevy of strip clubs. The man really was all class.

He divested himself of his clothes, turned the water on in the shower and then stood there with his hand beneath the spray until it grew warm. This was not how he had hoped to be spending his morning. No sir.

With Eva's sister and the boys just next door, he'd hoped that Eva would have accompanied him home last night. They would have shared a nightcap. Then, perhaps, they would have tumbled into bed, becoming nocturnal beings, exploring each other's bodies until the wee hours of the morning, only for her to fall asleep with her head on his chest. The two of them would enjoy one last tryst in the shower the next morning. A reprise of their shower that first night in the hotel room.

Fuck, that felt like a lifetime ago.

He missed her taste.

He missed her smell.

Fuck, he just missed her.

Shaking himself, then slapping his face twice to not only wake himself up, but also knock in some sense, he stepped beneath the warm water.

"Damn it, Eva," he grumbled, his cock springing to life at the memory of her on her knees the last time they were in the shower. More times than he could count, he went back to that memory, taking himself in his palm and wishing it was her hot little mouth.

It didn't take long for him to finish what needed to be done—what his body *required* him to do so he could function for the rest of the day—then he washed his hair, body and stood beneath the spray for a solid five minutes before shutting off the water and stepping out into the day.

"What the hell is going on with you, Eva?" he muttered to himself as he wiped the condensation off the vanity mirror. He was digging the thick beard he'd grown over the last few months, but it was getting a touch scraggly. He needed to tame the bush, particularly if he hoped to be diving face-first into Eva's bush—or in her case, well-groomed three postage stamps—anytime soon.

Once he was dressed for the day in a pair of dark gray dress pants and a snazzy navy long-sleeved shirt with tiny white polka dots—a Christmas present from his fashion-forward baby sister, Bianca—he headed downstairs for coffee.

It was now eight o'clock, a totally reasonable time to call someone, right? Particularly someone with school-age children who needed to be up with the crows, pouring cereal and fixing lunches. With peanut butter toast in one hand, he pulled up Eva's number on his phone.

She hadn't texted him back or left any voicemails.

Was she okay?

He would like to say "this wasn't like her at all," but he didn't know her that well, so maybe this was her MO. Maybe she was a flake; she'd just done a bang-up job of hiding it until now.

As much as he hoped that that wasn't the case, that she wasn't like his ex-wife—inconsiderate, thoughtless and selfish—it was tough to completely dismiss the niggly sensation of déjà vu that itched at the base of his skull.

Did that mean there was something wrong with him? Was there a reason he kept picking women like that? Women who treated him like an afterthought?

Shaking himself to relieve the thoughts of self-doubt and the dark spiral he could so easily have slipped into, he dialed her number.

Once again, it went to her voicemail.

"Eva, it's Scott again. Please just let me know you're okay. That you and the boys are safe. My overactive imagination is going all dark and twisty right now, and I'm beginning to fear the worst. Even if you don't want anything to do with me, please just let me know you're alive."

Should he say that he missed her?

No.

His message already sounded sappy enough.

He hung up but then brought up all their back and forth text messages. Hers had been flirty and fun. He thought for sure she was as into this budding relationship as he was. Had he read her wrong?

Did he read all women wrong?

He decided that one last, final text was all he was going to send her, and then after that, if she didn't respond, he was going to wash his hands of the whole damn thing. He could only be the worried and ghosted guy for so long before his nuts began to shrink.

Last text message, Eva. Just let me know you're alive, then I'll leave you alone.

Leaving his phone on the counter, he finished his coffee and then ran upstairs to go and brush his teeth. When he returned, with his jacket, wallet and keys, he found the light on his phone flashing.

I'm alive. That was all it said. That was it.

No apology, no explanation.

Well, all you asked for was proof of life, nothing more. What do you expect?

He expected an explanation. He expected to be shown some consideration.

All the rancor he thought he'd let go of from his ex came rushing back, hitting him dead center in the back of the head until all he saw was red. It was all he could do not to hurl his phone against the wall.

Fine. If that's how she wanted to do this, then fine.

They could be feuding neighbors rather than fucking ones. His parents had feuded with the Burns family next door for nearly forty years. If they could do it, so could he. He could watch as the wind carried her empty trash cans down the street, sit from his window and enjoy her struggles as she fought with her temperamental lawnmower. He could be petty. He could be mean. He could be inconsiderate.

And now that Eva had ghosted him this way, shown him such little consideration and care, he would be. It wasn't a good color on him, but who the fuck cared? Scott was done being the nice guy, the good guy. They really did finish last. It wasn't just a saying.

He was fucking done.

From now on, he would take what he wanted and then move on.

Because that's clearly what women wanted, how women treated him. Katrin, Eva. They were all the same.

And now he would treat them all the same. He had a feeling Eva Marchand was going to ruin him for other women when he first met her. He just didn't know that it was going to be like this.

It was Wednesday night by the time he had a chance to breathe out the angry breath he'd been holding in since Tuesday morning. Sure, he'd actually *breathed* all that time, but over the last thirty-six hours, he'd struggled to relax. Particularly when he arrived home super late Tuesday night after work and spied the minivan in Eva's driveaway and lights on in the house.

There was still no call or text message from her though. Not even a note taped to his door. Nothing.

What the fuck?

He'd called Mason on his drive home Wednesday night and sworn like a sailor who'd just lost his foot to a crocodile when he drove past her house and spotted the minivan.

"Don't assume anything, bro," Mason said over the phone. "You don't know what came up Monday, or yesterday. Maybe that was all she could text and she wants to hash things out in person. Give her the benefit of the doubt. Don't swear off women entirely just yet."

Scott's vision was so full of red, it was a challenge backing into his driveaway and not losing a side mirror to the hedge. "She's had more than enough opportunities to apologize and explain herself," he said through gritted teeth, turning off his truck. "I at least deserve *that*. I mean, who the fuck ghosts their neighbor? That has got to be the dumbest fucking thing on the planet."

"It is. You're right. Which makes me think she probably isn't ghosting you."

Scott disconnected the Bluetooth in his truck and put the phone on speaker before climbing out and shutting the door. "Ghosting me or not, what she did was fucking rude as hell."

"I agree. And she will probably agree too. Don't fuck this up by being a Dixon Dickhead."

"You guys like that nickname far too much," he grumbled.

"I have to hand it to Atlas. He really hit the nail on the head coining that term for you and Liam. Can't believe I didn't think of it myself."

Scott grumbled again.

His watch said it was closing in on nine o'clock. He usually worked late on the weeks he didn't have Freddie so that he could leave work early enough to get his kid from school or pick him up early from after school care. Didn't Eva say she was going to work late on Wednesday nights? Put her kids to bed and then have clients until ten?

He stepped around the hedge to see if there was any other vehicle in the driveaway. There wasn't one. But that didn't mean she didn't have a client. Uber was used frequently here, and they were also on a major bus route.

"You still there?" Mason asked, the sound of Willow warbling in the background letting him know that his buddy was home with his baby girl and probably his new love, Lowenna.

Scott nodded. "Yeah. But I gotta go."

"Don't do anything stupid, man."

He was already halfway down her driveway. "I'm not Liam."

Mason chuckled on the other end. "Yeah, but you're his brother. The dickhead gene might not be as strong with the second born, but it's still there."

He was nearly at her back door now. The one she used for her salon.

"I gotta go."

Mason exhaled, his irritation palpable through the phone. "Okay. Call me back and let me know how it goes."

"'K." Then he hung up, tried the door handle and stepped inside.

12

Eva was just handing Vanessa her change when the door to the salon opened. "I'm just closing up," she said before she saw who it was. Oxygen whooshed from her lungs as she breathed out his name. "Scott."

She should have known.

He wasn't going to let her get away with the brush-off she gave him.

Well, you were incredibly rude to him.

"Do you take walk-ins?" he asked, ignoring her earlier declaration that they were closed.

Vanessa, her final client for the evening and a longtime client at that, smiled and thanked her before skirting around Scott's big frame to leave, but not before giving him a head-to-toe eye fuck.

"Figured this was the only way I could get in to see you," he said, his voice holding a tight, bitter tone that made every muscle in her heart tighten until her chest hurt. "I need a cut, please." He wandered around her and then plunked himself into one of the two salon chairs she had. Vanessa's hair was still on the floor around the other one.

Well, at least if they were going to have the conversation, she might as well keep her hands busy.

His eyes tracked her across the room as she grabbed a black cape off the hook and draped it over his body, fastening it around his neck. The scent of him was already driving her mad, and the feel of his skin beneath hers, even that simple whisper of a touch as she brushed her knuckles across his neck, made her nipples tighten to painful peaks and heat rush into her lower belly.

Their gazes locked in the mirror ahead. His eyes seared her enough to leave second-degree burns. But the look wasn't entirely anger. No, there was also hurt buried down deep behind the intense brown. He was hurt, he was confused, but he was also really fucking angry.

And rightfully so.

Celeste had told her she'd messed up.

And every time Scott's messages would pop up or she'd ignore his calls, she knew she was digging herself deeper. She just couldn't get the image of him and Todd out of her head.

With just a hint of a tremble to her hands, she lifted them up and pushed them into his hair. God, he had great hair. Dark and thick. Soft and full. She played with it a bit, pulling it out at the sides and on the top to get an idea of how much needed to be taken off.

The groan from the depths of his chest made her pussy quiver, and the way his eyes softened and his nostrils flared as she watched him watching her in the mirror sent her pulse racing.

"We need to talk about Monday," he said, removing his eyes from her and allowing them to flit around her freshly painted and newly decorated salon and spa. She was proud of all that she'd managed to accomplish, setting her business up so quickly, getting her clients organized and scheduled. Everyone had been so accommodating with her move, most of them saying she was now closer to where they lived than before.

"Do you want your hair washed?"

He grunted, stood up and followed her over to the low chair and basin sink, sinking down and resting his neck in the groove.

She made sure the water was nice and warm before she put the spray over his head.

"I'm not leaving until we talk about Monday," he said. "You can wash my hair, condition it, shave it all off for all I fucking care, but I'm not leaving until I get an explanation. I *deserve* an explanation."

He was upside down glaring at her now, which, she had to admit, looked pretty hilarious. His brows pinched in a way that made him look both menacing but also sexy, and the way his slightly crooked upside-down nose crinkled was not only charming but also kind of cute. The man, for all the ire that swirled around him, was very kissable right now.

"You hear me, Eva? I'm not leaving."

She gave him one, barely-there nod, pumped shampoo into her hand and began to work her fingers into his hair. He shut up after that. His face relaxed, and his eyes closed.

She didn't want to make the comparison, but in a lot of ways, men were kind of like dogs. If you rubbed them in the right spot, they usually calmed right down. A part of her expected his leg to start twitching any minute.

She rinsed, then conditioned, rinsed again before wrapping his head up in a towel, guiding him back to her salon chair, his big, solid frame a wall of heat beneath her palm.

With a grunt, he plopped back down into the chair. Even though she was tall for the average woman, he was taller, and she had to hit the bar on the bottom of the chair to drop him down a bit so she could see of the top of his head.

The air grew more and more taut between them as she

combed out his damp hair and parted it. She avoided looking in the mirror at all costs, but sometimes she had to, and each time she brought her eyes up, there was the fire blazing back at her.

Swallowing, she brought the scissors up, the shake in her hand still there. She needed to rip it off like a Band-Aid. Tell Scott the truth, the whole truth and nothing but the truth. He had been nothing but kind to her. He deserved to know why she was acting like a wingnut. Then he could decide for himself whether she was worth the effort. Whether she was worth the headache.

"Do you know who you were having drinks with?" she whispered, holding his hair between her middle and index fingers and then cutting along the top.

"Todd Fletcher, my client. I told you that." Impatience was not only evident in his tone and glare, but it was damn near tangible in the air. "What does that have to do with anything?"

"I never told you my married name," she went on, ignoring his irritation. "It's Fletcher."

His furrowed brow slowly relaxed as all the color drained from his complexion and realization dawned across his handsome features, fear replacing any last traces of impatience in his eyes.

"Todd Fletcher is your ex-husband?" he whispered so low she was forced to read his lips in the mirror to understand what he was saying. His head began to shake as if he didn't believe her. Or as if he believed whatever *Todd* told him about her.

What *had* Todd told him about her?

A cold numbness tingled in her feet, but finally, she nodded. "Todd Fletcher is my ex-husband, yes. He is Kellen and Lucas's father."

Both of his hands shot up from beneath the cape, and he

snagged her wrists. Instinct kicked in and she jerked away from him, jabbing the end of the scissors into the back of his hand.

"Ouch!" He yanked his hand back and eyed her like she was a rabid beast that had just gone for the kill strike. "What the hell?"

She swallowed and took a step back, her hand still shaking as she set the scissors down on the vanity. "I'm sorry." Stepping back toward him, she took his hand in hers to survey the damage. He was bleeding.

Damn it.

Hot tears pricked the corners of her eyes as she snatched up a tissue from the box behind her and held it to his hand. "I'm so sorry, Scott. You just ... you startled me."

"And your first instinct is to try and sever my hand off?"

She rolled her bottom lip inward and held the tissue tight against his hand. "No ... I ... just. Instinct. I went into protection mode."

Once again, he gripped her wrist, squeezing until she lifted her head to look at him. "Am I someone you think you need to protect yourself from?"

No. Not you. Not you ever.

She shook her head. "No."

"But you're used to having to protect yourself from someone ... from *him*." It wasn't a question.

Her molars slammed together to keep her chin from trembling. "He wasn't violent with me, if that's what you mean. Todd, he just ... " She couldn't maintain eye contact any longer and glanced back down at his hand, lifting the tissue to see if he was still bleeding. He was. "The man has a temper. He yelled a lot, belittled and threatened. And he ... " A tear slid down the crease of her nose. Before he could take her hand, she shook herself free of his grasp, handed him the tissue and moved back around behind him, resuming her station with the scissors and comb.

"Eva ... " His deep voice drew her gaze up to the mirror, where dark eyes, curious and gentle, looked back at her. "What did he do to you?"

Swallowing, she began to cut his hair again. "A few years ago, when things with Todd really started to get bad but I was too scared to leave, I moved into the guest bedroom. I wasn't interested in being his wife anymore, at least not behind closed doors—and certainly not in the bedroom. I knew he was cheating on me anyway, so I figured he didn't care that I wasn't interested in sex. He didn't make much of a stink about it, thankfully, until one night ... "

His nostrils flared, and even in the mirror, she could see his pupils dilate. The hair on the back of his neck pricked up too. "What. Did. He. Do. Eva?"

"He came home after a work function, and he'd been drinking. He came into my room and tried to have sex with me. I pushed him off, but he became persistent, and then he ... "

"Eva ... "

She shook her head and bit down hard on the inside of her cheek until the metallic taste of blood spilled across her tongue. But not even that could keep the tears from flowing freely down to her chin, spilling over to her purple tennis shoes. "I didn't know that marital rape was a thing." Her laugh at her own stupidity was brittle. "Can you believe that? Celeste had to inform me that a husband can rape his wife." She continued to cut his hair, using the sleeve of her white T-shirt to blot at her eyes. "He hurt me ... during ... it. He was rough, and I had bruises and pain afterward. I ended up running out and getting the morning-after pill the next day because I wasn't on any birth control, and as much as I love my children, I couldn't imagine having another child with that monster."

"Did you report the bastard to the police?" Anger infused every one of his words, and his fists were now bunched and white-knuckled on the arms of the chair.

She shook her head again. "No. I didn't know that I had any kind of a case. And even so, it would have been his word against mine. I told you how much he lied about me to try to get custody of the boys. He would have lied about that too. After he ... " She couldn't even say it, not again. "After he *did* that to me, I had a long, hot shower and scrubbed myself. I wanted to rid myself of his smell, of his sweat, his spit and his semen. I washed away anything that could have helped a police investigation, had I known I even had a case."

Scott's eyes flared, his cheeks reddened and his mouth opened on a gasp at the same time he pivoted in his chair to face her. Thank goodness she wasn't mid-cut, otherwise she could have done some serious damage to his gorgeous hair. "He lied about you to me too."

A pit the size of Jupiter opened up inside her gut. Just like she feared, Todd had mentioned her to Scott. Oh God, what had he said? What lies had he filled Scott's head with? How many other people had he lied to?

"He told me you were an alcoholic, a pill-popper and a kleptomaniac," he said, more and more rage filling not only his tenor, but also the air around him. "And he was convincing enough that as much as I dislike the guy, I believed him."

Of course he did, because Todd was a charmer. He was a pathological liar, a vapid narcissist, a psychopath and the devil's spawn. But he was also incredibly convincing when he lied. It was part of the reason why she'd stayed with him so long. Each and every time she thought she'd worked up the courage to leave him, he'd go and convince her that he was a changed man, or that he *would* change, that he would do better by her and the kids. Or he'd convince her that somehow his anger was justified, that *she* deserved his ire because of her stupidity and poor choices.

She trimmed more of his hair, this time off the top. It took everything she had to keep her hands steady. "Now do you understand why I couldn't come inside the bar? Why the thought of you two chatting it up like a couple of frat bros made my anxiety go through the roof?"

He nodded slowly.

"I couldn't face you after knowing you'd just spent several hours with my ex-husband. It made my skin crawl just seeing you sitting that close to him, smiling and laughing."

"Well, all my laughter was forced. The man is a crude pig."

Now that was just an insult to pigs.

She combed her fingers through his hair, tugging slightly until he turned back around and faced forward. Their eyes locked in the mirror. "I'm sorry I didn't text you. I'm sorry I didn't call you back. I ... " She wiped the back of her wrist beneath her nose again and sniffled. "I just needed some time to think. Some space and to talk things over with Celeste ... and my shrink. I saw her yesterday too."

"Did it help?"

"It did. I was planning to come over and talk to you tonight after my client, actually. Clear the air and apologize." Her bottom lip wobbled, and she shook her head, her lashes now spiked from all the tears. "I'm really sorry, Scott."

Before she realized she was moving, she found herself hauled around the chair and in his lap. As she opened her mouth, he smothered her response by taking her lips roughly, plunging his tongue in and taking control. One hand fisted her ponytail, while the other held her jaw, angling her neck back so he had greater access and could push his tongue deeper into her mouth.

She melted against him, her body going lax and letting out its own sigh of relief now that she was back and safe in his arms. Where she was meant to be.

Her body temperature ratcheted up the longer they kissed, the more he pulled on her ponytail, and his pinky finger rested against the rapidly beating pulse in her neck.

She'd been so worried that she'd blown it with Scott, that her going all freaky-AWOL on him Monday night had ruined their chances. She knew he was mad by his last voicemail and text message, but at that point she still hadn't been ready to talk to him. She needed to see her therapist, get some coping tools and figure out the next steps. Todd was, after all, Scott's client—a big client, at a new job no less. It would be deleterious to his career to lose Fletcher Holdings.

But she also didn't want to lose Scott.

How could she keep him and he keep Todd?

Was that even possible?

After a few moments, he broke the kiss. His lips traveled down her cheek and over her jaw. "Eva." Her name on his lips was a plea. It cracked her wide open, causing her emotions to clench tight in her throat. "What are we going to do, Eva?"

She had no idea. No clue.

It was all so messed up now.

Even when she tried to start a new life with her sons in a new neighborhood, with a new man, Todd Fletcher still haunted her. He was a true demon, and if Allison DeWitt's books had taught her anything, the only way to kill a demon was to rip off its head and burn its body.

Tempting, but she'd never been one for bloodshed.

Against everything inside her that protested, she pried herself up off his lap and walked back around the chair. "I should finish your hair." Her voice was hollow and not at all sounding like her own. She resumed her job, the feel of Scott's silky hair between her fingers and the cool steel of the scissors in her hand reassuring and grounding. She loved her job. All she'd ever wanted to be was a hairdresser. Since the age of three, she loved playing with people's hair. She'd learned to braid and plait hair at a young age, and by the third grade, girls were lined up at recess waiting for her to braid or style their hair.

Aesthetician school had been a bit of a no-brainer after she finished hairdressing school and started working in a salon and spa. She knew she wanted to keep educating herself in the field of beauty and pampering. She wanted to have more to offer people, add more skills and expertise to her CV. So she worked her way through aesthetics school while cutting and coloring hair at The Yellow Owl Hair Salon in downtown Seattle.

Man, she missed it there.

The Owl had been a hip, fun place to work, and she'd made some incredible friends.

But Todd had done his job as an abuser and alienated her from all those friends. She didn't speak to any of them anymore. At one point she would have gone so far as to call them her extended family, and now? Now she doubted any of them would throw a bucket of water on her if she were to spontaneously catch fire. Todd had caused her to burn a lot of bridges and hurt a lot of people.

"That's what abusers do," her therapist had said. "They isolate their victims from friends and family so that all the victim has left, the only person they trust is their abuser."

And that's exactly what Todd had done. And he'd done it so well.

Thank God, Celeste hadn't given up on her and refused to leave Eva alone, no matter what Todd said about her sister. She was still working on repairing her relationship with her parents. Todd had destroyed the once close and loving relationship she had with them. There was a chance they hated her ex-husband more than she did.

She grabbed the razor off the vanity counter and tidied up the back of Scott's neck and his sideburns. The silence between them began to grow thick in the air. Their passionate moment from earlier already seemed like a lifetime ago. Now all that filled the room was the buzz of the blade and her thundering pulse in her ears.

Once she was finished, she circled around in front of him and hunched down a bit to make sure everything was even. Her fingers found their way back into his hair, and she flayed them out over the sides of his head, pulling the hair out to double-check the length.

Everything looked good.

Scott looked good.

It was habit that had her reaching for the soft, fuzzy brush from the vanity and brushing it over his neck and shoulders, sending the small hair clippings to the tile floor. Then she removed the cape from him and stepped back to grab the broom, but she didn't have the chance to reach it before his arm snaked out and he grabbed her around the waist, drawing her once again onto his lap.

Her chin trembled as he settled her into him. Heat poured off him like a nuclear reactor. If she wasn't careful, he was going to send her into a full-on meltdown. "I thought that Todd might have convinced you I was all those terrible things," she whispered, her fingers twisting around the hem of her white T-shirt. She was in her comfy but professional attire. Stylish dark wash denim capris, a plain white V-neck T, purple tennis shoes and funky, sparkly chandelier earrings. It was an outfit that said she tried, but she wasn't trying *too* hard because she was also a mother of two boys and it was a daring enough move for her to wear white, let alone get all glammed up.

She couldn't bring herself to look at him. Too many thoughts and emotions swirled inside her that the strength to lift her head, to look him in the eye failed her.

Luckily, it was Scott to the rescue. His knuckle found her chin, and gently, he tilted her head up. "I believed him about his ex-wife when I didn't know who she was. But now that I know it's you, that I *know* you, I don't believe a single word out of his lying, bastard mouth."

Relief flickered inside her. "Thank you."

"Haven't you figured out by now that we're inevitable, Eva? I don't know how you can't see that."

The flickering relief morphed into hot, licking flames of need. No man had ever been so patient and caring with her, while at the same time making her swoon and think a million dirty thoughts.

"I'm going to be honest with you," he said, clearing his throat. "I went through a lot of emotions when you ghosted me like that. First, I was worried. My overactive imagination had you upside down in a car, pinned inside as the engine caught fire and the fire department was unable to reach you."

"Well, that's rather detailed and morbid," she muttered.

"Blame Allison DeWitt and her epic attention to detail." He chuckled before his smile faded and his tone grew serious once again. "I was worried. I was scared, and I was sad. I really wanted to go out with you. Yes, the book signing of my favorite author would have been awesome, but that was just a bonus. Dating you was the real prize. And then when Mr. Gallagher said you ran home and then packed the boys up in your van, I started to think that maybe you were *all* at the hospital. Like everyone had come down with food poisoning or had ingested bad pork or whatever. I started to fear for your kids. Then I thought maybe Todd had kidnapped all of you."

Her eyes flared. That thought came to her more often than she cared to admit. Only Todd didn't kidnap her; he killed her and then took the boys. At least once a week she woke up in a puddle of sweat after having a nightmare much like that. And of course, those were the nights the boys chose not to climb into her bed, so she'd then have to pad barefoot through the house to go and check on them, often sitting on the sides of their beds for close to half an hour staring at their messy bedheads and angelic faces.

Todd would have to kill her before she allowed him to take her children away from her. He knew it, and she knew it. Which was why she had those kinds of dreams. Awful, haunting, gut-wrenching dreams.

"But then when you texted me back that you were alive ... " His voice grew wooden. "I became angry. I told you how Katrin treated me. Like a second-class citizen in my own marriage. I was never considered, never consulted or shown respect. Her communication skills were total garbage—and that's coming from me, a man, and we're not known for our outstanding communicating abilities. And that's exactly how I felt you were treating me. Like I wasn't worth a proper phone call, or at the very least a text message apologizing for bailing. Like I was an afterthought."

Totally understandable. If the shoe was on the other foot, she would probably feel that way too.

"I'm a good man, Eva. I'm not like Todd. Not at all. You're a woman worth waiting for, but I won't wait around forever, and certainly not so that I can just be walked all over. Dogs are great, but I'm nobody's lapdog." The sudden flare of his nostrils and narrowing of his eyes said that he had indeed been upset. She appreciated the fact that he had cooled down before coming over. Todd would not have shown such courtesy.

Her throat grew painfully tight as she fought back the urge to cry. She nodded stiffly. "I know what I did was wrong. Celeste said the same thing. So did my therapist. And I knew as I was doing it that I was wrong. I'm truly sorry for making you feel like you don't matter, because you do." She cupped his face with both hands and brought her head closer to his until their noses were only an inch a part. "You matter a lot, Scott. So much that it scares me a little. We haven't known each other that long, and yet ... "

"You feel this pull."

"Yeah, I feel this pull."

"Me too." His hands fell to the backs of hers as they rested on his cheeks. "We can take this as slow as you need to, Eva. I don't want to push."

"I don't want to go *too* slow." A cheeky smirk tugged at the corner of her mouth.

His own wily grin made her insides get hot and turn to goo.

"What are we going to do about Todd though?"

A warm puff of air from his nose landed on her top lip. His dark eyes held a mix of confusion and sadness. He pulled away from her and pushed his hand into his freshly cut hair. "I have no idea. I will probably lose my job if I try to ditch him." He shook his head before scrubbing his hand down it, pulling on his beard and chin. She found his hand and laced her fingers with his. He brought the back of her hand to his lips. "I'll have a chat with my boss in the morning and say that there is a conflict of interest surrounding Fletcher Holdings. Maybe he'll just give Todd to another executive."

If only things were that easy.

"I've missed you," she whispered, the intensity of the emotions she felt once again making her throat feel clogged and her chin tremble. With her free hand, she gripped the front of his shirt, her eyes now pleading with him. "I never meant to hurt you or worry you. I just ... " Her fist tightened. "Todd is a trigger for me. I'm not sure he ever won't be. Not until he's dead, anyway."

Which was probably going to be never, because the man wasn't human, and he never got sick. Not even a sore throat or the sniffles. Meanwhile it seemed like she and the boys came down with one plague or another every six weeks or so.

"But I should have called you, and I'm sorry."

"Water under the bridge, baby. Just shoot me a text next time, okay? Don't make me worry. My imagination runs rampant when I'm worried. I may be a happy-go-lucky guy on the outside, but inside"—he pointed to his head—"my imagination always goes to the worst—sometimes completely illogical—case scenario."

Her laugh felt forced, but being so close to Scott, feeling his warmth and safety surround her loosened all the muscles of her body, and eventually she chuckled freely. "I promise."

"Good." Unlinking their hands, he gripped her by the waist and flipped her around until she was straddling him in the chair. A squeak darted from her throat when she was roughly plopped back down in his lap and over a rather noticeable bulge. "Now, new topic. Better topic. Sexy topic." His grin made the air whoosh from her lungs. "I had plans for us, Ms. Marchand. *Big*, naked, dirty plans. I was forced to do those plans on my own."

Her eyebrows lifted. The thought of Scott touching himself was crazy-sexy, his big hand wrapped around his impressive length, sliding back and forth until hot, white cum shot from the center. She wet her bottom lip.

"Do you know how hard it is to lick chocolate off your own stomach?" he asked.

Her fantasy exploded, and her vision refocused on his face. He was grinning like an idiot. A handsome, sexy idiot.

"You ... chocolate?" she breathed, well, more like gulped.

"Ah, glad you're back. Your face went all blank for a second, and I thought you were either in a spontaneous coma or having some kind of silent female hysteria."

Her hands landed on his shoulders, and she steadied herself, locking her gaze with his. "Just imagining you *taking care of business*, that's all. It was hot." She lunged out and snagged his bottom lip between her teeth, tugging just enough to make him growl beneath her.

"Another time," he murmured, reclaiming his lip. "And we'll definitely have to incorporate chocolate another time too."

A pout pulled the corners of her mouth down. But not for long. That pout quickly turned into a gasp of surprise when she found herself—actually both of them—on the move. She wrapped her arms around his neck and locked her thighs on his hips as he stood up from the chair and walked them both over to the larger chair that had the overhead hairdryer above it.

He sat down but set her on her feet beforehand. "You owe me," he murmured, his fingers hooking into the belt loops of her denim capris. "I'm a forgiving man, but I'll be a *more* forgiving man if I get to see some skin." His eyebrows bobbed playfully. "Catch my drift?"

With an eye roll and a smirk, she reached for the hem of her T-shirt and made to pull it over her head, but his hands on her stopped her.

"Let me. It'll be like unwrapping a present."

Her nipples peaked beneath the thin fabric of her bra, and her mouth grew dry. She released her shirt and allowed him to slowly ease it over her head, his lips tracing a path of warm, wet heat over her lower stomach as the fabric left her skin.

Goosebumps chased his lips, and her breathing grew more and more ragged. His tongue now joined the party, and when he dipped it into her belly button, she giggled and squirmed, but his strength held her in place.

Together, they shed her shirt. Now she stood in her pale blue bra and denim capris.

The auburn storm that swirled in his eyes dissolved any and all of her fears. This man wanted her—her, Eva Marchand. He demanded nothing from her but honesty, and that she could do. She could give him honesty and consideration. Never again would she let Scott think he was an afterthought with her. Because he couldn't be further from such a thing. He was her first thought. When she went to bed at night and then again when she woke up in the morning, Scott was the first thing she thought of. He consumed her.

Long, strong fingers worked at the button and zipper of her jeans, the warm backs of his knuckles grazing her belly just enough to send hot zaps directly between her legs. With his help, she shimmied out of her pants and kicked them to the side. Now she was in her black cotton undies—thankfully not her laundry-day granny panties of yesterday—and her blue bra. Her underwear didn't match, but at least they were clean and didn't have any holes in them.

She'd given up long ago being one of those matching thong and bra kind of women. It was just too much work. She had her favorite bras and her favorite underwear, and unfortunately, not too many of them matched. But they were damn comfortable.

Scott didn't seem to give a damn either, the bulge in his dress pants evidence enough. With his encouragement and the way his hooded eyes devoured her like she was a juicy steak cooked to perfection, she stepped between his widespread knees. Beginning at her knees, his hands trailed up her legs, over her thighs and the curves of her hips, settling on the roundness of her butt cheeks. His breath on her belly made everything inside her tingle, and then when his fingers gently pulled her cheeks apart and one finger pressed against her crease, those tingles turned into quivers and jolts of both anticipation and pleasure.

"Not today, but I would love to see you truly come undone after I've given *this* some of my undivided attention." His tongue swirled around her navel again. "Whether you ever let my cock in there or not is irrelevant. There are *so* many ways I could make you come from just a little bit of ... " He licked her belly, then pressed his finger against her tight hole. "If you get my drift?"

Oh, she got his drift, all right. She got his drift, jumped onto his drift and wanted to ride his drift wherever the hell it was headed.

There wasn't a single thing she would say no to when it came to Scott and the bedroom. They'd only had sex that one night, but it was enough for her to know the man was a god. Especially when her last sexual partner had been Todd the Selfish Lover Demon Spawn.

"Hmm?" His hum and the buzz from his lips against her ribs was connected directly to her clit, and her hips jutted out toward him of their own volition. "I'll take that as a *yes*."

It was a *hell* yes.

"But not today," he reiterated. "Today ... *tonight*, I want just you. Just *Eva*."

From her ribs, he dipped his head again, but this time lower, his nose pressed right against her panties, directly over her clit. He inhaled.

She gasped.

"Ah, Eva. I've missed this. I've missed you."

Her fingers pushed into his hair, and she tugged just a little. "I've missed you too."

The twirl of his tongue over the fabric that covered her clit made her legs spasm, and she gripped his hair tighter to hold on, to keep herself up.

He chuckled against her, causing a warm gush of arousal to seep from between her legs. "Panties off," he murmured, the heat from his mouth searing her through the cotton.

She did as he instructed, with his help, of course. Thank goodness, she'd taken care of the playing field on Sunday right before their botched date on Monday. She was sporting her small strip of hair but nothing else.

His look was predatory. Hungry. Insatiable. And the way he licked his lips reminded her of a lion licking his chops as he stalked an impala on the savannah. Ravenous and willing to give the chase of a lifetime to get what he wanted. What he needed. What he *craved*.

And right now, Scott craved her.

Her ego did a little happy dance. It'd been far too long since a man had looked at her like that. And Scott looked at her like that a lot. Todd had actually gone so far as to call her post-partum body—just six months after she had Kellen —"absolutely disgusting." After that she ate nothing but chicken breasts and cucumbers for an entire month.

His hands on her thighs brought her back to the now; she blinked and smiled down at the man who gazed at her with nothing but adoration. No disgust or contempt filled his eyes. Just ... awe.

"Are you wet?" The deep, gravelly tenor of his voice was an aphrodisiac all on its own. He also didn't wait for her to respond and slid two fingers between her folds, where, of course, he found her slick and swollen. His nostrils flared and his eyelids dropped even farther. "Very."

She pulled a long breath through her nose and then slowly released it. "Scott ... "

"Eva ... " Those two fingers explored further, delving into her quivering heat, where she contracted around him. His thumb landed on her clit and her hips jerked.

"Scott," she pleaded.

The man was skilled with his fingers for sure, but she wanted, no, *needed* more. She needed him. All of him. Inside her. Not just a couple of fingers. No matter how talented those fingers were.

Would she come from this? Absolutely.

But it wasn't just about the orgasm. It was about the connection, the intimacy, the feeling of being one with another person who was beginning to mean a great deal to her.

"Scott, please." She was whimpering now.

With a growl, a grunt and the speed of a cheetah, his fingers were out of her, he was up out of the chair and she found herself pushed forward, hinged at the hips, hands on the armrests.

The zip and *swish* of his pants behind her was like sweet, raunchy music to her ears. Dribbles of her arousal trickled down her inner thigh, and her pussy clenched at the thought of having Scott inside her again. Then came the quiet tear of the condom wrapper—he was so prepared, showing up with protection—and before she could blink, wiggle her hips or ask him where he went, he was pressing the thick head of his cock against her dripping slit.

"Scott ... "

Although she'd been hoping for hard, fast and dirty, the laziness with which he eased himself inside her was a million times better. His girth coasted across every one of her neurons as he made his way into her body, giving each inch his undivided attention. Her eyes threatened to roll back into her head.

She could come just from this. Just from the first thrust. His fingers squeezing her hips and a low grunt said he was to the hilt inside her now. She was tight. The pleasant ache and throb between her legs as she adjusted to his size sent shivers sprinting down her limbs.

This was what heaven felt like. Ecstasy. Pure bliss.

That was until he started to move.

Oh God.

Now *that* was heaven. Every draw of his cock, followed by a hard plunge and a hip swivel that knocked her G-spot just right. She could hear angels singing, harps playing. Clouds were everywhere. It really was heaven.

"You're it for me, Eva." His dark timber made her core clench around his length. "I know this is all new, but new or not, I feel the pull, and I know you're it. I'm not going anywhere. You're stuck with me now."

"Scott ... " That was all she could say. His name was a plea on her lips. A plea for more. For harder, for faster, for it to never end.

The slapping sound of flesh on flesh was a new dirty music that filled her small spa space, and when his hard chest connected with her back and he hunched over her, changing the angle, she nearly lost her mind. And she really did lose her mind when his finger pressed against her clit.

Every muscle inside her went rigid, her toes curled on the tile floor, and her back bowed as the orgasm came crashing through her. Like the waves on a harsh sea, it pounded her, jostled her, rocked her to her very soul. Until she was nothing more than a boneless, buzzing pile of goo still standing only because Scott was holding her up. Keeping her safe, tight against his chest and his wildly beating heart. After a few moments, he stood back up, his pumping becoming more fervent, his cadence more erratic. He was close too.

She did her best to return to the moment, to regain some of her senses and be present for him when he came. Her eyes remained glued shut, her lips parted, skin tingling. She was still riding the high of her climax, enjoying the exquisite way his cock drove deep into her and then retreated over her sensitive channel. The potential for another climax bubbled deep in her belly.

Her breasts swayed heavily beneath her. Even in her bra, they jiggled with each one of his mighty thrusts. Her hard nipples ached for the heat and relief of his mouth.

The smell of sex, hairspray and Scott's own citrusy, manly smell circled around her, combining into one intoxicating scent that was uniquely their own.

"Eva, babe." He grunted. "I'm close."

His thumb shifted from her hips to the top of her crease, sliding just south enough for the hairs on her arms to tingle and her pussy to tighten around his cock.

"Come for me," she whispered, curious to one day find out what it felt like to have him show her the pleasure she could experience in that intimate, forbidden erogenous zone.

"Eva." Her name was more of a strained purr as he pumped into her harder and faster, his fingers tightening on her hip.

She squeezed her muscles around him as best she could. His breath hitched. He stilled, inhaled sharply, held it and then let it out in a moan of satisfaction as his cock began to pulse inside her.

"Oh fuck, babe," he ground out, hunching over her again and wrapping an arm beneath her, his fingers delving into her bra and tugging on a tight nipple.

That was all she needed to send her back over the edge. To send her back to heaven. Squeezing her eyes shut and gripping the armrests until her knuckles ached, she allowed the orgasm to consume her. To shred her very existence, take all the remaining muscles that worked, and pummel them until they were nothing but jelly. Moaning with each pulse of her orgasm, she milked his cock as best she could, pulling him deeper inside her as his own release began to wane.

She knew he was spent and his orgasm over when his warm breath swept across her sweat-kissed skin and his fingers on her nipple relaxed.

"Babe," he cooed, planting gentle, sensual kisses across her shoulders as he held her there in place, still safely nestled inside her. "So good."

"So good," she echoed.

A mewl of mourning slipped from her throat as he gently stood up and slid out of her. She missed him already.

While Scott went about zipping up and disposing of the condom, she went on the hunt for her clothes.

They took turns in the bathroom, then met up again under the bright recessed lighting next to her desk and computer. Neither of them was able to keep their grins at bay. And let's be honest, why would they want to?

He reached for her hand and brought her knuckles to his lips. "I'm glad we were able to *clear the air*," he said. His nose wrinkled, and then he grinned even wider. "Now that air smells like sex. Hot, hot sex."

She giggled foolishly.

He squeezed her hand. "I mean it though. I'm glad we talked. I'm glad we're not over."

She stared down at their entwined hands and nodded. "Me too."

"I'll talk to my boss tomorrow and see about transferring Todd to another executive," he said. "I can't ... " He shook his head and glanced down at her. "I don't even want to be in the same room as that man. I'm afraid of what I might do, now that I know what he did to you."

His protectiveness was touching, but he also needed to know how dangerous Todd could be. Scott did not want to cross her ex-husband. Todd's morals were questionable and his scruples lacking. Who knew what he could do to Scott, not to mention his career, if he got a bee in his psychopathic bonnet and decided to exact his revenge?

"We'll figure it out, babe," Scott said, releasing her hand and pulling her into his arms, his lips pressing against her forehead. "Todd is the least of my concerns right now. Let's just ride the wave that we're good, the sex was great and there is plenty more where that came from."

She chuckled against him, her hands splaying across the warm solidness of his back. "Okay. Just please be careful, Scott. Todd is dangerous."

He kissed her forehead again. "I will. Now, let's plan a date, because I meant what I said, woman, I want to take you out. Hot sex in hotel rooms and salons is great, but I want to be your boyfriend. I want to show you off to the world."

Heat flooded her cheeks, and she smiled shyly. "I'd love that."

13

"What do you mean it's a *conflict of interest?*" Remy, Scott's boss, asked snidely as Scott sat in Remy's enormous office the following day. "Since when?"

Since it's none of your damn business.

"Since recently. I, uh ... " He scratched the back of his neck as nerves prickled along his freshly shaved skin. "Since I discovered that the woman I'm seeing is actually Todd's ex-wife." Scott swallowed. "Their divorce was not exactly amicable."

And Todd is a motherfucking rapist bastard who should be behind bars right now.

Remy's normally rather pale complexion turned the color of a tomato fresh off the vine. "You're saying that our biggest client in I don't know how long is suddenly a conflict of interest because of a *woman?*"

Scott's hands gripped the armrests of his chair to keep himself from lunging at Remy for making such a remark, not to mention the irritated facial expression that went with it. "Not just *a* woman. Todd's ex-wife. This has no way of ending well. If you haven't noticed, the man is fiercely competitive, demanding and is used to getting his own way. If he gets a bee up his ass about me dating his ex-wife, what's to stop him from just up and pulling all his businesses from our service?"

"Uh, I dunno, how about a little something called a binding contract?"

Scott chomped down hard on his back teeth. How old was Remy anyway? Twenty-five? Twenty-eight? He was no more than a maggot. A grotesque, white, wiggly little flesh eater. And how in the hell did he get into a senior partner position?

Oh yeah, that's right. His daddy was the CEO.

Clearing his throat and loosening his grip on the chair, Scott made sure to keep his tone as respectful as was humanly possible when faced with an idiot who was possibly still in diapers when Scott was busy losing his virginity in the back of a Chevy pickup. "Yes, we do have a contract, and it *is* binding, but that doesn't mean Mr. Fletcher wouldn't try. There is an escape clause in the contract, even though I'm not sure my romantic life is grounds for contract termination. But the man has an army of lawyers at his disposal, and he doesn't strike me as the type of guy who's used to losing. It would come down to whether or not you want to waste our company money on lawyer fees during a lawsuit."

Remy worked the jaw of his baby face back and forth, his amber eyes closer to a catlike yellow, which combined with his orangey-red hair reminded Scott of his childhood cat Chester, a bit fat ginger thing missing half an ear and with a docked tail.

"Look, Remy." Scott sat forward in his chair and rested his elbows on his thighs, his gaze level with his dumb-dumb boss. "I'm not saying we cut ties with Fletcher Holdings. I'm just saying it would behoove us—behoove the company for me to be removed off the file."

"Or you just break up with this chick," Remy offered,

curling his fingertips toward his wrist and examining his nails. He appeared bored.

"Not an option."

Remy kicked his feet up onto his desk, reached for a dark blue stress ball and began tossing it up into the air. "Well, I want you on this project, Scott. You're a new hire, you're still on probation, and I want to see how you're going to handle this VIP client. You came highly recommended." His cheeks grew ruddy again. "And so far, I think you were a bit overrated. I've yet to be wowed by anything you'd done. I want you to prove me wrong."

Rage raced through Scott's veins, heating his cheeks and chest until he felt sweat begin to bead on his upper lip. He wanted to wipe it away, but his knuckles were lily white, he was gripping the chair arms so tight again.

Who the fuck was this guy anyway?

An entitled maggot, that's who.

Inhaling deep through his nose, Scott stood up and retreated to the closed door of Remy's office. "Then I will ask that you keep this information to yourself, please."

Remy tossed the stress ball back up into the air again. "I'm already bored with this topic, Scott. It doesn't interest me. Making money interests me. So make money from Fletcher Holdings, and that's when I'll be interested."

Exhaling through his nose because he was clenching his molars so damn hard, Scott gave his maggot-boss one nod, then opened the door and left. He needed to text Eva. He needed to let her know that things did not go as planned. Now they had to really be careful, because if Todd got wind of the two of them together, it could not only make Eva's life a living hell but it could be the end of Scott's career. And as much as he disliked Remy Barker, he really liked his new job at Dynamic Creative, and he really, *really* liked his new salary.

Once he was back in his office, he grabbed his phone off

the desk and brought up Eva's number. He'd taken a picture of her last night, all freshly fucked and looking unbelievable. That was now the photo that went along with her contact info. Fuck, she was gorgeous.

After staring at her for a full minute, he texted her the bad news.

Babe, my boss is an idiot maggot and won't let me switch off the project. I'm really sorry.

It was only about five minutes before she messaged back.

That really sucks. Did you explain the conflict of interest?

Yep. He's an idiot maggot. Doesn't care.

Todd is dangerous, Scott. If he finds out we're dating ...

I know, babe. We'll figure it out, I promise.

Fuck, he was getting tired of this texting bullshit. He needed to hear her voice. If she was with a client, she wouldn't be able to reply so quickly.

He ran his thumb along the curve of his chin as he punched dial on her number then put the phone to his ear, awaiting her sultry, throaty voice.

"Hello?"

God, that voice was what wet dreams were made of.

He smiled without meaning to—the natural side effect of hearing her feminine rasp—and swiveled around in his chair to look out the window of his snazzy corner office. "Hey, babe," he started. His view of the sound was slightly blocked by a shorter building in front of him, but he could still see the water and the boats in the bay. There was nothing quite like Seattle in the springtime. The sea sparkled, the trees were in full bloom, and the urge to mate was thick in the air.

Eva sighed. "I don't want you to lose your job, Scott."

He propped his feet up on the window ledge. "I won't. I'll just be careful. *We'll* just be careful."

She sighed again, and it was all he could do to not envision her sighing as he slid his fingers between her legs. She'd made a similar sound last night down in her salon. "I miss you already. Isn't that crazy?"

His dick jerked in his trousers. "Not crazy at all. I miss you too. What are you doing Friday?"

"Going out on a date with you, why?"

Well that made his chest expand and his smile hurt his face. "Just making sure you're available. Dinner?"

"Absolutely."

"Good."

The air between them grew quiet. His ears strained in an attempt to hear what she was up to. His office door was closed, but there were murmurs from outside sneaking under his door.

"Eva?"

"Hmm?"

"I can't wait to get you naked again." Even though he knew she was scared about her ex finding out about them, no way in hell was he wasting any time talking about him. Not when they could be talking and *planning* other things.

Fifty bucks said she was blushing.

And probably biting her lip too.

"And then once I have you naked, sprawled out on my bed, I'm going to run my tongue over every inch of your body. Leave no nipple unsucked, no hipbone unlicked."

All that came through on the other end was a quick inhale of breath followed by a low moan. Yeah, she'd done that last night too.

"Friday, come over for dinner. I'll cook for you."

"Mac and cheese again?" Her breathy voice made his cock do another twitch. He adjusted himself for more comfort.

"If that's what your heart desires."

"Mmmm ... what my heart desires ... what about my body?"

"I'll take care of it all. Your heart, your taste buds, your body. No part of you will be left unsatisfied. Unlicked. Untouched. Unsucked."

Her next words came out as more of a whimper. "Scott ... "

"Eva ... " A knock at his office door broke the spell, and thank goodness it did. He was sporting a full stiffy now, and that was not workplace-appropriate. "Listen, babe, I've gotta go. But I'll call you tonight and we can make plans for tomorrow, okay?"

"Okay."

"And Eva?"

"Yeah?"

"I'm going to fuck you until the cows come home." Then he ended the call, but not before he heard the satisfying gasp from the incredible woman on the other end. He adjusted his pants, spun around in his chair and slid his waist back under his desk to hide any remaining evidence of his arousal. "Come in," he barked.

The doorknob turned, and though he was expecting Remy the douchebag or his receptionist, Sondra, it was neither.

"Hey, dumbass, wanna grab lunch?" Liam asked, sauntering into Scott's office in his fancy suit, shiny loafers and very expensive smile.

Ah, just who he needed to see. His retainer-free lawyer on-call. Also known as his annoying but loyal big brother.

Double-checking that his cock was now back to its flaccid self, he snatched his wallet from the corner of his desk and stood. "I am if you're buying?"

Liam's grin grew. "Sure, I'll take my *poor* baby brother out for lunch. It's the least I can do, given that I probably make triple your salary. I have to help out those in need."

Scott rolled his eyes and pushed past his brother, who

was just a half-inch taller than him. "It is the *least* you can do."

Liam slapped him on the back and, laughing, followed Scott out into the reception area.

Scott jerked his chin toward Sondra and patted the counter above her desk twice. "I'm heading for lunch with Liam."

Sondra's cheeks pinked up as she settled her gaze on Liam. The woman had a very obvious crush on him, and Liam played that up by flirting shamelessly with her whenever he came to visit Scott. Not that Scott had worked there long, but Liam usually came by once a week for lunch, and when he did, he charmed the pants off all the women in the office.

As they made their way toward the elevator, Scott let out a long sigh, his shoulders slumping as the last of the air left his lungs.

"Ah, see." Liam tapped his temple. "Big brother intuition. I knew my little Scottie needed me. What's up? How can Liam fix your life this time?" They stepped into the elevator, and Liam hit *M* for the main floor.

Scott rolled his eyes again. "Awfully crowded in this elevator, you, me and your ego."

Liam tossed his head back and laughed.

They stepped into the building lobby, then out into the warm, late April afternoon. The sun was shining, the birds were chirping, and the breeze was mild.

It was a beautiful day, and yet the dark clouds that Scott felt approaching his life, lingering just behind him, were ominous and foreboding.

Despite the massive ego that joined them as a third party for lunch, maybe it was a good thing Liam had stopped by. He could pick his brother's brain on how to handle this Todd, Eva and Dynamic Creative situation.

"So, little Scottie, what's got you down?" Liam teased as he sipped his beer on the rooftop terrace of the fancy downtown Seattle harbor restaurant. It was a favorite spot of Liam's and a lunch hotspot for Seattle's upper echelon in the corporate world. Not only did the suit monkeys come here to eat, but they also went to be seen, network and hold meetings.

Scott scanned the harbor beyond them and watched as an enormous crane across the bay loaded shipping containers onto a freighter. He'd once heard that that was one of the world's most stressful jobs. That the crane operators only worked four-hour shifts but got paid for eight, it was so nerve-racking.

At that moment, after his meeting with Remy and knowing that he was going to have to see Todd tomorrow when he came in to touch base on things, Scott was seriously considering a job change, and shipping container crane operator didn't sound half bad.

"Hmm, Scottie?" Liam probed.

Scott hated that nickname, and Liam knew it. Which was why he used it.

"Unbeknownst to any of us," he started, "it would appear as though I am sleeping with and dating my new, very rich, very successful and very important client's ex-wife. And their separation was anything but amicable." He took a long pull off his own beer bottle. "He's also a terrible human being, and I'd like to rip his fucking face off."

Liam's dark brows shot up beneath the swath of light brown hair that hung perfectly over his forehead. His brown eyes, a shade darker than Scott's, went wide, and all the amusement left his face.

"You're shitting me?"

"'Fraid not. That's why she stood me up Monday. Saw her ex through the window at Prime and hit the bricks. Then she went all squirrelly thinking I was going to side with him." He began to pick at the label of his beer bottle with his thumbnail. Anything he could do to keep his hands busy, otherwise they would surely form fists and he'd end up punching a hole through the wall, breaking his hand in the process. Anytime he even thought about Todd and what he did to Eva, he saw red and wanted to break things—and one particular person.

Liam tugged on his chin, the thin layer of tidy scruff making a raspy sound against his fingers. "So what are you going to do?"

The waitress arrived with their Kung Pao steak sandwiches—a fusion dish the place had become instantly famous for—and then quickly retreated. Liam dug into his sandwich.

Scott merely picked at his fries, dunking them into the homemade sesame ginger aioli. "I went to my boss today and asked to be removed from the project. I told Remy it was a conflict of interest and that Fletcher Holdings would be better suited with someone else."

"And he didn't agree?"

"He did not. I even went so far as to tell him that I'm dating our client's wife, and he still didn't seem to care. The guy is a tool. Earned his position by kissing his father's ass." He took another pull off his beer, then nodded when the waitress wandered past and asked if he'd like another.

"Well, what are you going to do if this Fletcher guy finds out? Is he dangerous?"

Scott wiped the corner of his mouth with a napkin and nodded.

"Then you've got to find a way to either end it with Eva or come clean with Fletcher. Because even though he'll still be mad you're fucking his ex, I bet you he'll be even more pissed if he finds out from a source that *isn't* you." A dark blond streak in Liam's hair glinted in the afternoon sun as he flipped his head back, causing that swath he babied to bob over his forehead. Scott could practically hear women on the patio groan and swoon.

Scott's older brother was known far and wide as one of Seattle's most eligible bachelors. He was rich, he was successful, he was handsome, and he was straight. A winning combination for any red-blooded woman still looking for Mr. Right.

Too bad Liam was nobody's Mr. Right. Not anymore at least. He was determined to never settle down again. He wouldn't even consider having a girlfriend. Not after his ex, Cidrah, stomped all over his heart. Now Liam had his Wednesday night fuck buddy, Richelle, and the two kept it casual—or so he said.

"I can't be the one to tell him," Scott said before he dove into his sandwich. "The guy would probably fire Dynamic Creative and then kill me."

The meat from the sandwich hit his tongue, and he fought back a groan, losing the battle and squeezing his eyes shut for good measure. Fuck, it was almost as good as sex. Spicy, sweet, sour and salty. All the best flavor notes piled between two slices of homemade sourdough. Peanuts and ginger, sesame and soy sauce. It was all there, and combined with the perfectly cooked rare steak—if he hadn't just had incredible sex last night, he would have possibly ranked it higher than sex. But sex with Eva was unsurpassable, even by an awesome steak sandwich.

"Can she tell him?" Liam asked, forcing Scott to open his eyes and swallow his bite.

He shook his head. "Unless she did it over the phone or through an email. She has a restraining order against him. The guy has a temper. He, uh ... " Shit, was it his place to tell Liam what Todd did to Eva? That he raped his own wife?

No. Probably not.

"He just has a temper, from what she's said. He doesn't take no for an answer. He is competitive, demanding, easily offended and a narcissist. Eva also called him a psychopath, though he's never been properly diagnosed."

"Most psychopaths aren't," Liam muttered. "Though I'd bet you my fucking house, my car, and my right nut that I've worked with close to a hundred of them. More of them walk among us than we think. They're just not all ax-wielding murders."

"What do you suggest we do then? If I tell him, he'll fire the company, and then I'll be fired and then probably run down in the streets by an unmarked car. If she tells him, he might hurt her or take the kids."

"Does she have a lawyer?"

He nodded. "Yeah, apparently her lawyer was awesome. Got her full custody of her kids and a pretty decent divorce settlement. He also has to pay child support and alimony, which he tried to fight."

"Fucking scum."

"That's insulting to scum."

"Well, if you want my help, let me know. I can draft something up or work with her lawyer and the two of us can draft something up. We could send it to his lawyer. Do this all the legal way. Or as legal as we can. Don't you have a contract with him for work? He can't just fire Dynamic Creative, can he? I mean, I'm not a contract lawyer, but ... "

"Like I said, he's a man who doesn't acknowledge the word *no*. If he wants to break the contract, he'll find a way." He scratched his beard. "There's an escape clause in his contract, too. I'll have to relook at it to see what constitutes evoking it."

"Escape clause? Who has an escape clause?" A hand landed hard on Scott's shoulder and squeezed. Liam's eyes flashed up behind him, his brows forming a ridge.

Holy fuck.

Scott spun around in his seat to find none other than the devil they spoke of—Todd *Fucking* Fletcher.

"Hey there, Scott. How's it going?" Todd was all smiles in a black pinstripe suit that made him look like some kind of mob boss. He certainly looked demonic, the way his dark brows winged up at the corners and his hair was all slicked back high and hard with gel. His pale blue eyes pierced Scott. The man had no soul—it was clear now. Todd lifted one brow when Scott failed to reply, his gaze drifting over to Liam. He extended a hand. "Todd Fletcher."

"Liam Dixon," Liam replied, taking Todd's hand warily, his eyes flicking to Scott's quickly but then back up to Todd's, a forced smile tugging on his lips just in time.

"Oh, brothers?"

Scott nodded. "Yeah."

Todd's grin widened, then recognition dawned on his face. "Not *the* Liam Dixon of Wallace, Dixon and Travers?"

"The very same," Liam said, releasing Todd's hand and then taking a swig from his beer.

Scott's temperature was approaching inferno. His blood was magma, his skin on fire, his palms hot, sweaty and itchy as his hands bunched beneath the table, desperate to make contact with Todd's face.

This man had ruined Eva. He'd cheated on her. He'd raped her. He'd bullied her and demoralized her until she was a shadow of who she'd once been. Scott's fists through his face would be a drop in the bucket of what he truly deserved.

Murmurs behind them all and more men in suits smelling of cologne and money filtered out onto the restaurant patio. Todd acknowledged them as they wandered past. "Well, I won't keep you gentlemen. Nice to meet you, Liam. Scott, I'll see you tomorrow, hey, bud?"

Scott's jaw ached, he was gnashing his molars so hard. "Yes, meeting at eleven. See you then."

Then the fuckface took his leave of them and went to join his cronies, who all looked just as smarmy, slimy and psychopathic as him.

"Speak of the fucking devil." Liam coughed into his beer, tipping it up again and draining it. "Jesus fucking Christ."

"You got that right," Scott murmured. He stared down at his sandwich. Goddamn it. Now he'd lost his fucking appetite. He snagged the waitress's gaze as she passed. "Can I get this to go?"

She nodded and said she'd be right back with a to-go box.

"So that's the piece of shit there, huh?" Liam asked, still seeming to have his own appetite and diving into his sandwich.

"The steaming pile fresh from the dog's ass," Scott confirmed.

"Well, let me do some digging," Liam said, shoving his food into his cheek so he could continue to talk. "I've got a PI friend who owes me a favor. I'll see what he can dig up on this suit-wearing turd. We might be able to leverage your relationship if the man's hands are sticky."

Scott's interest piqued, and his stomach rumbled. He dipped a fry into his aioli before popping it into his mouth. "Really?"

Liam shrugged. "A man like that"—he shook his head —"no way he's clean. The question is: just *how* dirty is he?"

14

It was Friday night, and Eva bounced on pins and needles as she slipped out of the front seat of her van in her sweaty gym clothes and headed up the walkway to her front door. She had an hour to shower, shave, primp and preen before she was expected over at Scott's for dinner ... and *more*.

She'd dropped the boys off with Celeste before heading to the gym, and her sister was going to keep them overnight. Todd's parents had asked for the boys Saturday morning, so they would pick Kellen and Lucas up from Celeste's and then bring them back to Eva's later in the afternoon.

She had not only all night to herself (and Scott) but also all day tomorrow.

Were things finally beginning to look up?

Don't get too carried away just yet. You can do a happy dance but no party hats or streamers. Your ex is still messing up your life. Now he's your new boyfriend's VIP client.

The nearly too-hot-to-bear water sluiced over her naked skin as she stood beneath the shower and washed herself. Even though the bruises were long gone, the memories were still clear as day. When she washed her legs, she could still remember the dark blue and green marks on her inner thighs and her hips from Todd's vicious demands. The purple "cuffs" around her wrists from where he'd restrained her so tightly with his own hands, she didn't think she'd ever break free.

But even those were bearable, were mere specks of shame and abuse compared to the bite marks he left along her collarbone, shoulders and across her breasts.

From the moment he banged on her bedroom door to the minute he left her lying there in the bed, naked, crying and drenched in sweat and semen, she had feared for her life.

Sex with Todd had never been earth-shattering. He'd been a selfish lover from day one. But it had never been painful or violent. That night had been. Everything he did to her hurt. He was rough and mean, harsh and aggressive. He took from her, and then he left.

She'd lain in that bed trembling for a good twenty minutes, fearing that he might return and do it again. Thankfully, though, Todd had never been more than a one-trick pony, and he'd also been drunk. He'd most likely just gone to bed and passed out. It had taken every bit of energy she had left—which wasn't much, having just tried to fight off her husband—and she dragged herself to the shower. Then she put on heavy sweats and a big hoodie, and she began to plan her escape. It wasn't until three days later, when Todd was away for business, that she and the boys finally got away. She'd been forced to live and face her rapist for three days until then, unable to sleep out of dread he might burst into her room again. After all, her door didn't have a lock on it. She couldn't even barricade herself, in case one of the boys needed her. So she lay awake every night for three nights, praying he stayed in his own wing of the house.

At first, she wasn't sure he even remembered, because he never said a word about it. Never mentioned anything, never asked her how she was. He ignored her for the first two days, then on the third, when her sleeve slipped up her arm and the bruises around her wrist were exposed, he commented.

She'd flinched when he came up behind her and grabbed her wrist, her whole body going rigid from his touch. Unfortunately, that just made it all worse, and the rage that glimmered back at her in his pale, soulless eyes was a look that still haunted her dreams.

"You seem to forget your place, Mrs. Fletcher," Todd began. "You are my property. Bought and paid for." He ran his thumb over the diamonds that sparkled on her ring finger. "You are my wife and therefore obligated to perform your *wifely* duties. Refusing me is not an option, understand?"

All she was able to do was tremble. Tears burned at the back of her eyes, and her throat tightened to the point of excruciating pain.

"I've been pretty understanding and kind, letting you rebuff me for as long as you have, forced to find my pleasures elsewhere. But you've grown complacent, forgetting your *place*. Which is *beneath* me."

He was right up in her face now, his breath hot and smelling strongly of coffee. "Was the other night fun for you?"

Still trembling, she shook her head.

He released her wrists and gripped her by the shoulders, shaking her until her teeth rattled. "Answer ME!"

"N-no." Tears spilled down her cheeks now, into her mouth and down the crease of her nose.

He released her and shrugged. "Then don't fight me next time. You did that to yourself, you know. Every one of your bruises, your aches and your pains are your fault. Not mine. You made me do that. You made me assert myself. You made me remind you of your place, of *who* you are. You're *mine*,

Eva. You are *my* wife. *My* property and I will do as I see fit with what is mine. Understand?"

She swallowed, her chin quivering so hard she thought she might chip a tooth.

The grip of his fingers tightened around her biceps, and he shook her again. "Understand?"

"Y-yes," she whispered, now blubbering.

He released her, reached behind her for one of the grapes she'd just washed and popped it into his mouth. "Good. I'm glad we're on the same page." He bent down, pecked her on the cheek and stepped away. "I'm going to go pack. My plane leaves early tomorrow." Then he was gone.

Eva's knees knocked and her body shivered despite the heat of the shower as the memories flooded her. Tears mixed with the water, hot and salty.

"I can't let you win," she whispered. "I can't let you take any more from me."

Resolve settled in her belly, warm and sure. She couldn't allow Todd Fletcher to affect any more of her life, any more of the people she cared about. He had to go.

Now she just had to figure out a way to get rid of him.

Murder was out of the question. She looked awful in orange.

A hit man? No, she didn't know any hit men, and somehow that shit always made its way back to the source. She also wasn't rolling in dough—not after buying her house —so she probably couldn't afford a hit man.

She finished rinsing out her hair, wiped away the last of the tears and took a deep, fortifying breath. The memories of Todd would always be there, but if all her time in therapy had taught her anything, it was that the last thing Todd deserved after everything he'd done to her was a place in her mind. She needed to shrink him down to virtually nothing, put him in a tiny black box and shove him to the deepest, darkest recesses of her subconscious. The man did not deserve to be considered, remembered or thought about—ever.

But before she did that, she needed to figure out a way to really get rid of him. Either ship him off to prison forever, push him into a bottomless crevasse, or dig up something so dirty on him she could blackmail him from here to kingdom come to stay away from her, her children and everyone else she loved and cared about.

Shutting off the water, she said out loud to no one in particular, "I need a PI."

FORTY-FIVE MINUTES and four wardrobe changes later, Eva was smoothing down the front of her turquoise, flowy, boho, knee-length skirt and adjusting the off-the-shoulder sleeves of her white eyelet top. She'd decided to go with fun, flirty and just a little bit cheeky with her outfit. Show off her svelte shoulders and trim waist with the cinched elastic rusching below her breasts. When she'd sent a picture of herself to Celeste with her final outfit, her sister had texted back *Hot Mama!*

Not that her sister's opinion didn't matter, but she wasn't trying to seduce *her*. Even though she thought she looked pretty damn doable, if she did say so herself.

She kept her hair loose around her shoulders after a quick blow dry, allowing the natural wave to take over and the layers to gently frame her face.

A little bit of bronzer, blush and some tinted lip balm and she was out the door.

She was about to lift her hand up to Scott's door when the realization hit her. She was arriving empty-handed.

That wasn't right.

Shit.

If her mother had taught her anything, it was that you never, ever arrived to someone's house for dinner empty-handed. You brought something to contribute to the meal, alcohol or a host gift.

Shit. Shit. Shit.

As if she had pockets or a spare bottle of prosecco stuffed under her skirt, her gaze flew around the porch and her body. She glanced into her purse and brought out her wallet. Was cash a tacky host gift?

Yes. Yes, it was.

Shit.

She was down the steps and halfway across the driveway when Scott's door opened behind her. "Running away again?"

She skidded in her tracks, tripping on her cork wedges and needing to fling herself onto the hood of his truck to keep from bailing onto the asphalt.

With flames in her cheeks from the embarrassment, she righted herself using the hood of the truck and turned to face him, once again smoothing the front of her skirt down and adjusting the shoulders of her top. She cleared her throat, thankful that he couldn't glean how hard her heart hammered inside her chest. "No, not at all. I was just ... I forgot something is all." She pointed at her house as if his host gift was simply sitting on her kitchen table forgotten. It was not.

She didn't even have a dusty bottle of wine in her liquor cabinet that she could pass off. She had zilch. Zip. Nada. A big ol' goose egg.

"If it's condoms, I've got *plenty.*" His grin soaked her panties.

Now it wasn't just her cheeks that were warm, it was her whole damn body. She swallowed. "No, it wasn't that. Um ... " Realizing she was defeated, she hung her head. "I'm showing up empty-handed. I don't have any food, wine or a gift for you."

A heavy *clomp, clomp* on the porch steps competed with the lawn mower a few yards down, but she still couldn't bring herself to lift her gaze, that was until big, sexy man feet came into view on the pavement and his heat and scent lassoed around her.

A knuckle tucked under her chin as gentle as could be, and he tilted her head up until all she could see in front of her was Scott.

His lips were pursed as if he were trying to withhold a grin. "You're adorable, you know that?"

Rolling her eyes, she pulled away, glancing back down at his feet. "Don't make fun. This night is really important. I stood you up on our last date—which was also our first *real* date—so this do-over is really important. It's special, and I ... I should have brought you flowers or something."

His knuckle was back beneath her chin. His other hand sought out hers, and he brought the inside of her wrist to his lips. "Eva, listen to me. All I want is you. I have everything else. Food? Check. Wine? Check. Flowers?" His smile grew wry. "Why don't you step inside and find out?"

He released her chin and entwined their hands, leading her up the path back toward his house. A ripple of delight coursed through her. She'd always had a soft spot for the traditional gestures like candy, flowers and having the door held open for her—you know, chivalry. Even though she prided herself on being independent and no longer requiring a guy in her life, her belly still did silly little somersaults when a man showed her his gentlemanly side.

"Be with a man who always walks along the curb," her father had drilled into her and her sister since they were pre-teens. She hadn't walked along the road with Scott yet, but a part of her suspected he was definitely the type to make sure a woman never got splashed when a car drove through a big puddle.

He dropped her hand and brought his fingers to the small of her back, the heat of his palm searing right through the white cotton of her shirt and making sweat spring out from beneath her breasts. "Promise me you won't overthink tonight," he said, holding the door open for her. "We've already slept together. We've already eaten together. Don't think of this as our first date, if that makes it easier. Think of this as our ... " He wrinkled his crooked nose at the same time he reclaimed her hand and led her down the hall toward his kitchen. "Think of this as an anniversary dinner. Because *technically* it's been two months since that night at the bar. And I don't know about you, but I'd like to keep that night, that date as our official *they became a couple* date." He made air quotes with his free hand.

"You're considering that drunken night in the hotel—"

"Uh-uh, you weren't drunk, remember? I don't fuck drunk chicks. At least not the first time I fuck them. Now if you decide to get a little tipsy tonight and climb up my body like it's a jungle gym, I can't say I'll be as much of a gentleman as I was on our first date."

She snickered, the smile he pulled from her easing all her previous anxiety. It was hard not to relax and be herself around Scott. He just made it so easy.

They entered the kitchen, and she was immediately greeted by an enormous bouquet of spring flowers sitting on the counter in a vase.

"Zara at Flowers on 5th did up the arrangement for me. She's the best. I hope you like them." Unease flitted across his features, hanging in his eyes.

She reached for the vase, releasing his hand, and brought one of the flowers to her nose. "It's perfect. Thank you."

His smile was back, and this time it was cocky. "You can keep the vase too. Came with the bouquet."

"Thank you."

No longer unsure and back to being comfortable, large and in charge in his own element, Scott grabbed the bottle of wine off the counter. "It's been breathing for over an hour. Guy at the liquor store said this one is, and I quote, *totally bitchin', dude.*" He poured them each a glass and handed her hers.

"Was your wine connoisseur a twenty-one-year-old beach bum named *Seth?*"

One eyebrow ascended up his forehead. "Why Seth?"

She lifted one shoulder. "I dunno. It just strikes me as the name of a surfer with short blond dreads, piercing blue eyes and dimples like he's been shot in the face with a nail gun."

"That was very specific. There's gotta be a story here."

"I may or may not have had a fling with a twenty-one-year-old blond, blue-eyed nomadic surfer named Seth." She put her nose into the wineglass and inhaled. "My family rented a house on Cannon Beach in Oregon for a month the summer I turned seventeen, and Seth *washed up* on shore one afternoon while Celeste and I were sunbathing on the sand."

"And he was the love of your life that got away?"

"Not quite. He took my virginity, got my name stick-and-poke tattooed on his hip by some random guy around a bonfire one night, then vanished a week later."

Scott's lip twitched. "So what you're saying is that I have enormous shoes to fill if I want to be better than the vagabond surfer who deflowered you."

"I'm not sure I ever saw him *wear* shoes, but yeah, that's what I'm saying."

He lifted his glass. "Well, this wine guy was not named Seth. He was probably my dad's age with a ring in his ear, long gray beard, no hair on top, and socks with sandals. But despite his surferesque vernacular—and egregious footwear —he knew a shit-ton about wine."

"What was his name?"

"Joe."

Eva snorted. "To Joe, Seth and terrible bachelor and bachelorette parties."

"May Joe be right about his wine recommendation, may Seth still be alive and *not* suffering from Hep C, and may we never be invited to another bachelor or bachelorette party ever again." He clinked her glass with his.

"Hear, hear."

They each took a sip, their eyes locking over the rims of their glasses.

When the deep, dry red hit Eva's tongue, her eyes widened in pleasant surprise.

Scott's soulful brown orbs mirrored hers.

He was the first to speak, as she wasn't quite ready to swallow her sip. "Damn, Joe knows his shit. I will definitely be going back there to speak to Joe. Good ol' Joe. True definition of not judging a book by its cover. Or in this case, not judging a man by his heinous choice in footwear." He clucked his tongue before sliding it along his bottom lip and catching a drop of wine. Oh, what Eva would have done to be that drop of wine. "Maybe I should buy Joe a gift certificate to Macy's so he can go and find himself a nice pair of loafers."

She tittered into her glass, unable to look at the handsome man currently giving her fuck-me eyes as he took another sip of his wine.

Despite how hilarious their banter was and how much she was enjoying it, her mind kept drifting back to Scott's sexy bare feet and the promises he'd made over the phone. About licking every inch of her body ...

"I'm really glad we were able to make this work," he said, setting his glass down and stepping toward her. He waited for her to take a sip, then he took her wineglass from her and set it down next to his before he wrapped his arms around her waist and brought her chest against his. "I meant what I said on Wednesday, Eva. I'm in this. I want you. I want *us*. And I will figure out a way to make it all happen *without* losing my job."

Sighing and melting against him, she allowed her arms to drift up and rest on his strong, broad, capable shoulders. "Let's not talk about that tonight. I've put *that man* away. He's been shrunken down to virtually nothing, bound with duct tape and stashed in a tiny black box in the darkest, most untouched, unthought-about recesses of my mind. Please don't be the one to bust him out."

His smile was small and placid, but it nonetheless made her belly quiver with desire. "As you wish. *Voldemort* shall not be brought up again."

She was quick to press her finger to his lips. "Uh-uh. You can't even call him that. He who must not be named must also not be given a code name. Otherwise, he'll be set free from his box and I'll be forced to think about him again."

Scott's lips parted and his teeth snagged her finger, the smile on his face devious and wry. "Fair enough." His expression sobered, but his eyelids fell to half-mast and his nostrils flared. "Besides, there are far better things to discuss and think about tonight anyway, right?" He bit down on the pad of her finger just hard enough to draw a sharp inhale from her lungs. "Far *dirtier* things."

Excitement spiraled through her. They were nose to nose now, their breaths mingling. "Far *dirtier*," she echoed. She pressed her lips against his, the relief of finally getting to kiss him again hitting her harder than she'd been prepared for.

Scott was quick to take control of the kiss, his grip on her waist tightening at the same time he pried her lips open and wedged his tongue inside. He was a masterful kisser, taking his time, exploring, massaging and coaxing. Without warning or breaking their connection, he lifted her up around the waist, and she found her butt plunked onto the counter. His body encouraged her to spread her knees so he could step between them.

She was above him now, her hands in his hair and around his neck, tracing the delicate shell of his ear and feeling the rough, sexy scruff of his beard. She was probably going to have beard burn around her mouth when they were finished, but not an ounce of her cared. The man was too good a kisser, too amazing of a seducer for her to be anything but turned on and happy when she was with him like this.

She knew sex was on the agenda for tonight—and she couldn't be more excited—but even if it wasn't, she would be plenty content just making out with Scott all night. He was *that* good of a kisser.

His hands now cupped the sides of her butt as she sat on the cool granite of his counter. It would be so easy to have sex right there. She was, after all, in a skirt, and she could tell he was turned on. So was she. Her nipples were hard and her panties held a puddle.

Did she dare?

Slowly, her hands traversed down his neck, the strong cords sticking out, his pulse racing. She found the front buttons of his short-sleeved dress shirt with the light blue chambray, and she worked the first button free from its hole. Then the next, and the next.

She was halfway done when his fingers on her made her pause. "What's the plan?" he murmured against her mouth.

"I thought the plan was pretty clear," she whispered back, not liking the unsettling feeling that creeped into her chest. Was she reading things wrong? Why had they stopped?

"We have the whole night." He brought her fingers away

from his buttons and up to his lips. "This thing between us is real, Eva. I don't want it to just be about sex."

She blinked double-time at him, not believing what she was hearing.

He nipped at her finger again. "Believe me, all I want to do is have you naked in my bed all night, but I also want to get to know you better. I feel like I've only really scratched the surface of Eva Marchand, and I want to go deeper."

A groan she had zero way of fighting bubbled up from the depths of her chest. "When you talk like that, it makes it very difficult for me to not tear off your clothes and ride you like a mechanical bull."

Goddamn it, that smile of his. "I know. It's all part of the seduction."

She rolled her eyes and pulled away from him, needing the space and the reprieve from the heat, otherwise she might spontaneously orgasm from not only his smell, touch and kisses but also his words. The man was a walking, talking orgasm machine. "So." She cleared her throat and reached for her wine. "What's for dinner?"

"I'm glad you asked." Taking his wine with him, he left her sitting there on the counter and walked over to the stove. He lifted up the lid to reveal an intriguing-looking sauce. "Roasted brussels sprouts, steamed green beans, seared duck breast with a fig sauce." Her belly growled with sudden starvation. "And for dessert?" He opened up the oven door to reveal what appeared to be a delicious-looking torte of some kind. "Cherry almond torte."

And here Todd struggled to boil water.

She mentally slapped the back of her hand. He who must not be named but also not be thought about. She needed stronger duct tape, and this time she needed to wrap it around the box as well.

Back into the depths he went, bound, gagged and without

any airholes. She even took a stapler to the lid of the box just for good measure. No way was he getting out of there tonight again. No way, no how.

"You okay?" He was back between her knees, worry clouding the various shades of brown in his eyes.

She nodded and sipped more of her wine. "Better than okay."

"You're not allergic to anything I mentioned, are you?"

She shook her head. "Nope. No allergies."

"You're sure you're okay?"

She rested her wrists back on his shoulders and nuzzled her nose against his. "I am. I'm just in a bit of shock—awe, really—that you cooked and that you cooked like freaking Gordon Ramsay to boot."

"I consider myself more of an Emeril Lagasse kind of guy, personally." He pecked her hard on the lips. "Bam!"

Eva tossed her head back and laughed, which only gave him access to her throat, and he dove in without quarter, his teeth raking along the sensitive tendon until shivers sprinted the length of her spine.

"You're really good at this whole seduction thing," she murmured, allowing her eyes to flutter closed as his mouth continued to explore her neck.

"It helps when you can't get enough of the person you're trying to seduce."

"You know all the right things to say, too."

"Easy to say when you mean every word."

She slid her hands into his shirt where the buttons she'd released just moments ago remained open. His skin was warm and soft, but the muscles beneath were hard and solid. Warm breath slid over the shell of her ear, and a hand slowly crept up her shin and under her skirt. Like a heat-seeking missile, his fingers found her throbbing, wet pussy, and they deftly pushed her damp panties to the side.

"I think I might need an appetizer," he whispered before sliding his tongue around the curve or her ear. He sank to his knees. "First, I *eat*, then I'll feed you, okay?" He glanced up at her, waiting for her reply.

All she could do was nod.

Then he dove beneath her skirt and made her come faster than she'd ever come before.

15

THEY WERE HALFWAY THROUGH DINNER, and Scott still had so many more things he wanted to know about the amazing woman in front of him. He'd been asking her questions nonstop since he ducked out from beneath her skirts and finished preparing dinner. He wanted to know everything.

He knew what made her come. That was, well, easy. But what made her tick? He knew she was a stellar mom and a great hairdresser and aesthetician, but what other passions did she possess? Had Todd eradicated them all from her life when they got together, forcing her to choose between her passions and him, or did she have things she enjoyed that she clung to during her shitty marriage that allowed her to feel some sense of happiness during all the chaos and abuse?

"And that about covers my childhood, preteen years and high school years," she said sarcastically, after regaling him with stories and tales from her youth. "I had a pretty quintessential childhood. Loving parents, annoying but wonderful younger sister. Nothing too devastating to report, I'm afraid."

She picked at the food on her plate, which he'd already

learned was a tell for when she had a lot on her mind. He would hedge to guess that the *lot* went by the name Todd Fuckface Fletcher.

She popped a brussels sprout into her mouth. "What about you? Fill me in. What does your ex-wife do?"

His brows narrowed. Why would she ask about Katrin?

She read his confusion and quickly followed up. "I only ask because if she's like a dental hygienist or something, I'll make sure I avoid that dental office. That's all. I'm not going to go stalk her or anything." She took a sip of her wine. "No. I'm not a stalker, not *at all*." The last words were said with a saucy smile and a sarcastic tone.

He loved her sense of humor. It was so refreshing after the enormous horse pill that was Katrin. She never found anything truly funny, only *amusing*.

"She's a jeweler," he replied. "Has her own business. Does well at it too. Works with precious metals and gems."

Hard concentration caused her brows to furrow. "Wait, is she Katrin David?"

Scott's fork paused midair. "You know her?"

"I know *of* her. I mean I know of her stuff. She's very talented."

He nodded. "That she is."

"I think my mom has a pair of her tanzanite and white gold teardrop earrings. They're very beautiful."

Just like the last thing Eva wanted to talk about was her ex, the last thing Scott wanted to talk about was his ex. Not that Katrin was comparable to Voldemort or even half as evil as Todd; she still wasn't who he wanted to focus his energy on. He needed to change the subject.

"So I thought I might explain just what my plan for this evening is." He put the fork to his lips and tugged off the melt-in-your-mouth duck breast with his teeth. "If you're interested?"

Even in the muted candlelight, he could tell she was growing flushed. Licking a drop of sauce from her lips, she nodded. "I would like that."

"Excellent." He sipped his wine. "First, I'm going to slowly undress you until you're wearing nothing but the soft, supple, beautiful skin you were born with."

"Then you're going to peel off my skin and wear my face as a mask?" she interrupted, followed by a chuckle. "I'm sorry, I couldn't resist. Intense moments like this make me go goofy, not to mention the wine, and I think I'm still a bit loopy from that orgasm earlier." She took another sip of her wine, eyeing him over the rim of her glass.

Goddamn it, the woman just continued to get more appealing.

"Actually, yes. That *had* been the plan. But now you've gone and ruined the surprise, so I'm going to have to rethink my psychopathic face-wearing scheme." He tapped his chin with his finger and glanced up at the corner of the room. She was giggling across the table at him. "I guess I'll just have to massage your body. Oil it up. Knead your muscles until they're the consistency of pudding."

"It puts the lotion on its skin or else it gets the hose again," she said between fits of laughter.

He shook his head, grinning. "Will you let me finish? You're ruining the mood. You're botching my plan."

"Your plan for cannibalism and face-wearing?"

"Yes." He cleared his throat and gave her a stern look, which only prompted a giant sassy grin from her. Now he wanted to sweep his arm over the table, send all the dishes clattering to the floor and have his way with her right then and there.

"Sorry, sir," she said, not an ounce of sincerity in her tone. "It won't happen again."

"Hmm, *sir*. I like that." He bobbed his eyebrows. "Now, where was I?"

"Massaging me until I am Jell-O, *sir*."

"Right. But I believe it was pudding. I'm going to strip you bare, lay you on your belly and massage you until you're moaning, begging for me to take you. But I won't."

She whimpered and made a sexy little pout.

He resisted the urge to roll his eyes and continued. "Once you're begging me to take you, claim you, *fill* you, only then will I roll you over onto your back, spread your legs and dive in to claim what is mine. I've already had one taste of you, Eva, and I want *more*."

Her squirming in her seat was fuel for his fantasy. Her cheeks were ruddier than ever, and the way her chest lifted and fell rapidly told him she wasn't far off from begging now.

"I'm going to lick your clit until you scream, until you can't take it anymore. And when you're ready, you're going to roll back over onto your belly, position yourself on your knees, and I'm going to lick your ass."

Eva's jaw damn near hit the table.

He resumed eating, cutting into his beans and casually adding, "Well, I did say I was going to lick *every* inch of you, didn't I?"

She swallowed again, the sexy line of her throat bobbing in a such a way that his cock was rock-hard beneath the table in a matter of seconds. "Scott ... "

"If you don't like it, we'll stop. But I want *all* of you, Eva. I want to show you pleasure you haven't even dared to imagine."

The breath she released was slow, as if she were trying to regain control of a frantically beating heart. No way was her heart beating faster than his. Because even though he was trying to appear calm, cool and in control, the thought of getting more of Eva tonight made his pulse race.

"M-maybe let's finish dinner first," she offered, draining her wineglass, then moving on to her water. "You may be too full afterward to—"

Scott let out a whoop of a laugh, interrupting her. "To eat ass? Was that what you were about to say?"

Her lashes covered her eyes as she glanced down at her lap. "Yes, but then I thought better of it when I said it in my head."

"Don't ever be afraid to speak your mind around me, Eva. Ever. I want to hear all the dirty, weird, random thoughts. They're what make you *you*." He reached across the table and took her hand, bringing her knuckles to his lips. "Okay?"

She nodded and brought her gaze back up to his face. Amusement, embarrassment and arousal all swirled behind the intense mossy green of her eyes. "Okay."

He kissed her knuckles once more, then gave her back her hand. "Now, I agree, let's finish dinner. We need to fuel up."

Her smile was closed-mouthed now as she shook her head. Using her fingers, she popped a perfectly charred brussels sprout half into her mouth. "You're incorrigible, you know that?"

"Incorrigible, infatuated. Take your pick."

"Can I pick both?"

"Abso-fucking-lutely."

DINNER WAS OVER, and what a dinner it was. And the dessert —if it was even possible—was better than the dinner. Eva had even gone back for seconds, batting her eyelashes coquettishly at Scott until he served her up a second slice of the torte. Not that he needed much convincing. He had a second slice too.

Tingles ran rampant through her when he took her hand

after they'd finished cleaning up the kitchen and he led her upstairs to his bedroom.

It wasn't like they hadn't had sex yet. They'd had crazy-hot sex a few times, and yet the way her nerves were taking hold of her body, it was if she were some innocent virgin preparing for her deflowering.

Though this was not how Seth had gone about it. Seth had lived in his van on the beach. Her first time had been no less romantic though. On a giant blanket on the beach under a star-filled sky. Yeah, he might have been a hippie nomad who never wore shoes, but Seth had made her first time special.

She'd been less nervous then than she was now, though. Maybe it was because Scott had been so descriptive about his intentions. And that she was so damn curious and so damn turned on when he revealed his plans that she was not so much nervous as she was anxious—champing at the bit to experience all his promises.

They reached the top of the stairs and he stopped, turning toward her. "All kidding aside, Eva, I want you to really enjoy tonight. So if there *is* anything you don't want to do, just say so and we'll stop. You mean a great deal to me, and I don't want to spook you."

Her heart constricted inside her chest, and those tingles picked up their intensity. But she pushed that all aside, lifted up onto her tiptoes and pressed her lips to his. "Careful, Scott Dixon, or I might just fall in love with you."

She was up and into his arms, squealing, before she knew what was happening. His strides were long and true, and they were inside his very manly, very tidy bedroom in no time. "Didn't you know, Eva," he said, staring down at her, "that's the plan?"

"I thought licking every inch of me was the plan," she said with a giggle, looping her arms around his neck. They were standing at the foot of his bed now, the dark brown duvet with blue trim just demanding to be chucked to the floor in a heap as they got all tangled up in the sheets.

"That's all *part* of the plan of getting you to fall in love with me." His brows knitted together, and his gaze grew serious. "It's a very complex plan, you know. Many layers." Then he tossed her onto the bed like she was no more than a stuffed animal. She squealed again as her butt made contact with the mattress and she bounced.

He pounced on her after the second bounce, stopping her from doing a third and pinning her body beneath his. She grinned up at him, her arms finding their way around his body, her hands fanning out across the solid expanse of his back.

"First," he purred, "I'm going to take off all your clothes, as promised."

His lips landed on her shoulder at the same time his fingers began to peel the sleeves of her top down over her arms. Every kiss was exquisite, every light, gentle brush of his fingers divine, sending a ripple of pleasure careening through her only to end up smack dab between her legs, where her soaked pussy now throbbed for him.

"Then, I'm going to spoil you," he murmured, trailing his wet, hot tongue over her collarbone and down to where the swells of her breasts now tumbled out the neck of her top. He was still pulling her shirt down and over her body, inch by luscious inch. "Massage away your aches and pains. Dissolve your stress and worries. And, if you happened to have an orgasm while I'm doing it, all the better."

Her shirt was now all the way down around her waist, her strapless bra doing a piss-poor job of containing her breasts, since she was on her back. It took little effort on his part to relieve her breasts of her bra entirely, and within an instant, her nipple was in his mouth.

A sharp inhale caught in her chest when he scissored his teeth over her tight, sensitive bud, the other nipple between his fingers being equally tortured.

His tongue meandered across the valley of her breasts to the other nub, and he raked his teeth over that one too. "Arch your back, babe," he murmured against her skin.

She did as she was told, and he made deft work of her bra clasp, tossing her bra to the floor. Her shirt came next, then her skirt. He was getting down to business. She was left in nothing but her panties now. Pale blue, but a noticeable darker blue where she was unable to control her arousal. With his mouth still teasing her breasts and his fingers roaming her naked body, she was already close to coming. Until the heel of his hand cupped her mound, that is. Then she was *really* close to coming.

He pressed gently, then harder.

"I love that you get so wet," he purred, slinking down her body, his lips never more than an inch away from her flesh. He hovered over her mound now and her hips voluntarily leapt off the bed toward his face and his heated breath.

"Eager, are we?" He kissed her clit over her panties, and of their own volition once again, her hips jerked up to meet him. He chuckled and kissed her again.

She groaned, her fingers making their way forcefully into his hair. She tugged. "Scott ... "

"I have a plan," was all he said, hooking his fingers into the sides of her underwear and sliding them down her legs. "Just wait. The wait is half the pleasure. Half the fun. Don't you think?"

She groaned in frustration and shook her head, her hair splaying out all around her in an arc of fire. "I'm not sure I agree," she said through gritted teeth.

"Anticipation can be an incredible aphrodisiac," he said,

bringing her panties up to his nose and inhaling, shutting his eyes.

She gaped at him.

When he opened his eyes, his grin was downright wicked, almost a little frightening. But it wasn't *actually* scary. More like thrilling. Like when you get spooked on a rollercoaster or in a haunted house.

"Roll over, babe," he ordered, climbing off the bed and walking over to the dresser against the far wall.

She did as she was told and shut her eyes. She'd gone hard at the gym earlier, and her muscles were tired. If she wasn't about to have some earth-shattering sex in a moment, she could very well fall asleep. And she nearly did until Scott reapplying his weight on the bed caused it dip on one end.

She opened her eyes to find the room lit by close to a dozen candles. It was beautiful and romantic, and she felt herself fall just a little bit more for the man. Todd had never done anything like this for her—no man had.

Scott was doing just as he promised. He was spoiling her.

He wasn't naked, but he'd removed his pants and was now in just sexy black boxer briefs, and his dress shirt was on but open. With a bottle in his hand, he straddled the back of her thighs. "Just relax," he whispered, squeezing some yellow-tinted oil into his palm. The scent of it wafted over her shoulder, and it smelled magnificent.

Leaning over, he pushed the heels of his palms into her shoulder blades, which somehow proved to be a button for her to shut her eyes again because she did. And then everything went a little blissfully blurry for a while.

Scott's powerful hands kneaded and prodded, massaged and caressed her tired, aching muscles until they really were nothing but pudding by the end. He had magic fingers, strong and capable. She caught herself groaning a couple of times from how good it felt, only for his thumbs on the back of her neck to lull her back into that fuzzy state where you're not quite asleep but not quite awake either.

After he'd devoted an immeasurable amount of time to her back, shoulders and buttocks, he slipped off her thighs.

"Do you want me to roll over?" she asked groggily.

"Not yet." With the speed of a sloth, she pried one eye open and craned her neck around to look at him. He stood at the foot of the bed and squirted more of that delicious-smelling oil into his hands. "I'm not done." Those hands were back on her, starting at her feet and gliding up her leg on either side. All the way up to the apex of her thighs.

When his fingers brushed her pussy lips, she trembled beneath his touch, and her breath hitched.

Up and down he raked his hands along her leg, drawing out the last of her energy with each stroke. And with each pass, his fingers probed just a little bit farther, until when he switched legs, his fingers pushed inside her just a tad.

She clenched around him when he breached her, desperate to keep him there just a bit longer, but he would click his tongue and retreat from her heat, sliding his hands back down her leg.

Just when she thought she was going to pass out from the buildup of anticipation mixed with the relaxation of the massage, he removed his hands from her completely.

She was unable to stop the whimper that rattled up from her chest and past her lips. Her body was in instant mourning. The loss of his touch was nearly too much to bear.

But she didn't need to grieve for long. His hands wrapped around her ankles, and she found herself briskly flipped over to her back. With an *eek* and an *oof*, she stared down the length of her body at the man before her and the impressive black mountain of his boxer briefs.

Involuntarily, she licked her lips. His pupils dilated, his nostrils flared, and he slid his tongue along his bottom lip.

"Spread your legs, Eva." His rough voice had her complying instantly. "So wet, so pink," he murmured.

Holy Jesus.

"Remember the plan?" he asked, his chest lifting and falling at a quick pace.

She nodded.

"Good." Then he dove between her legs face-first, taking her clit between his lips and sucking like it was a goddamn lollipop.

Eva's hips shot off the bed.

He hooked his arms beneath her legs so her thighs now rested on his shoulders. Alternating between licking and sucking, he brought her to the edge in no time. Then when he added that finger inside her, she really thought she was going to pass out.

"Remember the plan, Eva," he purred against her clit, laving at it with the flat of his tongue. The buzz of his words against her plump, sensitive folds sent a new pulse of electricity through her.

He reached up and tugged on her nipples with each hand until they were tender, stiff peaks.

Her hips leapt off the mattress again..

"Eva ... " he grumbled into her cleft.

"Right, right," she breathed. "Okay, now." Her bottom lip snagged between her teeth at the thought of his mouth on her in the way he'd described. What if ...

What if you love it?

Well, yeah.

Scott lifted up onto his knees and waited for her to roll over to her belly once again.

"On your knees, babe," he encouraged gently, his fingers brushing her calf. "Spread your legs."

She swallowed but complied, doing as instructed, her cheek pressed hard into the mattress, her most intimate parts on full display. She felt incredibly open and vulnerable.

"Oh, Eva." It didn't matter when he said it, the way Scott pronounced her name made butterflies take wing in her abdomen. But when he said it now, while they were in bed, and that tenor of admiration accompanied his seductive pronunciation, she almost came on the spot.

"Scott ... "

Wet warmth sucked on her pink folds from behind. He drew each one into the soft heat of his mouth only to release it with a gentle pop. She moaned into the mattress, resisting the need to churn her hips or reach beneath her and rub her clit. His tongue dipped between her labia and flicked her clit. She spasmed. Then that tongue began to travel. Through her slit, over her perineum and up her crease.

"Holy shit," she breathed.

Around and around her tight rosette, Scott swirled his tongue.

"Oh God."

She didn't think she was going to enjoy it, let alone this much. The man was a true savant of all things dirty, wicked and wonderful. Not ceasing from his tongue magic, he trailed his fingers up her inner thigh until they found her dripping pussy. He slipped two fingers inside, pumping and pressing on her G-spot.

Bright lights flashed behind her closed eyes.

He pulled his fingers free and flicked her clit, toying with the swelling nub like a cat with a mouse.

"Scott ... "

His tongue in her crease picked up speed, his fingers on her clit began luscious concentric circles, and she was gone.

He'd carried her boneless body up to the cliff top, then hurled her off the summit. Only she didn't fall, she flew. Up farther into the ether, Eva sailed as the waves of the intense orgasm ricocheted through her, blooming from the epicenter of her core outward to her limbs, her fingertips, her toes and the crown of her head.

And just when she thought she was on the downward coast, enjoying the euphoric fog that accompanied an orgasm so life-changing, another one hit her out of nowhere, and like a second wind, she flew back up in the stratosphere.

16

When Scott returned from the bathroom after washing his face, Eva was right where he left her: on her belly with her face in the pillows, her legs flopped out and spread. If he tilted his head slightly, he could see her slick, plump, pink folds between her legs and a puddle of wetness beneath her on the tan sheets.

Had she fallen asleep?

He certainly hoped not, though he couldn't necessarily blame her if she had. He could have sworn he heard her snoring a few times during her massage. That was partly why he would slide his fingers inside her, just to wake her up.

He knew she would like having her ass licked, and he was so glad that she gave it a try. Though, by the way she came twice in a row, he might have a created a monster. Not that he minded. He'd eat Eva's ass every time she asked him.

"Babe?" he whispered, pressing a knee into the bed and climbing on beside her, smoothing his hand down over the luscious curve of her ass. She twitched beneath his palm, but the sigh that followed on the heels of that prompted him to do it again.

Groaning, she turned to face him, pressing her other cheek into the mattress. Long lashes fluttered open. Her yellow-green eyes shone bright, contrasting beautifully with her pinked-up complexion and wild just-fucked hair. She was, without a doubt, the most exquisite creature he'd ever seen.

"That was ... "

His grin made his cheeks hurt. "Yeah?"

She nodded. "Yeah."

"Good."

Her gaze slid to his very eager, close-to-painful erection in his boxers. A small bit of leaked precum had turned the fabric a darker shade of black. "Is it my turn yet?" She licked her lips.

Fuck, she was incredible. "Anytime you want to wrap those lips around my cock, babe, I won't say no."

With a groggy-sounding groan, she pushed herself up to sitting, then reached for the elastic of his shorts. He helped her, lifting up so she could tug his boxers off as she slid to her knees on the floor. Her face fell to his lap, and she took his cock into her mouth, instantly deep-throating him.

"Fuck." His fingers pushed into her hair.

She bottomed out over and over again, taking him quickly to the edge of completion. And even though he knew he would be able to provide Eva with cock a few times that night —she just made him get it up nearly on command—he did not want to come in her mouth. Not yet anyway.

She cupped his hairless balls and tugged gently before moving her head down to one and taking it into the decadent heat of her mouth. She sucked on his sac, using her other hand to continuously pump his cock from root to tip.

"Babe." He tapped her head. "Not like this."

She hummed a response, and his hips jerked into her face.

He tapped her head harder. "Babe, no, seriously."

Enormous green doe-eyes flicked up to him. She released his sac and pouted. "Really?"

"Yeah, really. I don't want to come like this yet."

Her pout grew deeper before morphing into a big grin. She stuck her tongue out and, using the flat of it, ran it up the length of him, finishing with a hard suck on the head before she released it with a sassy, sexy *pop*.

"You are a wicked little thing," he growled, helping her to her feet and then throwing her to the bed.

"Whatever turns you on, stud." She smiled, her legs flopping open.

He grabbed a condom from the drawer of his nightstand and slid it on. "Babe, everything about you turns me on. Absolutely everything."

He prowled up the bed toward her and without even waiting, slid inside her. Their mutual groans of satisfaction filled the room, accompanied quickly by the sound of flesh slapping flesh and the heady and distinct smell of sex. Musky and loaded with pheromones, it drove his libido ever higher, and his thrusts picked up vigor.

He pushed up onto his knees and gripped Eva behind the thighs, angling his cock inside her so that he hit her right in the G-spot every time he fucked her. Then she'd feel every inch of him along her ridges as he pulled out.

Her bottom lip was hung up between her teeth and her eyes closed as she rubbed her clit with one hand and pulled at her nipples with other. He loved that she had no qualms enhancing her own pleasure. She knew what she liked and wasn't afraid to work with him to achieve the ultimate goal.

He released one of her thighs at the same time his cock slipped all the way out. With his fist around the base, he guided the head of his shaft through her folds and up to her clit, where her fingers worked double-time. Her eyes flashed open when she felt him, and she smiled. He rubbed her nub with his cockhead a few times, her fingers taking a break, her eyes focused on him.

"Back inside me," she whispered, pushing his cock away with her hand and guiding him back into her drenched slit. "It's where you belong."

Well, if those words didn't hit him like a sledgehammer to the solar plexus. Probably because that's exactly how he felt too. He belonged inside her. He belonged *with* Eva.

Her sigh reverberated through him when he pushed his dick back inside her and resumed his thrusting.

"Yeah, just like that," she murmured, her fingers once again doing circles around her clit.

He looped his hand back beneath her thigh and continued to pump, the urge to come growing each time she squeezed her muscles around him.

"Close," she whispered, shutting her eyes again, a sheen of perspiration glistening on the top of her chest and forehead like diamond beads. Was it weird that he wanted to lick those beads? He didn't fucking care.

"Me too, babe," he grunted.

And then she did something that he'd never witnessed another woman do before. At least not in real life.

She started to slap her clit with her fingers. Yes, slap.

"Oh God," she cried.

With her fingers pinned tightly together and her palm open, she tapped her clit over and over again, her body jerking and squirming erratically.

"Oh God, Scott."

"Right there with you, babe." He was mesmerized by her hand and the slapping. It was so fucking hot.

Another couple of hard, deep pumps, combined with Eva's incessant slapping, and he was coming.

Scott grunted and stilled as he dug his fingers into the

backs of her thighs. "Fuck!" he ground out. His cock pulsed inside the condom. Thick spurt after thick spurt shot out of him as his orgasm reached its crescendo.

"Yes!" Eva's head tilted back in the pillows and her hand stilled midair as her body went rigid and a gorgeous red bloomed across her chest and up her neck. Scott's gaze fell down to where they were connected, to her insanely swollen clit and pussy lips and the gush that rushed out of her, coating the outside of the condom and dripping all over his balls.

The woman continued to be full of surprises. He had never met a woman who liked to slap her clit as she got herself off, nor had he met a woman who got as wet as Eva did. Another thing that was hot as absolute fuck.

With a sigh, she relaxed her muscles and adjusted her head to look at him, her smile knocking every last bit of air clear from his chest. "Wow!"

He grinned down at her, content to still be inside her, despite his quickly deflating cock. "Yeah, wow!"

He released her legs and pulled free of her, removing the condom and tying it off. He glanced at the cum inside. He'd really blown a load; it was a fucking full condom.

"Holy crap, that's a lot of cum," she remarked with a smirk, sliding her legs over the side of the bed and standing up. "You always blow a load like that?"

Scott snickered and followed her to the bathroom. "No. You just *bring it out in me.*"

She rolled her eyes. "Is that a compliment?"

"It was meant to be." He tossed the condom in the trash, then quickly rinsed his dick in the sink.

"All right, then, I guess I'll take it. Now get out. I need to pee, and even though you've licked my asshole, we're not yet there in our relationship where I'm cool peeing in front of you."

Scott scoffed. "But I want to be a part of your life in *every* way."

She tossed a washcloth at him from the shelf they were all stacked on. "Get out. We need to leave a little bit of mystery."

Grinning, he caught the facecloth and set it down on the counter. "All right, fine. But hurry up, because I'm not done worshiping that body of yours. The night is young, and my balls aren't empty." He closed the door.

"Will you cross-stitch that on a pillow for me?" she called through the door.

"Birthday present!" he called back.

MORNING CAME BEFORE EITHER of them was ready, particularly because they'd fucked until the wee hours of it, only to collapse in a pile of sweaty limbs and tangled sheets, with chests heaving and faces smiling sometime around 4 a.m.

But, much like Eva, Scott liked to sleep with his window open just a bit, and the birds in the tree outside his window didn't know that it was the weekend and had failed to sleep in.

Groaning, Eva glanced at the digital clock on Scott's nightstand. It was roughly nine thirty.

Okay, fine, it was a respectable time for the birds to get breakfast, but for the achy-limbed Eva, who'd been fucked to within an inch of her sanity last night, it was far too early to be waking up.

A warm, wiry-haired arm snaked its way over her waist, the palm cupping her breast. He tugged her against his chest and his ...

"Someone's *up* early this morning," she chided, wiggling her butt against him.

"Always sporting at least a half-chub when you're around,

babe," he murmured, biting her shoulder. "You have all day, right?"

"Mhmm."

He encouraged her to roll over so they were face-to-face, but she was reluctant.

"No, no, no," she protested, drawing the sheet up over her mouth. "Morning breath."

He tugged it away from her face. "I happen to love your morning breath. I want to wake up to it every day. No hiding, okay?"

Her lips twisted. "You do *not* love my morning breath."

His grin was infectious. "Well, no, but I'm not one to *not* kiss you because of it. Besides, *if* we kiss, then our morning breaths will mingle, creating one super morning breath. Then our breaths will be the same and we have nothing to worry about. It's like garlic. One person eats it; the other dies a horrible death. They both eat it, no problem." Inching closer, he nuzzled his nose against her. "Make sense?"

Her eyes slid to the side and she grew quiet for a moment. This all felt so surreal. In reality, she hardly knew Scott, and yet this man already meant a crazy-scary amount to her.

"Eva?"

She allowed her gaze to drift back to his face, where flecks of gold sparkled in the dark brown of his beautiful eyes.

"You okay?"

Sighing, she brushed her lips over his. "You are just making it damn near impossible to not fall in love with you, Scott Dixon. I am powerless to your charms."

If she was wearing panties, his grin would have caused them to fly right off. He rolled her onto her back and settled between her thighs, her body relaxing beneath his weight.

They kissed like they had all the time in the world, because although they didn't have *all* the time in the world, they did have the morning and afternoon to spend in bed.

Though something told her that that was nowhere near enough. She wanted Scott in her bed every night.

Hands roamed and fingers explored. She was close simply from the grinding and the way the head of his cock knocked the stiff peak of her clit over and over again. He hadn't even slipped inside and already she was close to losing her mind.

Without breaking their kiss, he opened his nightstand drawer and went on the hunt for a condom. They'd used a fair few last night. She was a bit surprised he was able to get it up again so soon. They'd only been asleep for a few hours when the sounds of daybreak woke them.

His lips paused over hers, and he stilled. "Shit," he murmured against her mouth. "Out of condoms."

"What!"

His chuckle and the way his body lightly shook on hers, brushing against the hard tips of her nipples, sent a shock of electricity right down between her legs. "Fear not, my horny little lass. I have an unopened box in the bathroom. Hang on." He sprung up off her body, his long, hard cock *thwacking* against his belly from the motion as he stood up. The room was full of light now, even with the drapes drawn. He made a detour to the bathroom and pulled back the curtain to peer outside. "Nope, they're not home yet."

"Who? My boys? They shouldn't be."

He let the curtain close and turned to face her. "No, the cows."

"What cows?"

He was in the bathroom and back out in under a second, a full box of condoms in his hands. "I told you last night that I was going to fuck you until the cows came home, and I just needed to double-check that they weren't home yet." That smile ... it was most definitely going to be her undoing, if it wasn't already.

Rolling her eyes, she covered her face with her hand. "Oh, for crying out loud." Her body trembled as she laughed.

"That's what you'll be doing in a sec." He opened the condom box, pulled out a foil pack and sheathed himself. "Now, where were we?"

Nibbling on her bottom lip, she cupped her breasts and mashed them together before tweaking the nipples between her thumbs and forefingers. "I think you were about to fuck me."

He held up one finger. "Ah, yes. Thank you. I almost forgot." With one knee into the bed, he climbed back over her, his cock now locked at her cleft, which was exactly where it belonged.

"Until the cows come home?" he asked, inching forward just a touch so that his cockhead breached the entrance of her channel.

"Until the cows come home."

With a mighty *moo* that made her laugh, he surged forward, claiming her fully with one hard, deep and oh-so-satisfying thrust. She lifted her hips up and locked her ankles around his back, enjoying the new angle and the way his pelvis hit her clit.

She bowed her back and he latched onto a nipple, and just as she gasped from the pain-laced pleasure of his teeth scraping her bud, the definitive sound of multiple car doors slamming and children calling out "Mom!" eviscerated any arousal she might have had.

Scott stilled at the same time she did.

"Mom!"

"Mom!"

Okay, that second voice was definitely Lucas. He had a very distinct timber. For seven, it was unusually deep. She'd even gone so far as to have his hormone levels checked to make sure he wasn't maturing too quickly. He was fine. The kid just sounded more like Mufasa rather than Simba.

"Is that?"

"My children," she answered, pushing him off her.

He climbed off willingly, going back over to the window, where he pulled back the drapes again and peered out. "And your ex-husband, it would appear."

Ice flooded her once-bubbling-hot veins.

Why the hell was Todd dropping the boys off? That was not the plan. He wasn't supposed to set foot on her property.

She was up and off the bed, searching for her underwear among their piles of haphazardly divested clothes, before she even knew what she was doing.

"Where are my underwear?" she breathed out through as a vice of panic began to slowly squeeze around her chest.

"Here." He passed her the panties, and she slid into them.

Scott was busy searching through the clothes too and came up with her bra, shirt and skirt before she did. She was dressed in no time and barreling down his stairs, her heels in her hands, muttering, "Shit, shit, shit," under her breath. She flung open his front door and was halfway down the porch steps before she lurched to a stop.

How the hell was she going to explain her whereabouts?

"Run around to the backyard," Scott offered, standing in his doorway wearing nothing but the same pair of jeans he'd had on last night. "There is an old gate between the two properties. It hasn't been used in ages, but it still works. Say that you were in the salon cleaning with the radio on and didn't hear the boys."

That was an excellent suggestion, but she didn't have time to admire his quick-thinking skills. She needed to get next door. The boys were still calling out "Mom!" every ten seconds.

With bare feet and sex-head bed-head, she booked it to

the backyard and the gate within the fence Scott had mentioned. It squealed like a stuck pig when she heaved it open, but the upside was that it opened at all. She didn't slow down but made sure to keep an eye on her yard, in case one of her sons, or God forbid her ex-husband, saw her sneaking through the fence.

So far, she was in the clear.

Out of breath, she slowed her roll when she approached the house, smoothing her hair away from her face and hoping it didn't look as wretched as it did most mornings. She tucked her heels onto one of the deck steps and continued on around the house to the front, where her sons' voices were growing more panicked.

"Hey!" she said, spying Kellen first. Tears brimmed in his eyes, but when he saw her, his face lit up like the Christmas tree at City Hall.

"Mom!" As if being chased by the monsters he believed lived under his bed, he beelined right for her, nearly knocking her over as he collided with her legs. "Where were you? We were so worried. Lucas! She's here. I found her."

She heard her eldest son's footsteps smacking against the stepping stones that curved around to the other side of the house, his face appearing seconds later. But unlike his little brother, who was not afraid to show his emotions in front of his father, Lucas's face became calm, almost steely and stoic as he slowed down and walked toward them. Todd turned the corner a moment later.

"Where were you?" Lucas asked, his tone riding the edge between irritated accusation and fear.

"I was just in the salon cleaning with the radio on. I didn't hear you guys. I'm sorry." She cupped his cheek and bent at the waist to peck him on the head. "Why are you guys home so early? Why is your dad dropping you off?"

A glimmer of frustration flitted behind Lucas's bright

blue eyes. "Grandma and Grandpa took us to breakfast. Dad came too and then Grandma was having trouble breathing, so Grandpa took her to the hospital. So Dad brought us home."

Was Lucas thinking what she was thinking? Why didn't Todd take his sons and go *do* something with them for the afternoon? Why didn't he act like a father and be involved in his sons' lives? Or why didn't Todd just take the boys back to Celeste's house? He knew damn well he wasn't supposed to be within five hundred feet of her, and they sure as hell were standing closer than five hundred feet.

She cleared her throat and pried Kellen's arms from around her legs, wrapping her arms around each of her sons' shoulders. "Well, I'm very happy to see you both. I missed you."

"We missed you too, Mom," Kellen said, his eyes red-rimmed but his face bright.

"Interesting that you said you were in the salon. I peered inside the window of the salon and didn't see you in there. Didn't hear the radio or see any lights on either. I also knocked," Todd said, his face so fucking smug she wanted to backhand him into next year.

She shrugged, attempting to appear casual and unfazed. "I was under the stairs. It's a small storage space *off* the salon."

His brows barely lifted, but his jaw tightened. He didn't say anything though.

"Is Freddie home?" Kellen asked. "Can we go play with him?"

Prickles of unease snagged in her gut. "He's not home, honey. He's still at his mom's house."

Kellen's face fell.

"Who's Freddie?" Todd asked.

"He's our new friend and neighbor," Kellen said, his smile

back. "He's *really* cool. Has a big soccer net in his backyard, and his dad makes *great* mac and cheese."

Todd's nostrils flared. "His dad, huh?" His eyes roved over her body from head to toe and back again.

She tucked her hair behind her ears once more and straightened her posture.

For all his enormous faults, her ex-husband was not an idiot. She watched him do the calculations in his head. They'd already established that Freddie's parents weren't together. He was at his mom's house. Now Todd knew that Freddie's dad lived next door. All it would take was a couple of assumptions, and her ex-husband would be enraged—as was his MO.

"So you were in the salon, huh?" Todd asked again, having come to his own conclusions, the evidence of them written in the ire on his face.

She didn't owe him anything, least of all an explanation. "Why are you here, Todd? You know the rules. Celeste does the hand-offs. You should have dropped the boys back with her if you didn't want them. This"—she pointed back and forth between them—"is not five hundred feet."

He rolled his eyes, giving her the look she'd seen nearly every day of their marriage. It was the look he gave her when he was trying to make her feel stupid and small. "Come on, Eva. You know as well as I do that that fucking restraining order is a joke."

"Is it?" she countered, taking a couple of steps back for good measure, bringing her boys with her.

"Yes. I could have my lawyers contest it and win in a heartbeat. Both you and I know it."

"Then why haven't you?" She swallowed down the fear that had grown into a hard ball at the back of her throat, her grip tightening on her sons' shoulders.

"Because I'm a good guy."

She fought the urge to laugh.

"I wouldn't need a restraining order from a good guy."

Anger flashed in his eyes but quickly dissipated. "I have a meeting I need to get to." He nodded at his children. "Later, boys."

"Bye, Daddy," Kellen said, waving happily. The poor kid, he still held on to a few shreds of love for his father, while Lucas was older and not only saw how Todd treated Eva in the last years of their marriage but also knew how uninterested Todd was in his sons. He'd given up hope on Todd a long time ago, holding nothing but contempt for him now.

Todd's eyes landed on Eva. "Say *hi* to Freddie and his dad for me." Then he headed to his Mercedes SUV, revved the engine and peeled out of the driveway.

Eva let out the breath she'd been holding, though it did nothing for the anxiety that cannoned through her. Did he know?

Did he know *who* Freddie's dad was? Or was he just being an assuming jackass, deducing that she hadn't in fact been in the salon but over at the neighbor's, but he didn't know *who* the neighbor was.

God, she hoped it was the latter.

She and Scott still needed to figure out a way to handle Todd, and him finding out that they were together this way could not be further from ideal.

She also still needed to find a PI and hire the guy to dig up some dirt on Todd.

"Can we go inside?" Kellen asked, slipping out from beneath her arm and grabbing his backpack. Lucas did the same.

"Of course." She followed the boys to the front door, punched in the keycode and turned the latch. Her eyes flicked back to the street when the niggling feeling that eyes were on her made the hair on the back of her neck stand up.

But there was nothing nefarious in sight. A faint whistle had her shifting her gaze skyward, and that's when she saw him.

He was still shirtless, and even from a distance, she could tell Scott was on high alert. He waved at her, and she waved back.

"You okay?" he called out the window.

She nodded. "Yeah."

"We'll figure it out. I promise."

All she could manage was a grim smile and another wave. As much as she wanted him to be right, he couldn't promise that kind of thing. Todd was a powerful man with money and connections. This might just be one problem that couldn't be fixed—aside from Eva breaking up with a man who in a very short span of time meant more to her than she was willing to admit.

17

SATURDAY NIGHT FOUND Celeste and Eva curled up on Eva's couch beneath a microfleece blanket, a rom-com on the television and wine in hand, mulling over the Todd dilemma. It was only a matter of time until Todd figured out who lived next door to Eva—if he hadn't already. He had friends who were cops. He had friends in city planning. He had friends who were hackers. All it would take would be one phone call to one of his *buddies*, and Scott's name would pop right up.

"Maybe just tell him," Celeste offered, taking a sip of her wine. Her sister had come over for dinner. Sabrina was at a sleepover with a friend, so Celeste offered to stay the night at Eva's, as Eva didn't really feel like being home with the boys by herself right now, not after her jarring altercation with Todd.

"And run the risk of Scott losing his job? I can't do that."

"Yeah, but like you said, he's going to find out anyway. Might as well hear it from you, no?"

Eva exhaled and finished the final sip of her wine. "If the

PI I hire can't find anything, then I will, but I may need you to be there too when I tell him. You know—as a witness."

"PI's can take a while to dig up shit," Celeste said, reaching for the wine bottle on the coffee table and topping up both their glasses. "You might not have that time. And let's just say that the PI *does* find something, if it's dirty enough, you can't keep that information to yourself. You'll have to go to the police with it."

"Well, then Todd will go to prison. Problem solved. I either blackmail him or I send him to prison." She hated the idea of stooping to the horrendous method of blackmailing, but Todd pushed her to do things she never ever thought she would or could do. What was a minor felony in the grand scheme of things?

Celeste's lips formed a thin line, which meant she wasn't entirely on board with Eva's plan. Oh well, neither was Eva, but she didn't have any other plans coming out of her ass at the moment, so she needed to roll with the one she had. She glanced at the television, where the happy couple on screen were involved in a cheesy home-reno montage set to music.

"Fast forward through this garbage?" Celeste asked.

Eva nodded and was about to reach for the remote when her phone on the coffee table buzzed a text message.

It was from Scott.

BBQ tomorrow at Zak's place. Kids invited. Please come. You and the boys. I'm grabbing Freddie early.

"Who is it?" Celeste asked, her nose wrinkling and pushing her glasses up an inch on her face. She usually wore contacts but had taken them out an hour ago to give her eyes a rest.

"Scott. He's invited me and the boys to a BBQ at his friend's house."

Celeste's mouth made an *O*, which then seemed to

prompt her to yawn. "You going to go? Is this the single dads club he's in? You ready for that big step? Meeting his friends?"

"Well, now that you say it like that, I don't know."

She was about to text him back when her phone buzzed again with another message from him.

Liam hired a PI to dig up some dirt on Todd. He has some interesting information for us, wants to speak in person tomorrow at the party.

Now it was Eva's turn to look like a codfish.

"What is it?" Celeste asked, impatient and grabbing Eva's phone from her. She read Scott's messages. "Holy shit." She handed Eva back her phone. "I wonder what he dug up?"

Eva shook her head, equal parts stunned, terrified and thrilled. "I have no idea, but whatever it was, if Liam wants to speak in person, it can't be good."

Celeste clicked her tongue. "Oh, Todd, you're about to get your ass handed to you. And it's about damn time."

Eva texted Scott back. *Sure. BBQ sounds great. And why didn't you tell me your brother hired a PI? I was going to hire one.*

He texted back right away.

I didn't want to get your hopes up in case the guy didn't find anything. Sorry, I should have told you. To be fair though, my mouth WAS pretty occupied last night and this morning.

Heat flooded her cheeks.

"He sexting you?" Celeste asked. "Can I see?" She went to reach for Eva's phone, then stopped. "Wait, do I want to see? Is he into some kinky shit?"

Well...

Eva's gaze slid sideways.

Celeste scrunched her nose. "Never mind. Forget I asked."

Eva texted him back. *You're forgiven. Text me in the morning about the BBQ and we can convoy.*

We can put Freddie's booster in your van and all go together. Even better.

"You've got it bad, you know," Celeste teased. "You're smiling like an idiot and twirling your finger in your hair like you did when we were kids and you were on the phone with a boy."

Eva's hand paused, and she glanced at the coil of hair wrapped around her finger. She hadn't even been aware she was doing that.

"You going to the BBQ?" Celeste asked.

Eva nodded. "Yeah. I'm excited to meet his friends. That's where he is tonight, at his brother Liam's for their poker night. I think it's really cool, a bunch of single dads getting together to support each other. Mind you, apparently the majority of them are no longer single, but it's still a really great concept."

"I should start us a single moms club," Celeste offered. "Like a book club, but without books, because who the fuck has time to read? And instead we sit around drinking wine and bitching about how much we love our little crotch fruits but that they ultimately drive us to drink the wine we're drinking."

"I'd join that club," Eva said, clinking her sister's glass.

Celeste nodded. "Then it's done. I hereby decree that the first meeting of The Single Moms of Seattle will come to order." She glanced around. "Do you have a gavel?"

"Sorry, lost it in the divorce."

"Damn." She grabbed a paperweight made of pewter shaped like an alligator—a weird wedding gift from Eva and Celeste's equally weird Great Aunt Ruth. She banged it twice on the end table. "There, it's official. Now we need to recruit."

"Flyers?"

"No, we'll need to vet people. I'll think on it. Maybe hold auditions. See if the women are a good fit. I mean, we can't just invite any ol' riffraff into our exclusive club. If they don't consider wine a food group, they have no place in our organization. We can't have sober chicks judging us the whole time."

Eva nodded, giggling. She bumped shoulders with her sister. "I love you, Celly."

"Love you too, Eves." Then they snuggled up close under the blanket like they did when they were kids and watched one of the most awful movies Eva had watched in a while, but it didn't matter, because the company she kept was awesome.

"Ready to go?" Scott asked as he slid in behind the driver's seat of Eva's van and adjusted the seat to accommodate his long legs.

Three little boys with enormous grins beamed back at him in the rearview mirror. He'd gone and picked up Freddie from Katrin's that morning, and his son was more than happy to come back to Scott's early. Katrin seemed to be ready for her week off to start too. Scott didn't probe far into her and Freddie's week together. He'd get what he needed from Freddie, and as long as Katrin kept their son safe, Scott had to back off and let his ex-wife parent their son the way she chose to parent him.

Wise words from his therapist that had taken a while to sink in.

Freddie was asking about Kellen and Lucas before he even got into Scott's truck, wanting to know if he could play with them when he got home. Scott had burst out laughing at his son's glee when he revealed that they were all going over to Uncle Zak's house for a BBQ and that Jordie would be there, as well as all the other kids too.

Thankfully, so far anyway, all the kids seemed to get

along. Perhaps it was because they were being raised together, so therefore they were becoming more like family than friends. Either way, all the dads were grateful there was no bad blood between any of their children.

Eva's smile was small and forced as he backed out of her driveway. Just like Scott, she was probably anxious as hell to find out what dirt Liam's PI had dug up on the slimy Todd.

It had been all Scott could do on Saturday to not run out into Eva's driveaway and punch the living shit out of Todd. This man was certainly testing Scott's self-control in ways he never thought he would have to be tested. It'd been hard enough facing him later in the week after his lunch with Liam and their run-in. Every word he spoke to his VIP client was forced out through clenched teeth and fists beneath the table. He was a tightly wound cord close to snapping by the time Todd and his executive assistant, Braxlan (yes, you heard that name right!), left the office.

"What the hell's got your panties so tightly wedged up your ass?" Remy had asked with a cocky grin.

"You know what!" Scott snapped, knowing he shouldn't speak to his superior like that but also not giving two fucks at the moment how he spoke to the maggot.

Remy rolled his eyes, continuing to grin. Now Scott wanted to punch two people in their stupid faces. "He didn't seem to know, and if he does know, he didn't seem to care. Relax." He smacked Scott on the shoulder and headed out of the conference room. "You need to do some tai chi, Scottie. It relaxes the fuck out of me."

He reached for Eva's hand across the center gap between the driver's seat and the passenger seat. Their fingers laced and rested on the armrest. "It's going to work out, I promise."

The line of her mouth turned grim. "You can't promise that. He's dangerous, Scott. We're playing with fire here. I'm so sorry I got you involved."

He squeezed her hand at the same time he pressed his foot on the brake when they came to a red light. "Hey, I'm involved because I want to be. You're worth every headache, every risk, okay? Besides, whether we were together or not, I would still have found the guy a tool to work for. Any way I can ditch him, I will. And if we happen to put him in prison as the fallout of all of this, then hey, *bonus!*" He offered her a thumbs-up to try to dilute the mounting tension.

The boys in the back were bantering playfully back and forth. Freddie was giving Kellen and Lucas a rundown of all the other kids they were going to meet at the BBQ.

"Now, Gabe is one of my best friends, okay? He doesn't really talk though, but that's okay. We're such good friends, I know what he's saying without him even needing to talk."

"Why doesn't he talk?" Kellen asked.

Scott glanced in the mirror to see Freddie shrug. "Dunno. He just doesn't." His nose scrunched for a moment. "I mean he *does* talk. He says *Tori* and *Dad*—sort of, but that's about it." He shrugged. "You'll see."

Eva's eyes shifted to Scott so he could fill her in.

"Gabe is Mark's little guy. He is on the autism spectrum. Great kid. Nonverbal though. Mark's girlfriend, Tori, was and *is* Gabe's intervention therapist. The little guy has come leaps and bounds developmentally since she started working with him."

Eva's head bobbed in understanding.

"And now, Mira and Jayda are sisters but also cousins," Freddie went on. "It's complicated, but not really."

Again, Eva's eyes shifted to Scott.

"Mira is Adam's daughter with Paige. They're separated, but amicably. Paige is with Mitch, whose daughter, Jayda, is Adam's niece via his girlfriend, Violet."

"Okeydokey, then," she breathed, glancing out her window at the passing houses. Zak lived in a really nice neighborhood. Not as elite as Liam's neighborhood on Lake Washington, but it was still pretty fancy. His buddy did well for himself with his gym franchise, and now he was dating a lawyer. When Aurora paid off her student loans and made partner, they'd be rolling in the dough.

"Hey Dad?" Freddie called from the back at the same time Scott pulled into Zak's driveway. It was already lined with vehicles.

"Yeah?"

"How do monsters like their eggs?"

Scott groaned and put the van into park. Freddie was obsessed with corny jokes. The kid lived for them. He lived to make people laugh. With a wry smile at Eva and unbuckling his seatbelt, he replied, "I don't know, bud, how?"

"Terri-fried!" Freddie paused for the laugh, his mouth open, his hands making gun shapes and poised at his dad. "Get it? Terri-*fried.*"

Lucas and Kellen both erupted into giggles.

"Terri-*fried,*" Kellen snickered, shaking his head and unbuckling his belt. "That's hilarious."

Eva was smiling now.

His jokes might be corny as hell, but Scott's kid really did have a way of making people smile.

They all bailed out of the van. He grabbed the fruit and dip platter Eva had made, his six-pack of beer and the container of seven-layer dip and chips he'd grabbed from the grocery store. The boys took off at a run up the driveway.

"Front door or back gate, Dad?" Freddie called.

"Back gate," Scott replied, wishing he could take Eva's hand to reassure her, but his arms were loaded.

"Did Liam give any indication what his PI found?" she asked, falling in behind him as they traversed the stepping stones in the lawn that led to the gate separating Zak's front and back yards.

"No. He just said that his PI dug up some stuff, and it's best if shown and explained in person." He held open the gate for her. She wore simple white denim capris and a sexy yellow and blue check short-sleeved button-up shirt with a black tank top beneath it. Her makeup was minimal, and she wore aviator-style sunglasses with brown lenses and gold metal frames. But it was that raspberry red lipstick she always wore that made him crave a kiss from her juicy pout. She was every bit a spring beauty, with bright eyes and a healthy flush to her cheeks.

She walked past him in her black flats but paused on the path until he shut the gate. Murmurs and the sound of squealing children drifted around the side of the house, followed by the sudden shrill cry of a newborn.

Ah, Brielle must be awake.

They turned the corner into the thick of the party just in time to hear Freddie telling a swarm of children one of his jokes. "What do you call a moose with no name?"

Mira bounced up and down on her toes. "What?"

"Anony*moose!*" Freddie said, slapping his thigh and laughing. But he wasn't the only one. A bunch of the other kids were giggling uncontrollably too, including Gabe.

"I don't get it," Mira said, scratching her head.

Jayda whispered in her ear, then Mira's face lit up, and she joined in with the children's glee. Since meeting nearly a year ago in dance class, Adam and Mitch's daughters had become inseparable.

They were greeted by everyone, one at a time, the women introducing themselves first, starting with Aurora. Even though she didn't live with Zak, she stayed at his place more than her own, so she was essentially co-hosting the party. Then came the men.

Scott mentally prepared himself for his "brothers" and their assessment of his love interest, particularly since a few of them—his brother Liam for sure—were still jaded about love. Emmett had been opinionated about introducing a new woman to children too early into the relationship, and his views had actually put his relationship with Mark in hot water, but the man seemed to have cooled down a fair bit. Especially since his own woman had met his daughter, Josie, on day one.

But, thankfully, not only were they all kind to Eva and her boys, his woman fit into their little crew seamlessly. In no time, she, Zak and Adam were playing bocce ball in the lawn, and she was kicking both their asses.

"You a professional bowler or something?" Adam asked, shaking his head in bewilderment as Eva lobbed another dynamite toss at the target ball, knocking his ball clear into the hedges.

Her grin was warm and beautiful. "Not quite, but I did pitch for my softball team all through high school. We made nationals."

Zak rolled his eyes. "Of course you did. Damn it, no fair. Next game should be a bench-pressing competition."

Scott scoffed, "Eva's got a hidden strength inside her, man. She might surprise you and kick your ass there too." He slapped Zak on the shoulder. "Besides, you coach Aiden's baseball team. I would have thought you'd be better at this."

"Baseball is overhand, softball is underhand," Zak grumbled, though he was more just putting on his frustration for show. "She has the advantage."

Eva simply grinned wider, directing her smile Scott's way.

They'd been at the BBQ for several hours, and the excitement of the day seemed to have died down a fair bit, when Liam approached Scott and Eva standing next to the gazebo softly chatting.

"There you two are," Liam said, beer in hand. "Are you enjoying the party?"

Scott nodded, as did Eva, but he could tell she was eager to hear what information about Todd the PI had managed to dig up.

Liam's face sobered and he took a pull from his beer, letting out a satisfied *ah*, before he spoke again. "Now that our bellies are full, we've had some drinks and you annihilated Zak and Adam at bocce ball, maybe we should step into the house for a minute and chat."

Scott could practically hear Eva gulp next to him. Or maybe that was him gulping. Either way, a huge knot bobbed in his throat as they followed Liam into Zak's kitchen. The kids—even the older ones—were all out in the driveway doing chalk art with a couple of women—drinks in hand—supervising. The rest of the group took up various pockets throughout the yard or house, caught up in conversations.

"In here," Liam said, jerking his head toward the empty living room. They followed him. "You might want to sit down," he offered to Eva.

She shook her head, her body stiff, jaw set tight. "I want to stand. Now please, tell me what your PI found out about Todd."

Liam's lips flattened. He dug into the back pocket of his jeans and pulled out a manila envelope that had obviously been folded once lengthwise. "It would appear that your husband—"

"*Ex*-husband," Scott corrected, not blinking as Liam unfolded the envelope and began pulling out papers and a few photos.

"Right. Sorry. Anyway, I have copies of all of these at my office, just so you know. But it would appear that your ex-husband's businesses are not what they seem. They are in fact fronts for *other* businesses. His strip club runs a pretty pricey escort and prostitution service out the back. He launders money through the gentlemen's club and his nightclubs to fund his other ventures, like illegal arms dealing."

Eva's hand flew up to her mouth to smother her gasp.

"His casinos have some shady shit going on in them too, though my PI is still digging to get more details. From what he can tell though, high rollers are given access to some underground betting. McGregor, my PI, thinks it might be dog or cockfighting—possibly even people fighting. At least that's his guess. They go into the casino but then disappear, emerging hours later, sometimes through a door around back."

With each word Liam spoke, Eva's head began to shake faster.

"And lastly ... " Liam exhaled, handing her a photo of Todd with his arm around a woman who looked not much older than her niece Sabrina. "He was spotted two nights ago with *this* woman. They climbed into his town car together. Now McGregor wasn't able to get a real name for the woman, but none of us believe that she's old enough to be in a bar or casino, let alone *dating* a thirty-seven-year-old man."

"I doubt there's much *dating* going on," Scott muttered.

Even with the tight, revealing clothes and makeup, the woman with Todd looked no older than thirteen or fourteen. Was he not only running a prostitution ring, but an underage prostitution ring at that? Could the man get anymore disgusting?

Did they want to know the answer to that?

"I think I'm going to be sick," she whispered, handing the photo off to Scott. Her cheeks had lost all their color, and her eyes no longer held that spark he loved. Her sunglasses were pushed up into her hair, and she mindlessly reached for them, her hands shaking as she cleaned the lenses on the hem of her shirt. He could practically see the fear clawing at her as she came to terms with the fact that she had been married to this man—and probably while he was doing all of this shit. She had *loved* this man. He was the father of her children, and he did despicable things, cruel things. Evil things.

Scott already knew it to be true after what he'd done to Eva, but now more than ever he was convinced that Todd Fletcher was the walking definition of a soulless, psychopathic demon.

"So what do we do now?" Scott asked, taking the notes and photos from his brother and putting them all back into the envelope.

"Now, we go to the police," Liam said. "There's too much illegal shit going down for us to just sit on it and use it as leverage for your relationship. Hopefully, the guy gets found guilty and sent to prison, then we don't have to worry about him for twenty-five years—if he gets life."

Eva's thumb was wedged between her teeth, and she stared straight ahead at nothing in particular. "But you said your PI is still working on getting more information about what's going on in the casinos?"

Liam nodded. "He is, yes. He might bring in an associate, and then Quincy can pose as a high roller and potentially get an invite. McGregor is like ninety percent sure it's dogfighting. He could have sworn he heard dogs barking when he was scoping out the back of the building."

"That's fucking disgusting." Scott's words came out through clenched teeth. He focused on his brother but kept his arm tightly wrapped around his woman. Her body was iron-stiff. "So then maybe we should sit tight until McGregor gets back to you with more information. The more dirt we have on Fletcher, the more ammo the prosecutor has to fire at him, right?"

"Yes," Liam confirmed. "That's right. And everything the PI has uncovered so far would hold up in court. We could put Fletcher away for a long time with what we already have on him."

Eva had gone silent, her gaze once again focused intently on nothing in particular.

He pecked her on the side of the head. "Eves, you okay?"

She blinked up at him, her head shaking slowly. "Would you be?"

Good point.

He squeezed her tighter. "We'll get through this, okay? Liam is helping. McGregor is on it. We just need to lie low for a bit longer until McGregor gets us the rest of the information, then, with Liam, we'll take it to the police."

Her jaw trembled, and tears welled up in her beautiful eyes. "Only twenty-five years, Scott. What if it's less? What if he gets a lighter sentence or community service or just a fine? Even if it's ten years, eventually he'll get back out, and then he'll come looking for me. For *us*."

He wrapped her up in his arms, determined to absorb as much of her pain and fear as he could. His chin rested on the top of her head, the fruity and feminine scent of her shampoo driving his senses wild. "We'll cross that bridge when we come to it, okay?" He glanced at Liam. His brother was normally one of the most confident men, sure in his plan and downright arrogant about how successful of a lawyer he was. But right now, the look on his face gave Scott anything but faith in the justice system. Liam was well aware of how connected and powerful Todd was and that Eva's concerns were not unfounded. Todd could get a puny sentence, and then he'd be out and he'd be furious.

Liam cleared his throat. "Do you mind if I ask who represented you during your divorce? If you weren't happy with them, I'd be more than happy to make some recommendations."

"Richelle LaRue, of Epstein, Singh, Rosales and Marsh. She was phenomenal. Have you heard of her?"

Holy shit, was Eva's lawyer Liam's Wednesday night fuck buddy? What were the chances?

Liam's lip twitched and his brown eyes glittered. "I *have* heard of her, and you're right, she is phenomenal. Good job landing her as your attorney."

She managed a grim smile. "Thanks. I guess she's been through a nasty divorce herself, so she sympathized with my plight. Got me the best deal she possibly could."

Scott fixed his brother with a questioning look, but Liam's quick head shake shot it down, and Scott swiveled his eyes back to his woman.

A cacophony of noises in the kitchen prompted her to pull out of his arms. "We should go check on the kids," she said, wiping her eyes with her thumbs. "Mine are probably wondering where I am."

"I'm sure they're all having a blast on the grass," Liam offered, his tone chipper but his face still stoic. "Zak's got a soccer net set up, and Tia brought out her bubbles for the littler kids."

Scott was reluctant to let her go, not only because her touch and presence at his side grounded him, but he also felt the need to protect her, to remind Eva that he *would* protect her. He would be there for her, be her knight in shining armor and keep her safe from her satanic ex.

They rounded the corner into Zak's enormous, state-of-the-art kitchen to find all of the women standing around the island, wine in their glasses, as they ogled the blue-eyed baby Brielle in her mother's arms.

All eyes turned to face them.

"Leave us," Tori, Mark's girlfriend, ordered, lasering her

sapphire gaze on Liam and Scott. "We want to meet Eva without either of you around." She poured a lovely looking rosé wine into a stemless glass and handed it to Eva. "From the sounds of things, you might need something stronger."

Eva accepted the glass and pounded it back. "Yeah, I think I might."

18

"They're their children too," Paige said, curling her legs beneath her on the sofa in Zak's living room. "Let the men watch the kids. We have things to discuss." She thanked Isobel for the flask and took a hit, her eyes flaring as her mouth pinched into a tight pout. "That shit is strong." She passed the flask to Eva.

"You didn't hear this from me," Tori started.

"Or me," Isobel added.

"But we may know a guy who knows a guy who has a moonshine still in his garage. I add a splash of blueberry syrup to make it palatable," Tori said. She put her hand next to her face and whispered. "It's our uncle. But you didn't hear it from us."

"And it hasn't made anybody go blind yet?" Zara asked, clucking her tongue as if she'd just bitten into a lemon, her eyes blinking double-time.

Tori and Isobel shook their heads, their similar dark brown ponytails swishing behind them. "Pretty sure he's been making it for close to twenty years, and he's never made a person go blind," Isobel said.

Eva put her nose to the mouth of the flask and sniffed it. She reared back when the alcohol fumes hit her nostrils.

"I swear it'll take the edge off," Tori said.

"And put hair on your chest," Isobel added with a giggle.

Well, she was certainly on edge. Maybe one little sip. Just to relax her. To get her mind off Todd and his money-laundering, dirty-pimping ways. She cringed at the thought of him being a pimp and running a prostitution ring or a dogfighting circuit. He fit the bill for that kind of business though. Soulless and cruel. Not caring at all who he extorted as long as the lion's share of the money wound up in his pocket.

The urge to vomit was real and strong when she thought back to that picture of him with his arm around that woman who was probably not a woman at all. She was probably a teenager. A runaway. Somebody's daughter. Somebody's baby.

She tipped the flask up and took a long, fortifying pull.

Then she started coughing.

Holy shit, that stuff was strong.

"Yeah, you kind of need to sip it," Isobel said. "It's not like tequila where you can take a shot."

Eva usually sipped tequila too.

Her throat burned, and her vision went spotty.

Oh God, was she going blind? Was she that one in a million person who was actually going to go blind from drinking moonshine?

"Breathe." Aurora chuckled next to her and pounded her a couple of times on the back. "The feeling won't last, and your vision will return."

Snickers drifted around their circle.

She passed the flask to Aurora. Without flinching, the young woman took a sip, then passed it over Eva to Violet.

Cradling a snoozing and nursing Brielle in her lap, Violet

shook her head. "I'm nursing and only comfortable having wine." She held up her free hand, her eyes turning worried. "Not that I don't think your uncle knows what he's doing, it's just I was only approved to drink wine or beer by my doctor. They don't really include the effects of moonshine on your breast milk in the New Baby handbook."

"They might in Arkansas," Lowenna added, tittering at her own joke. She'd been quiet up until now, sitting next to Violet and staring fixated at Brielle. According to Tori, who seemed to be the ringleader, Lowenna was the newest addition to their little group. She was with Mason, and the two had started dating around Valentine's. But she was welcomed into the fold with open arms, according to Tori, because with Lowenna came an endless supply of chocolate.

"We don't know *everything* that's going on with you," Tori said, sipping on her wine and uncrossing, then re-crossing her legs. "But we know enough. The guys talk, and then they talk to us. We know that your ex is a dick and he's now Scott's VIP client."

Eva exhaled deeply through her nose and nodded. "Yep. Huge conflict of interest that Scott's boss just doesn't seem to care about."

Heads shook around the living room.

"That's stupid," Zara muttered. "Though, apparently, so is Scott's boss, so it makes sense, I guess."

Eva hinged forward from where she sat on one of the couches, squished between Violet and Aurora, and picked up a piece of chocolate from the tray. It looked heavenly. Pink and shimmery, almost too beautiful to eat.

"Smoked peach jam with peach oolong ganache," Lowenna said. "A new flavor that we're trying out. Let me know what you think."

Eva popped the lovely little morsel into her mouth and crushed it between her teeth. Her eyes slammed shut, and her head tilted skyward. A moan she had zero control over erupted from the depths of her chest, and her toes curled in her flats.

"Yeah, we all have that reaction when we try a new flavor of Lowenna's," Violet said next to her. "Orgasmic, right?"

Eva opened her eyes, heat filling her cheeks as every woman's gaze said the same thing.

"It's okay," Isobel assured her. "Even if that's your *O* face, we don't judge. Seemed pretty tame to me, honestly. You should have seen Tori's chocolate climax when Lowenna brought out her raspberry caramel bonbons atop pistachio gian ... guan ... ?" She glanced at Lowenna.

"Gianduja," Lowenna finished. "It's a paste usually made with hazelnuts and sweet chocolate, but I tried it with pistachios and it turned out—"

"Fucking amazing," Violet, Paige and Tori all said in unison.

Lowenna's gray-silver eyes sparkled, and her cheeks turned a pretty shade of pink. "Thanks."

Next to her, Violet shifted and fanned herself with one hand. "This baby is a furnace," she said. "Just like her father, she retains heat like a black car."

"May I?" Eva asked, giddy at the thought of getting baby snuggles. It'd been too long since she held a wee one in her arms. Too long since she felt the calm of innocence enfold her.

"By all means." Violet propped a noodle-limbed Brielle in her arms and then did the transfer like a pro.

Eva nestled the baby in the crook of her arm and made sure Brielle's arm wasn't trapped between them. The little girl never even cracked open an eyelid. She was off in baby dreamland. Her lips pursed into a tight nursing pout, and once in a while she'd do a sucking motion—like she was dreaming of the boob. Then she'd squeak, squirm and settle right back down.

"This might be better at taking the edge off than the moonshine," she said, slipping her finger beneath Brielle's hand and waiting for the baby to grasp it. She did.

"I know, right?" Violet said, pulling her gray T-shirt away from her body and flapping it a few times to cool herself down. "But a break from them is nice once in a while too."

"So you and Scott are neighbors?" Zara asked. She seemed to be the oldest woman in the bunch. Not that she didn't still hold the vibrancy and beauty of youth like the rest —because honestly, the woman was a stunner—it was more the air around her that spoke of maturity and grace. Like she knew what she wanted out of life and wasn't afraid to speak her mind or go after her goals. Whereas the other women seemed more caught up in the drama and dysfunction of life —just like Eva was.

"We are," Eva replied. "Though we met prior to the boys and I moving in next door."

Isobel popped a chocolate into her mouth. "Oh? We haven't heard this story."

Ah, she might as well just get it out and over with. It was only a matter of time before they found out, and besides, she really liked these women. They were open and honest, funny and kind, and the way they welcomed her into their tight fold warmed her heart to no end.

She reached for another chocolate and this time bit down on it with her front teeth to savor the sweetness. Her eyes glazed over.

"Cinnamon pear and caramel," Lowenna said to the chuckles of the other women.

Eva swallowed the little bite of ecstasy and began with her story. "We met at a bar. We were both there with terrible parties. We ditched them and went back to my hotel room."

"Oooh," Zara cooed, "that's like Emmett and I. We got busy the first night we met too."

Eva's neck nearly snapped off, she whirled it around so fast to look at the woman beside her. Zara most definitely did not strike her as a one-night-stand kind of woman.

Well, she wasn't. She's still with Emmett.

True enough. But she still didn't strike Eva as the type of woman who slept with a man she just met. Not that there was anything wrong with that—power to the feminists and all that—but Zara just seemed slightly more ... reserved? Was that the right word?

"Yeah, we met three times on the same day, all by happenstance, and then the fourth time we met was at a New Year's Eve party. We had sex on a wine barrel in Riley and Daisy's wine cellar." The rueful smile that tugged at one corner of her mouth accompanied by the gleam in her sky-blue eyes said that she was not only proud of her torrid little escapade but also interested in doing it again.

You go, girl.

Respect.

"Nothing wrong with getting the sexual compatibility test out of the way *right* away," Aurora said. "Zak and I were the same way. Though I pined after him for six months before he even noticed me. So in my mind it wasn't a first-night thing. We'd been having sex in my fantasies every night for a *loooong* time. It was like clockwork by the time I got the real thing."

Everyone chortled. Then it seemed there was a collective agreement of momentary silence where wine was replenished, a couple of women got up to go to the bathroom, and Lowenna brought out another box of chocolates.

Once they were all seated back down in their "trust circle of bodacious bitches," as Tori called it, all eyes swung back to Eva.

"Then what happened after you guys slept together in your hotel room?" Violet asked. Eva still held a snoozing Brielle, and she was content to do so. The baby in her arms had brought her blood pressure right down. The new mom sipped her wine. "I need sexy stories, desperately. I'm not getting much below-the-belt action myself these days, what with the nocturnal feeder here, so I'm living vicariously through you randy ladies."

Eva shrugged gently, careful not to jostle Brielle. Though she probably could have sneezed during a Metallica concert and the baby wouldn't have roused. "I left the next morning without saying goodbye because I didn't want it to be awkward and also because I'd never done that before and I was freaking out. Then we went six weeks never thinking we'd see the other person again before he showed up in my driveway as we were unpacking the moving truck."

Isobel clasped her hands and tucked them beneath her chin, batting her eyelashes dramatically. "And it's been true love ever since?"

Yes.

"Something like that," Eva murmured.

"Well, we're really happy to add another woman to the group," Tori said cheerfully. "Scott's a super guy, and he seems so happy." She twisted her lips. "I mean happier than he normally is, because he's a pretty happy guy. A big goofball, really."

"Have you seen that side of him?" Isobel asked.

Eva chuckled and nodded before glancing down at a now snoring Brielle. "It's my favorite side."

It was closing in on seven thirty, and all the kids were in Zak's living room happily watching a movie while the grownups sat around Zak's enormous dining room table drinking and laughing.

Even though it was a school night, everyone was having such a great time that not one person had made a move to gather their children and leave.

Scott lifted his arm and wrapped it around the back of Eva's chair, allowing his hand to fall to her shoulder. She leaned into him. The ease and familiarity between them and the level of intimacy they were both comfortable with—particularly in front of others—beguiled him. But he also really liked it.

He liked being in a relationship. He liked having a special woman in his life who he could share his ups and downs with. He and Katrin had a few inside jokes between them, and when one popped out, it was like a little firework going off inside him each time. And now he and Eva would have those moments and secrets between them as well. Only she struck him as the type of woman who loved a good laugh, unlike Katrin, who you really had to work at getting to crack a smile. Eva smiled freely and easily, and more than once during the BBQ, he'd caught her laughing so hard she had tears in her eyes.

He'd never seen Katrin laugh that hard—ever.

"More wine?" Aurora asked, easing herself out of her chair and heading to the kitchen. All the women nodded or said, "Yes, please."

A few of the guys were still drinking beer, but others—like Liam—had moved on to scotch. Scott had stopped drinking because he was driving, but that didn't mean that Eva couldn't enjoy herself.

"Oh, damn it!" Aurora grunted and grumbled in the kitchen. "The cork busted off in the bottle. What the hell?"

"Try again with the corkscrew, Rory," Zak offered,

standing up and wandering over to help his damsel in distress.

"Don't break the bottle, you big jock," Aurora joked, swatting him away when his meaty fist looked about ready to crush the neck of the bottle.

"Push the cork *into* the bottle," Eva suggested, craning her neck around to see the commotion in kitchen.

"But then how will we get it out?" Aurora asked.

"Leave that to me," Eva said. "Use a knife to push the cork in, fill everyone's glasses, and then when the bottle is empty, bring the bottle a thin dish towel over to me."

"Ooh." Liam's brows lifted. "Party tricks."

Eva grinned. "Something like that. I was a server for a couple of years, and one of the waiters who had worked there forever used to do tricks for his tables." She thanked Aurora for her now full-again wine glass, then accepted the empty bottle with the cork stuck in it and a dish towel.

Scott's hand dropped from her shoulder as she scooted her chair in closer to the table, all eyes on her. Pride swept through him. Everyone seemed to like Eva, and she fit in with their little makeshift crew seamlessly. Her boys were thick as thieves with Freddie and Jordie already, with the four kids making plans to have sleepovers during the summer.

He took it all as another sign that she was meant to be in his life, meant to be by his side. Their sons got along. He and Eva were once again on the same page. Now all they had to do was *deal* with the toxic sludge that was Todd Fletcher, and then they could all ride off into the sunset in her soccer-mom minivan. Complete with orange slices and Capri Sun pouches for all.

Using the corner of the dish towel, Eva made a small Pope hat-shaped open-mouthed cone and fed it into the neck of the bottle. She shook the bottle until the cork bounced its way into the open part of the towel, then she tugged, securing the cork in the towel and up into the neck.

"Well, shit," Zak murmured.

"Cool," Mark breathed.

Eva pulled hard, grunting when the towel and cork became stuck in the middle of the bottleneck.

"Need a hand?" Zak asked.

Eva shook her head, grunting again. "Just a sec. I'll get it."

Scott had to admire her persistence. She was determined to see her trick through, even though there were men with rippling muscles all around the table. And he didn't mean himself, per se. Zak and Aaron were practically busting out of their T-shirts. Both were muscly redheaded men with arms full of tattoos. Aaron was a former Navy SEAL turned contractor, and Zak owned a gym. Either one of them could probably bench-press a Smart Car and not think twice about it.

Another grunt, tug and *pop*, out came the cork in the sleeve of the towel.

Several people around the table gasped. A few clapped.

Eva's grin warmed Scott from the inside out.

"So cool," Isobel whispered.

Eva handed Aurora the bottle and cork. "There you go." She then opened the towel up completely on the table, and while laughing at Mitch's joke about Eva being hired to do tricks for all their dinner parties, she began to roll the towel.

"Do you have any other tricks up your sleeve?" Tori asked, sipping her wine. "Like can you pull a tablecloth out from beneath the dishes without breaking anything?"

Eva shook her head, then for no reason, she dabbed at her mouth with her napkin.

"Bwaha." Aurora snorted. "Is that another trick?"

Eva made a face of angelic innocence as she dabbed at

her mouth again. "Whatever do you mean? Is there something on my mouth? Perhaps a bit of *cream?*"

That's when Scott noticed that she had rolled the dish towel into the shape of a penis—an erect penis—and was dabbing at her mouth with the head.

She just kept revealing more remarkable layers of herself to him—to all of them—and he just kept falling harder and harder for her when each layer was revealed.

"That's hilarious," Adam said with a chuckle, patting Brielle's butt lightly, the baby fast asleep on his shoulder. Mason held a sleeping Willow in the same position, Aaron a snoozing Sophie on his broad shoulder, and Atlas, who had been more quiet than normal, held his cousin's daughter— and his new foster child—Cecily against his chest after feeding her a bottle. Their little family was certainly growing. So much so that it wasn't a *little* family of single dads and their kids anymore.

Eva's smile was demure, but her eyes glittered as she unfurled the towel and passed it to Aurora. "Another trick I learned from my waiter friend Damien. We had a lot of fun at that restaurant."

Laughing, Scott wrapped his arm back around Eva and tugged her against his side, planting a kiss to her temple. "It means so much to me that you came to meet all my friends," he murmured against her hair. "Everyone loves you."

She blinked up at him, her smile small but hopeful.

She was everything he'd ever wanted in his life. In her eyes, with her in his arms, he saw his future. And not just for the next week or month or even year. He saw Eva in his life and in his arms for years and decades to come. He saw their old, wrinkled and liver-spotted hands linked as they sat in matching rockers in their nursing home watching the ducks in the pond outside. He saw their grandchildren coming to visit them, their great-grandchildren too. He saw a life with her.

"Thank you for inviting me," she said, keeping her voice low. The two of them now had their heads together, oblivious to the conversations going on around them. "I really needed this. A chance to get out of my head, make some new friends. I really love the women. I love everybody. They're great."

"Eva ... " He blew out a breath and touched his forehead to hers. "I love you."

The look in her eyes said it all.

Too soon.

Fuck, he knew it.

He knew it, but he didn't know better and went and said it anyway.

"Uh ... " She shifted away slightly, her gaze sliding to the side, where Freddie, Kellen and Lucas came walking toward them, all three of them rubbing their eyes and yawning.

"Mom, can we go home?" Kellen asked. "I'm tired."

"Me too," said Freddie.

"Hey, Freddie. Got any jokes?" Liam asked, his eyes following his own son making his way into the kitchen. Jordan climbed up onto Liam's lap.

Freddie nodded. "Want to hear a construction joke?"

"Sure do," Liam said.

Freddie yawned. "Sorry, I'm still working on it."

Laughter pinged around the table.

One by one, tired children with sleepy eyes and heavy feet trudged their way into the kitchen, locating their parent and either climbing up into a lap or snuggling into their side.

"I think that's our cue to call it a night," Mark said, hoisting an exhausted-looking Gabe onto his lap. He brushed hair off the little guy's forehead. "Hey, buddy. Bedtime?"

Gabe nodded and closed his eyes, resting his head against his father's shoulder.

"We should get these kids home," Eva said to Scott, her voice distant despite the fact that she was right next to him.

Fuck, had he completely botched everything with his overeagerness?

Probably.

Damn it.

She stood up, and he expected her to escape his side, following her children to make sure they didn't leave anything behind, but he found her hand on his shoulder and her mouth next to his ear. The warmth of her breath on his neck made his cock jerk in his jeans.

"I'm not there yet," she whispered. "But I'm close. Really close. I've fallen for you, Scott. I just need to get everything else sorted first before I can take that next step, okay?"

He released his breath slowly through thinly opened lips, his thundering pulse in his ears slowing down to a calming *thump, thump.* "Okay."

Her lips fell to his neck, and then she was gone.

Liam elbowed Scott once Eva was out of earshot. "I won't represent you if you guys get a divorce. Richelle is her attorney, and we've made a promise to never go up against each other again." Scott made a noise in his throat that said he wanted his brother to back off. But either Liam didn't give a shit or he was oblivious, as he just kept yammering on. "I can make some recommendations for you, though."

"You're a dick," Scott said flatly.

"But you love me anyway," Liam said, all grins.

Scott rolled his eyes. Liam had really come through for them with his PI. Now they had ammunition—and it was still building—to make sure Todd didn't come near Eva or the kids.

He slapped his brother on the shoulder deliberately just a touch too hard. Liam made an *oof* noise. "That I do. Night, bro, and thank you."

19

It was closing in on nine o'clock by the time Scott tucked Freddie into bed. The boys had found their second wind when Scott parked the van in Eva's driveway, and all three little rascals took off into Eva's backyard for a rousing game of tag.

Just as well. It gave Scott and Eva a chance to talk while the boys burned off the last bits of their energy—and the churros that Paige had brought for dessert.

They hadn't really spoken since they left Zak's house. The ride home had been quiet all around. Even the boys seemed lost in thought.

He couldn't tell if it was worry or sadness that wrinkled the corners of her expressive green eyes. Or fear that caused the tight press of her lips. Either way, Eva was lost in her own head as she put dishes away and began to toss granola bars, boxes of raisins and apple sauce squeeze pouches into two open lunch boxes on the counter.

Even though she'd responded to his confession with kindness, it still ate away at him that he'd told her he loved her. How stupid could he be? That was not the time, place, nor enough time into their relationship to reveal such a thing.

And yet he had.

Idiot.

He needed to clear the air further. Things were still hazy, and he feared that if they didn't talk about it, a fissure between them would form, and with everything going down with Todd, that fissure would turn into a crevasse so wide, no bridge could span it.

Clearing his throat, he stepped deeper into her kitchen. "Can we talk about what I stupidly blurted out earlier tonight?" He rocked back on his heels and shoved his hands into the pockets of his jeans.

"Whatever do you mean?" she asked with a big grin, her eyelashes batting flirtatiously. Even with the Colgate smile, he could tell she wasn't entirely on board with the happiness she was projecting. The twinkle in her eye wasn't there, and the corners of her mouth began to droop seconds after she tossed on the smile. She was plagued by everything Liam had revealed. And why wouldn't she be? That was a lot to take in, a lot to process. Scott was still processing it.

He leaned against the counter and eyed her carefully, not wanting to spook her but wanting to let her know that she didn't have to put on a happy face for him. She could be herself. She could be scared, angry, or any other emotion she wanted. He wasn't going anywhere. "You know what I mean, Eva. I'm sorry if I spooked you."

"Ah, you mean the part where you told me you loved me?"

He nodded, his gut twisting until he thought he might puke. "Yeah, that."

"You didn't spook me. Surprised me, sure. But I'm not spooked. And I'm not going to run, if that's what you're worried about. I told you that I'm not quite there yet, but I'm close. I'm on my way. Only a few paces behind you." This time, her smile was small, but the twinkle in her eyes was back. "I've fallen hard and fast for you, neighbor. I just need to unload a bit of the baggage that refuses to get lost in transit. I keep trying to ditch it roadside, and it keeps winding up back on my doorstep."

She ditched the bowl in her hand and stepped into his space. They were toe to toe, not quite touching, but close. Close enough he could feel her heat, feel her warm breath on his parted lips. Her unique and sweet feminine scent wrapped around him, and he resisted the urge to shut his eyes and inhale deeper.

She sucked in a deep breath to continue but must have thought better of it and sighed, pressing her hands to his chest.

The air between them—not that there was much room for it—suddenly turned thick. He tilted his head down so they were even closer now, so close her ragged breath washed over his lips when he opened them to speak. "I won't pressure you to say it back. I'm a patient man, and you are definitely someone worth waiting for."

Fire ignited in the yellow flecks of her eyes. She pushed up onto her tiptoes and surged forward, capturing his mouth in a heated, driven and purposeful kiss. Her nails raked up his shirt, and her fingers curled around his neck as she deepened their lip lock and tugged him down to her.

They kissed and kissed and kissed until ruckus at the patio door caused them to abruptly pull apart, seconds before their sons came barreling into the house.

"Ready to go?" Scott asked, ruffling Freddie's hair and coming up with a sweaty palm. The little guy was panting, and his cheeks were rosy. Hopefully that meant his son would sleep well after all that fresh air and running around.

Freddie nodded. "Can I come back over to Kellen and

Lucas's tomorrow to play? After school and then after dinner?"

Scott grinned, his gaze slowing lifting from his son's tired but eager expression to Eva's face. She was smiling.

It was such a bonus that their kids got along so well. They could have had a real problem getting to know each other if their kids weren't compatible.

"We'll have to see, buddy," he said. "But something tells me we'll be seeing a lot of Kellen and Lucas."

Freddie made a face that was the equivalent of *no shit.* "Well, yeah, Dad. They live next door."

Scott rolled his eyes.

Eva chuckled.

With his hand on his son's shoulder, he guided Freddie back toward the sliding patio doors. "Say goodnight to your friends."

Freddie waved enthusiastically at Kellen and Lucas. They waved back, their faces equally exhausted and rosy-cheeked.

Scott paused with his body half inside the house, half on the deck, his eyes landing on Eva's face. "Until tomorrow then?"

The smile that slid across her face made his pulse race. "Until tomorrow. Goodnight, Freddie. Goodnight, Scott."

Holding hands, Scott and Freddie descended the sundeck stairs to Eva's backyard. "Can we take the back gate, Dad?" Freddie asked, yawning.

"Not tonight, buddy. But next weekend I'll clear the bushes in front of it, fix the broken boards and grease the hinges. It can become you kids' secret passageway between the houses."

Freddie beamed up at him as they wandered down Eva's driveway toward the sidewalk. "That sounds cool. The guys and I want to build a fort this summer. Maybe we can build one that is so big, it's in my yard *and* their yard."

Scott chuckled. "I look forward to the blueprints." As they rounded the corner around the hedge back onto Scott's property, a Mercedes-Benz SUV drove by, slowing down in front of them. The windows were tinted so he couldn't see who was inside.

Was that Todd's vehicle from yesterday? Now he couldn't remember if the guy drove a Beamer or a Benz. He shook his head. Liam was the motorhead that took after their mechanic father, not him. He liked vehicles well enough, but he couldn't tell a make or model without looking at the company emblem on the front or back of the car. Liam and their father could tell a Chevy from a Ford by listening to the rev of the engine.

Freddie yawned again. "Race you to the door, Dad?"

Scott released his son's hand and gripped his shoulder. "You're on. On your mark, get set ... GO!" Then he playfully held his son in place, shoved him backward and, with a *whoop*, Scott took off toward his front door, a giggling Freddie behind him yelling, "No fair. You cheated!"

MONDAY MORNING, Scott propped his feet up on his desk and cradled his phone between his shoulder and ear as he jotted down notes on his yellow notepad. McGregor, Liam's PI, had texted him before sunrise to say that he had new intel on Todd and for Scott to call him ASAP.

That's exactly what Scott did.

"This is great, McGregor, thank you," he murmured into the phone, doodling on the page to keep his fingers busy. "So your guy was able to get into the underground dogfighting ring?" He shook his head. "Fuck, man, that's just sick."

"Liam's been forwarded everything. He suggests you and Ms. Marchand take all the information to the police together, with your lawyers," McGregor said into the phone. A straw at the bottom of a cup slurping up the last dregs sounded like a chainsaw on a metal fence in Scott's ear, and he pulled the phone away from his head and cringed.

He waited until the noise ceased before he spoke again. "Yeah, that sounds like a plan. Best to look as professional as possible. Thanks again."

"No problem. I'm going to keep digging for a bit, see if I can find out any more about that young woman he was with last week. If you can even call her a *woman*. Girl, was more like it."

"Fuck, man. Yeah, the more we can nail this guy with the better. Talk soon."

McGregor hung up without saying goodbye at the same time there was a knock at Scott's closed office door.

"Come in," he barked, sliding his feet down to the floor and turning the pad of paper over before the person entered.

The doorknob turned, and in sauntered Todd.

Scott's palms bunched into fists, and his pulse kicked up speed.

"Hey, Scottie-boy," Todd said, his eyes thin slits and his dark, thick brows pinched. The chipper tone to his voice did not match the expression on his face.

"We don't have an appointment, Todd. What can I do for you?" He was determined to keep his rage out of his voice. If Todd caught even a whiff of what they had planned, the whole thing could be derailed faster than a train on an icy track.

"Don't need an appointment. Not a VIP like me, right?" Unbuttoning the bottom button of his suit jacket, he sat down in the seat on the other side of Scott's desk and cocked the ankle of one leg on the knee of the other. Scott couldn't get a read on the man. His face said fury, but his tone said jovial. What was his angle?"

"What can I do for you, Todd?" Scott repeated, unwilling to bite and give the man any kind of sense he was as important as he was.

Todd sneered. "You never told me you lived on Hollyhock Avenue."

What the ... ?

How did he know where Scott lived?

Scott's eyes narrowed, and he focused on Todd's smirk of evil. A muscle in Todd's jaw twitched.

Oh, fuck.

He knew.

"You sleeping with my wife?" Todd asked, deadpan.

Scott was equally unflappable. "I have no idea what you are talking about. Who the hell is your wife?"

Todd's nostrils flared. His eyes darkened. "You know what I hate even more than a liar, Scottie? A liar who is also a thief."

Scott swallowed down the lump in his throat and willed his heart to stop hammering in his chest. He shook his head and tried his damnedest to smile through the fear. "What are you talking about, Todd? Thief? Liar?"

"I know you're neighbors with my wife. I know you're fucking her. How *long* have you been fucking her?"

How did he know?

When Scott didn't answer, Todd continued. "The kids told me. Which is just another thing that I hate, the fact that I had to hear this from my children and not someone I considered not only a colleague but a friend. I thought we were friends, *Scott*. So imagine my surprise and then my hurt to find out that my *friend* is sleeping with my wife. My *friend* stole my wife. Sneaking around behind my back, all the while smiling to my goddamn face. Pretending that you have my best interests at heart. That you're going to make me a bunch of money." He lunged forward in his seat, his volume raised as he spoke, "All the while you're fucking my fucking wife!"

"*Ex*-wife," Scott gritted out. "And I haven't stolen a damn thing." He knew he was better off not biting and instead taking the high road and remaining silent—Todd was, after all, a client, a VIP client at that—but the man was just so infuriating, the way he continued to lay claim to Eva, to call her his *wife* as if their marriage still existed, as if he still had a chance in hell with her.

Todd lips curled. "Ah, so you *do* know her. You're okay with my sloppy seconds? That stretched-out pussy of hers turn you on?" He leaned back in the seat again and casually examined his nails. "You know, Scottie-boy, I'm not so sure Dynamic Creative is a right *fit* for Fletcher Holdings. Particularly if I can't *trust* the man I'm supposed to lay the fate and financial success of my company with."

"What's this?" Remy popped his head inside Scott's office because, of course, Todd hadn't bothered to shut the door. "Y-you're thinking of leaving the company? Wh-why?" Remy was stammering the way he always did when he was nervous.

Where was your stress ball now, Junior?

Todd flicked his pale eyes up to Remy. "I'm firing Mr. Dixon here because the man has been sleeping with my wife."

Gasps from outside the office ricocheted through cubicles, followed on the heels by murmurs and whispers.

Oh, great. Now Scott was a new link on the company gossip chain. Damn it.

"B-but you're not firing *Dynamic Creative,* are you?" Remy asked, beads of sweat emerging on his reddening forehead like a diamond-encrusted headdress. "What if we just transferred you to another team leader? Another entire team, perhaps? I could even be the team leader. You'll be my *V*-VIP client. My *Very* Very Important Client. Please, Mr. Fletcher, give us another chance."

Todd tilted his chin toward Scott. "I will if you fire this asshole."

Remy nodded. "Done. Scott, I'm sorry, but you're fired. You're still within your three-month probation with the company, and after new information has come to light, it would appear that you and Dynamic Creative are just not a good fit." His enormous Adam's apple jogged in his throat, and he mopped up his forehead with the bottom of his tie. "I'll need you to pack up your things immediately."

Scott's jaw was clenched so tight, he wasn't sure he'd have any molars left after all was said and done. There was so much that he wanted to say, that he *needed* to say, but now was not the time.

McGregor was still digging, and Liam wanted to compile all the evidence they had against Todd in one organized, easy-to-read (and convict) package. And he needed time to do that.

But fuck. Scott hadn't anticipated he'd lose his job over all of this. Probation, maybe, but his job?

Goddamn it, Remy was a weaselly little tool.

Todd lifted his brows. "Well, Dixon, better get a move on." He turned back to Remy, who looked like he was about ready to shit his pants—or already had. "Unless you'd like *me* to escort Mr. Dixon out to his vehicle."

Remy swallowed again. "That won't be necessary, Mr. Fletcher. Mr. Dixon here is a reasonable man. I'm sure he won't be a problem." His amber eyes shifted to Scott. "Right, Scott?"

Scott nodded stiffly. "Right. No problem from me. Though I will say I'm disappointed in you, Remy."

Remy's baby face turned deep red, and he blinked a bunch of times. "In *me?*"

Scott shoved his hands in his pockets. Otherwise he would probably strangle Remy and then punch the living daylights out of Todd. "Yes. I came to you last week to let you know that there was a conflict of interest with me continuing to lead the new marketing team for Fletcher Holdings. When I told you, albeit reluctantly, that I was dating Mr. Fletcher's *ex*-wife and should be removed from his team, you dismissed me. You said it was a non-issue and that I was underwhelming you. Boring you. And now that it has become an issue, now that Mr. Fletcher has found out before I or his *ex*-wife had a chance to tell him ourselves, I am being fired. I have done absolutely nothing wrong, and even though I am within the three-month probationary period, don't think I won't fight this."

Remy's face went from red to white in under three seconds. His throat bobbed again as if he had a large chunk of bread stuck in there and couldn't get it out.

With a bored expression on his face, Todd stood up from his chair and buttoned the lower button on his suit jacket. "Ignore him, Remy. Let's say you and I go grab lunch? Talk more about this new and improved team you have planned for me?" He slapped Remy on the shoulder and wheeled him toward Scott's office door, but not before craning his neck around and pinning a steely, psychopathic glare on Scott. "I'm prepared to pay Dynamic Creative's legal fees and give them my best lawyer on retainer if you fight this, Dixon. You will *lose*." His gaze narrowed. "Everything." Then, with a sinister laugh that made Scott's skin crawl, he ushered Remy out into the lobby and toward the elevators.

"Oh my God, Scott, I just heard." Sondra rushed in once Fletcher and Remy were gone, concern in her honey-colored eyes. "They can't fire you."

"Oh, but they can." He pulled a few pieces of paper out of

his big blue recycle bin and began to load up all his personal effects into the box.

"But they just can't!"

Scott didn't bother looking up again, though he knew by the way the air in his office grew thick that there were other people milling around the door, watching him pack up his things.

"What are you going to do?" Sondra asked after he was all packed and had said his goodbyes.

"I have a few plans," he said, resting his hand on her shoulder. "This won't be the last you see of Scott Dixon, trust me. I just need to take care of a couple of things first."

Sondra wiped a tear from her eye with one of her bejeweled fake nails. "We're going to miss you."

"I'm going to miss you guys, too." He pulled her forward for a hug. She smelled like peppermints and Pantene. When they broke their hug, there were more tears in her eyes, which caused her mascara to run.

He reached for a tissue off his desk and handed it to her. "Can you do me one last favor before I go?"

"Anything, honey," she said, nodding and blotting at her eyes.

"Can you find me Remington Barker's home number, please?"

Sondra's eyes grew saucer-size. "Coming up!" She was all grins now as she skittered her body back behind her desk and her nails began to do their thing on the keyboard.

She handed him a pink heart-shaped Post-It note less than thirty seconds later.

"You going to call the big guy?" she asked, a new sparkle to her eyes.

He took the piece of paper and glanced down at it. "Well, when *my* son is behaving like a horse's ass at school or on the playground, the teachers or other parents come and talk to me. Let me know that my son's behavior is unacceptable. Then I sit Freddie down and we talk about what it means to be a *good* person."

"I think Remington Senior skipped that talk with Junior," Sondra said, tossing a hand on her hip. "Maybe having a father-to-father chat with Mr. Barker Sr. is just what Remy needs from you."

Scott tapped his knuckles twice on the counter. "My thoughts, exactly, Sondra. My thoughts exactly."

20

"HAVE A SEAT," Eva said with a smile, patting the backrest of the chair beneath the hair dryer.

Mrs. Ferguson from down the block shuffled over with her foils in her hair and sat down. "Thank you, dear."

"Would you like a magazine or a *Reader's Digest?* It's going to be about twenty minutes."

"That would be lovely, thank you, honey."

Eva handed sweet, old Mrs. Ferguson a stack of magazines and *Reader's Digests,* then she turned on the hair dryer and returned to where Mrs. Clark was sitting with her feet in the footbath, waiting for her pedicure.

She was going to have to dedicate every Monday to the seniors in her neighborhood. Ever since the ladies on the block found out that Eva was a hairdresser and aesthetician, they'd been calling nonstop to book appointments. But as Eva had quickly learned, an appointment, whether it be hair, nails or a lip wax, was never *just* an appointment. It was an update—on everyone else in the neighborhood.

And when she ended up with more than one little old lady in her salon at a time, it became a full-on gossip pool.

Eva knew more about people in the neighborhood she'd never met than she did about people she'd known for years.

Sitting down on the stool in front of the foot spa and Mrs. Clark, she reached for a towel. "Have you picked your color, Mrs. Clark?"

The elderly woman smiled, causing the corners of her eyes to form deep creases. She held up a bottle of vibrant orange. "I'm going daring this time. It's called Orange Dreamsicle."

"Sounds perfect." She gently lifted Mrs. Clark's feet out of the foot spa and dried them with a towel.

"So you're seeing that nice Scott Dixon next door, huh?"

Eva paused her hands and glanced over her shoulder at Mrs. Ferguson.

"Oh, she can't hear us. Even if she didn't have that fan-thing going in her ears, she's as deaf as a mole rat is blind." She leaned forward and rested her hand on Eva's arm. "It's just us, dear. You can tell me. I won't say a word, I promise."

Eva resisted the urge to make a *pfsst* noise.

Yeah, right. Mrs. Ferguson wouldn't say a word ... until she got home. Then she'd be on the horn to half the block.

"Mrs. Clark ... " But she wasn't able to finish before the back door swung open and in walked the gossip-topic himself, all sexy and professional-looking in his long-sleeved white button-down, his gray trousers and his silver tie. But his eyes were what caused her to stand up and approach him. Real, deep-seated fear stared back at her.

"Well, now," Mrs. Clark said behind her.

"What's wrong?" she asked him, ignoring Mrs. Clark.

He gripped her by the elbow and brought her back outside. "Not here."

She poked her head back into the salon. "Just a moment, Mrs. Clark."

"Take all the time you need, dear," Mrs. Clark sang, her

tone knowing and her eyes mischievous. If that woman had a cell phone, she'd probably be Tweeting about the fact that Scott had just shown up on Eva's doorstep and hauled her outside.

But she couldn't worry about that right now. What made her blood run cold was the lack of color in Scott's face and the increasing look of panic in his eyes.

"He knows," he said, once she shut the back door. "He knows. He came to the office today and confronted me and then Remy fired me."

Her head began to shake, and she found herself muttering, "No, no, this can't be happening." Over and over again until Scott grabbed her by the shoulders and then drew her in tight to his chest. Holding her. Keeping her safe until she stopped shaking. "Breathe, baby. Breathe."

She did as she was told.

Once she'd calmed down a bit, he held her by the shoulders but pulled away to look her in the eyes. "Eva, babe, listen to me."

She blinked at him, but everything in her head was fuzzy.

"It's going to be okay. I called Liam on my way home. We're going to go to the police station this afternoon and submit all the evidence we have. Todd won't be a threat for long."

"He'll just post bail or get one of his rich friends to post bail. Then he'll be a threat again." She was shaking her head again, her vision blurry, Scott's face just a bunch of mottled shapes and colors in front of her. "One of Todd's best friends is a cop down at the precinct. Todd will know what we've done before we even get into our cars. I need to leave. Go get the kids from school and leave town. Somewhere where he won't find us. Otherwise, we'll never be safe."

Tears stung her eyes as the fear bled through her body, and she began to shake.

"Oh, baby." He grabbed her and pulled her close. She trembled uncontrollably in his arms. "It's okay, babe. It's okay. He won't hurt you. You or the boys. I won't let him." He rubbed her back and whispered shushing noises to soothe her, but they were of little comfort. "I'm going to call Remington Barker, the CEO of Dynamic Creative, and let him know what's going on. His stupid maggot of a son is running the company into the ground, and whether I get my job back or not, Remington needs to know."

Hiccupping a sob, she pulled out of his arms and wiped her eyes with the back of her wrist. "I need to call Celeste, have her pick the boys up from school and keep them. She lives next door to a retired police officer, and he's aware of our situation."

He nodded. "That sounds like a good idea." His hands ran up and down her arms.

"Sh-should I call the police? They can't all be under Todd's thumb. Maybe I'll talk to a good one, an honest one."

His lips twisted in thought. "Let's wait to hear from Liam."

Her eyes drifted to the closed door. She needed to get back to her clients. "Okay."

"I'm going to go call Remington, then I'll come back over and sit with you so you're not alone. We'll wait until Liam calls, then we'll meet him down at the police station. You can point out Todd's lackey, and we'll make sure we avoid him. Sound good?"

Inhaling deeply through her nose, she bobbed her head, her brain not really computing everything he'd said but doing its best to make sense of it all. "Okay."

He leaned forward and pressed his lips to hers, his scent and warmth a balm to help heal the slashes in her heart that the terrible news had created. "We'll figure it out," he whispered against her lips.

All she could do was nod. "I ... I need to get back inside."

"Okay. I'll go call Remington, then I'll be back. I don't want to leave you here by yourself."

She didn't say another word but stepped back inside, her heart in her throat, her blood ice-cold and her stomach so small and twisted, she wasn't sure she'd ever be able to keep anything down again.

Todd knew she was seeing Scott.

The man was a jealous, possessive psychopath.

He was coming for her.

"WELL, I appreciate your call, Scott, I truly do," Remington Barker said into the phone with a pained sigh. "Truth be told, I've had my own set of concerns about young Remy at the helm of Dynamic Creative. It was my baby, after all, and I thought that *my* baby would take it to the next level." His tone turned disappointed. "A shame I was wrong, but such is life."

"I'm not calling to beg for my job back, sir," Scott said, sitting at his kitchen table and twiddling a pen around and around through his fingers. His nerves were teetering on the edge, and his stomach had formed a hollow pit. "I can find other jobs. But I respect you, sir. I respect what you've created, and I know that you wouldn't want the reputation of your company sullied by the fact that you represented a lowlife like Todd Fletcher."

"No, I wouldn't. You're completely right. Todd Fletcher needs to go."

Straight to hell.

He'd debated telling Remington Barker about what they planned to take to the police, but in the end, he decided it was a good idea. Remington Barker had more integrity in one of his few remaining gray hairs than Todd Fletcher or

Remy Barker had combined. Mr. Barker could be trusted with this information. And the sooner the company kicked Fletcher Holdings to the curb, the better. The last thing they needed was to get tied up in a scandal. And what Todd Fletcher had his greedy mitts saturated in was certainly scandal-worthy.

"And you need to come back."

"Sir ... "

"No. Hear me out, Scott." He hummed. "Better yet, come to the house now. I'd rather we hammer out your new title and job description in person. Leave Todd Fletcher and my son to me."

Now?

He wanted to discuss Scott's new job role *now*?

Continuing to have a conversation with himself, Remington Barker prattled on. "Yeah, that sounds like a plan. Come by. I'll have my assistant draw up the contract right now, and we can sign it and move forward."

Shit. Scott did not want to leave Eva right now. He was getting twitchy enough not being under the same roof as her that very moment, knowing how vulnerable she was.

"Uh, sir, can it wa—"

"How does Chief Operating Officer sound to you?

Scott choked on his spit. "You want me to be COO?"

"I do. I know you applied for the job, and it should have been yours from the get-go. I tried to put my faith in my son and his hiring abilities, thinking I could trust his instincts when it came to bringing on new employees. Seems the boy has poor instincts all around, and I'm sorry."

Scott swallowed. "Well, thank you, sir."

Remington grunted. "Your resume speaks for itself. You have *years* of experience in the advertising and marketing field—more than a lot of those young 'uns in there combined. I should have put my foot down when Remy said you weren't right for the COO position. The boy's still too green. Belongs in the mailroom, not running things."

Scott resisted the urge to say, "Well, duh," and remained quiet, since Remington Barker didn't sound like he was finished.

"You came highly recommended from your last firm. Even though I'm mostly just a figurehead now, I still have eyes and ears to the ground and walls in Dynamic Creative. I know how smart and savvy you are. I never should have hired my son in the first place, but my wife—God rest her soul— insisted I take care of him. Come on by, Scott. I'll put the kettle on and have Gordon draw up the papers. We need you back in the office tomorrow, posthaste."

Scott stumbled over his words, not really saying anything in particular but making a heck of a lot of noise doing it. Finally, he managed a coherent sentence. "Well, thank you, sir, but I have a bit of a family matter to attend to today. Would you mind if I came by tomorrow morning?"

Besides, didn't the board of directors have to vote on a new executive being hired? He knew Remington Barker held power in his own company, but a position like COO needed to be voted on.

Remington grunted again. "Fine, fine. I was just going to go have a nap anyway. But I guess I'll need to organize a meeting with the board of directors, do this the *right* way." He yawned over the phone. "First, though, I must deal with my *son*." His tone was the opposite of enthused. "See you tomorrow, Scott." Then he hung up.

Scott didn't know whether to throw up or whoop in celebration. He'd just been given a crazy promotion, but it was one he deserved.

Finally, he was being considered. His opinions mattered. His voice mattered.

It was about damn time.

He'd have to plan how he'd rub it in Remy's face later. Right now he needed to get back to Eva.

With one hand on the doorknob and his keys in his other hand, his phone began to ring again. He didn't recognize the number. But that didn't mean much these days. Hell, his mom's number came up *private* because she was worried about the government knowing too much of her information.

On the fifth ring, he answered. "Hello?"

"Cute kid. Looks older than his picture on your desk, though."

What the fuck?

"Who is this?"

He didn't recognize the voice. It was deep and raspy, like the man smoked a couple of packs a day.

"Mr. Fletcher would just like you to know that should you or Mrs. Fletcher decide to take matters to the police that we have eyes on all the children." The sound of traffic and children playing on a playground filled the background.

Was he *at* Freddie's school?

Lead dropped in Scott's stomach.

"Red shirt, brown pants, white sneakers that light up?"

Freddie had begged Scott for those sneakers when they were school-clothes shopping. He'd even offered to do chores in exchange for money to help pay for them.

The thought of his son being watched by some lowlife thug made everything inside Scott turn to ice. His fists bunched, and his jaw ached.

"Listen, you sick fucker," he ground out. "You stay away from my kid, you hear me? You tell Fletcher to stay the fuck away from my kid."

The recess bell rang, and then sound of children grew louder.

"I don't *want* to go anywhere near your kid, Dixon. I just follow orders."

He needed to get to his kid. He needed to *get* his kid.

But he didn't want to leave Eva.

"Just passing along the message, Dixon." Then the line went dead.

The moment the line went dead, he called his brother to let him know what had just transpired, and Liam advised him to go and get Freddie from school.

Next, he called Eva and let her in on what happened. She was still with clients, but the fear in her voice shook him to his core.

"I'm going to get Freddie, and I need your sister to go and get the boys. Liam is setting up a safe house for Celeste, you and the kids to stay at until we get this all sorted." He knew his words were of little comfort, but at the moment, they were all he had.

"I want to come with you," she said, her voice choked.

"Not a good idea, babe. Liam's going to get surveillance on your house. Said it will be there within the hour. Once Celeste and the kids are in the safe house, I will come back to get you and take you to them. Until then, stay quiet, keep the blinds drawn and don't open the door for anyone."

Maybe Mrs. Ferguson and Mrs. Clark could stick around until he got back so that she wasn't alone.

"I'll be back as soon as I possibly can," Scott said, turning on the Bluetooth in his truck and pulling out of his driveway.

"I know you will," she whispered.

Shoving down his desire to run back into the house and scoop her up into his arms, he tossed the truck into gear and took off down the road. "Just hang tight, okay, babe?"

"Okay," she breathed.

Then he disconnected the call and headed toward Freddie's school, his gut twisted in such tight knots, he thought he might puke. Lead filled his feet as he gunned it when the light turned green. He just hoped to God that Todd Fletcher

had the sense and decency to stay the fuck away from Eva—
at least until Scott got back.

EVA LOCKED the door behind Mrs. Ferguson and Mrs. Clark—
two of the chattiest and loveliest ladies she'd ever met. But
boy, did they like to gossip. Eva had been finished Mrs.
Clark's pedicure for nearly forty minutes, but the woman was
still sitting in the spa chair gabbing away while Eva finished
up with Mrs. Ferguson's hair. Then the two women stuck
around for another fifteen minutes talking each other's—and
Eva's—ears off.

You would think the two women hadn't seen each other
in weeks if not months, but the truth was they were next-door
neighbors and saw each other multiple times a day. Eva
wasn't sure there was anybody in the world she would have
that much to talk about with—not even her sister.

But, finally, they said their goodbyes, promising to return
again soon, if not for hair and nails, then for tea.

Eva smiled through the turmoil inside her and said she
looked forward to it.

Once she locked the door, she plastered her back against
the cool wood and let out the tight, pained breath she'd been
holding for far too long.

She didn't have another client for a couple of hours,
which was a blessing, because she really needed to sit down
with a cup of tea and chill the hell out. Shutting off the lights
in the spa, she ascended the staircase inside to the upper
level of the house. Had she locked all the doors before she
started work?

A *clunk* outside had her freezing where she stood.
Holding her breath, she waited, counted to twenty in her
head and then took a few more steps up.

Was the surveillance team outside now? Would she know it if they were?

The creak of the door sounded more like an airhorn blowing as it crashed into the stunning silence of the house. From the top of the stairs, she could see out the big picture window in her living room, and there were no other cars in her driveway besides her minivan.

Exhaling, she went to double-check the lock on the front door—secure. Then she checked that the small nanny cams she'd installed a few weeks ago were still working. There would come a time when she would have to leave her kids upstairs—awake—while she went downstairs to work, so she installed a few tiny cameras throughout the house to keep an eye on things. It also helped when she worked evenings in case one of the kids woke up and started wandering the house. She'd been a sleepwalker as a kid, and Lucas was definitely showing signs of being an active, restless sleeper as well.

When her phone in the back pocket of her denim capris started to ring, she nearly jumped clear out of her skin. Her pulse kicked up, and she might have peed a little.

With a hand on the wall and her chest heaving, she checked to see who was calling.

It was Celeste.

"Hey! I got the boys, and we're on our way to some guy named Aaron's house. His wife and baby are with her sister. Apparently, this Aaron guy is a retired military type?" her sister said, sounding distracted. The murmur of Kellen and Lucas in the back of the car gave Eva the reassurance she so desperately needed.

"Hi, Mom!" Lucas called.

"Hi, Mommy!" Kellen said.

After Scott's call, Eva had called her sister and asked her to pick up the boys from school immediately. Even though

Todd was not permitted to pick them up from school, that didn't mean he wouldn't try. He'd tried before. She's also called the school and put them on high alert, just in case Todd did try something.

She wandered into the kitchen and began to make herself a cup of tea. "Hi, my loves. Is everything okay?"

"Yeah," they both called.

"So cool getting out of school early," Kellen said. "I want to do this every day."

Eva groaned. "Maybe not every day."

"What if you just called the police and made an anonymous report?" Celeste suggested. "Like how people do for Crime Stoppers, you know?"

"I don't know. Maybe it's because Liam's PI has a bunch of photo evidence that will help add validity to the testimony? I have no idea."

"What are you talking about?" Lucas asked.

Crap. Right. Little ears who heard everything.

"Sorry," Celeste muttered.

"It's fine," Eva breathed. "Liam has a plan. I don't want to muck that up."

Celeste sighed on the other end. "Fair enough. I'll text you when we get to this Aaron guy's house."

"Okay, thanks." She closed all the drapes in the living room, which made her feel claustrophobic. "I hate this feeling. I thought I was over this feeling."

"I know, sweetie. And you will be, for good. Now that we know he's not only a psychopathic narcissist but a crook, he'll get what's coming to him. Chin up, sis."

"Yeah, thanks." Eva pulled back the drapes just a touch and glanced out into her driveway and the street. Nothing nefarious seemed to be in play. In fact, it was a beautiful, warm spring afternoon. "I'm being paranoid," she murmured to herself, letting the curtain fall back into place.

She had forgotten about her plan to make tea and was headed back to the kitchen when the phone in her back pocket began to ding and warble again. She didn't recognize the number.

"Hello?" She held her breath.

"Eva? It's Liam."

A rush of air whooshed out of her mouth. "Oh, Liam, it's you."

"Were you expecting someone else?"

"No ... I ... I'm just on edge right now."

"I know. I know. It'll all be over soon. Scott went to go get Freddie, right?"

"Yeah."

"And your sister has your kids and is on the way to Aaron's?"

"Yes."

"Good. I've got a two-man surveillance team that should be there by now."

She knew she should be relieved now that she had trained bodyguards keeping an eye on her and the house, but there was only a little less ice in her veins. Todd was smart, and if he or any of his hired thugs wanted to get to her right now, they could.

"Okay, listen," Liam continued, "I decided to submit all the evidence we've accumulated against him to the police myself. There was no sense dragging you down there. If they wish to gather statements from you, then they will be in contact. Besides, Scott mentioned that Todd has friends at the precinct, and if you're there, they might tip him off quicker."

Her stomach was now in her throat. "When did you submit the evidence, Liam?"

"About an hour ago. I meant to call you earlier, but I got tied up with work calls."

An hour.

"Who did you hand the information off to?"

"The senior staff sergeant, why?"

Her heartbeat slowed down a few notches. "Okay, I don't think he's in Todd's back pocket."

But he could be. She and Todd hadn't been together for a while. Hadn't been amicable for even longer, which meant she had no clue who his friends were anymore. He could have the whole police department on his payroll by now.

"Guy seemed pretty hellbent on taking care of Fletcher himself, so hopefully he doesn't waste any time."

"Yeah, hopefully." But then she started to wonder. Even if the senior staff sergeant accepted the information, that didn't mean *he* personally was going to bring Todd in for questioning. Most likely he'd pass it off to a junior officer. "When you were there, Liam, was there a cop with short-cropped, almost black hair, big, *big* arms that looked like hams squeezing through sleeve holes, and a big scar running through one side of his top and bottom lip?" It was a shot in the dark that Kip Croy would be mulling around the precinct. He was probably off patrolling somewhere, but even so, she had to ask.

Liam hemmed and hawed for a moment. "Yeah, you know, come to think of it, there was. He was hanging out by the coffee maker when I went in to speak with the senior staff sergeant. Why? Is that the guy?"

Her stomach shrank, and a sinking feeling took over her body. "That's one of them. Been friends with Todd for years."

"Shit. You don't think he ... "

"I do."

"Fuck."

"Yeah. My guess is that Todd already knows, and Kip Croy is doing everything in his power to delay his friend being hauled in for questioning."

"Always important to have friends in the right places," came a voice behind her.

Eva gasped.

"Eva? Eva!" Liam called out. "What's wrong?"

She whispered into the phone, "It's Todd. He's here. Call the police, please." Then she hung up, put the phone back in her back pocket and scanned her living room for anything she might be able to use as a weapon.

21

DAMN IT, she knew she should have double-checked the lock on the sliding glass door. The boys were always coming and going through that thing, so she usually just kept it unlocked. Her gaze fell on a brass candlestick on her mantel, and she snatched it, stowing it behind her as she crept toward the dining room.

She hadn't been hearing things, had she? That was Todd's voice. She'd recognize it anywhere. The question was: Was it real, or was she going crazy and only imagining her ex-husband's voice?

Her mind immediately went to the nanny cam she had in the kitchen, and the other one in the living room. If she got out of this alive, at least they would have video evidence of him entering her home and violating his restraining order. If she didn't get out of this alive, they'd have her murder on tape.

If she got out of this alive ...

Her murder on tape ...

God, no woman should ever have to think like that.

Gathering every last bit of bravery she had inside her, she

entered the kitchen to find Todd in a sleek black suit, blue tie and white shirt, leaning against the counter. His arms were crossed in front of his chest, a look of not only impatience on his face but barely harnessed rage. "There's the fucking slut."

Clenching her molars so her chin didn't tremble, she kept herself tucked tight against the wall, making sure that she wasn't in any corner and had at least two exits.

"Y-you need to leave, Todd. You shouldn't ... you *can't* be here. I have a restraining order, remember?"

He rolled his eyes. "And I have a business to run, but you're doing a damn good job fucking that up, aren't you?"

She shook her head. "Scott and I met before we were neighbors. We didn't know he was your client. This is all a big coincidence."

"But you're fucking him."

"We're divorced, Todd. You're not my husband anymore. I am free to be friends with whomever I choose, to date whomever I choose." She needed to keep him talking. If Liam had called the cops, she needed to give them time to get there.

Todd pushed off the counter and took a couple of long strides toward her, the fury on his face letting her know he was even closer to losing it. Her back was already to the wall. She couldn't retreat any farther. Turning her body sideways, she slid away from him, the candlestick still behind her.

"Stay away from me, Todd. I filed a restraining order for a reason."

His mouth turned up into a sneer that made the hair on her arms lift up and her blood turn frosty in her veins. "I never laid a hand on you until you gave me reason to."

"You fucking raped me," she blurted out, her jaw wobbling with each word. The candlestick behind her scraped against the wall, and she tightened her grip on it.

Todd rolled his eyes. "A husband can't rape his wife."

"You're wrong." Her heart hammered in her chest. The sound of her pulse was like a drum in her ears, which made it tough to tune in to other sounds around her—like the slam of a cop car's door or voices of rescue outside.

Where were the police? Where was her surveillance team?

He took another step toward her, cutting off one of her exits, so she was now forced to sidestep into the kitchen nook, which left her cornered and without an exit.

She whipped the candleholder out from behind her back, brandishing it in front of her like a sword. "Don't come any closer, Todd." Every word was said with a quaver. Her grip on the candlestick began to slip as her palms grew sweatier and her knees threatened to buckle.

It was if the devil himself were staring back at her.

She didn't even see it coming, his hand. But when it landed across her face with a harsh *crack* and sent the candlestick flying one way and Eva flying the other, the first thought that entered her mind was *I'm going to die.*

"You fucking slut," he roared, attacking her where she kneeled on the kitchen floor, cupping her cheek. She was beneath him in seconds, his hands around her throat, his weight on top of her. "Trying to ruin my business, everything I've worked for. Kip called me. You had me followed! That fucking lawyer is trying to get me arrested."

Bright lights and black spots clouded her vision the more she struggled against him, the more he cut off her airway. Her legs thrashed beneath him. Her hands scrabbled and scratched at his arms as the desperation to live, to not let him win seeped into every cell of her body.

This was not how her story was supposed to end. Not this way. Not like this. Not after she'd finally found the courage to leave Todd, to make a better life for her and her sons.

His thumbs pressed down harder on her throat. He was going to crush her windpipe.

Her head tossed back and forth on the harsh, unforgiving kitchen floor, hair covering her face and eyes, getting stuck to her cheeks from the spit flying out of his mouth and dropping on her.

She'd seen Todd mad, seen him enraged, but this was a whole new level. The man was deranged. Unhinged. A true, honest to goodness psychopath.

And he was going to kill her.

"T—To—" she sputtered, her fingernails scraping down his exposed forearms. But her energy was depleting. She had no more oxygen, no more fight left in her aching limbs to continue to battle him.

He was going to kill her. He was going to win.

And then, just as fast as he'd attacked her, he was off her. His hands left her throat. His weight no longer crushed her torso. Todd was flying across the room, landing with a thud and a crash against her china hutch. A few plates fell from their stands inside.

Eva gasped for air as if she'd just come up from the bottom of the pool. Her lungs burned with each breath. Her fingers fell to her throat. It hurt to swallow.

"Eva!" Scott scooped her into his arms and cradled her boneless body in his lap, her head against his chest. "Oh God, I didn't think we'd get here in time."

She blinked back the tears and lifted her head to see not only Scott, but Liam standing behind him, along with what appeared to be half a dozen cops or more. Three were attending to a dazed and confused Todd, their handcuffs out and at the ready.

"Along with your call, there were four other 911 calls within the span of five minutes," she heard one cop say behind her. He was speaking to Liam. "All the calls came from within this neighborhood. Next door, across the street. We haven't seen a neighborhood watch program like this in a long time."

"Where the fuck was the surveillance team I hired?" Liam asked, anger in his tone.

"Got stuck behind the pileup on Glenn and Ridgemont," an unfamiliar, deep masculine voice rumbled. "Sorry, man. Traffic was at a standstill. We were sandwiched in."

Liam muttered something else, but his ire seemed to have faded.

Another unfamiliar voice fell next to Eva's ear. Still in Scott's arms and catching her breath as she attempted to make sense of it all, she lifted her head to find a friendly-looking male police officer crouching down beside her. "Are you okay, ma'am?"

"Should get her checked out by the paramedics," Scott said, anger lacing his tone. He cupped her chin gently, the fingers of his other hand trailing down her throat with a feather-light touch. His gaze softened until he pivoted his head around to stare at a now standing Todd, his hands behind his back, a police officer reading him his Miranda Rights. Scott's jaw tightened iron-hard. "Get that fucker out of here before I—"

"Get him out of here," the cop next to them said, jerking his chin at the other officers. He glanced at Scott. "Leave the law to us, Mr. Dixon."

Scott's lips pursed until he zeroed his baby browns back on Eva. "Do you need help up, babe?"

She shook her head, but he helped her to her feet anyway, never leaving her side or letting go of her. His touch was the reassuring boon of comfort she sorely needed at the moment.

"We're going to need to get statements from you, Ms. Marchand," the officer said. "You as well, Mr. Dixon. We understand Mr. Fletcher has been working with your company?"

"Let's go next door to my place," Scott said, his hand cupping Eva's elbow and leading her to the front door. "We can get her cleaned up and give statements over there."

The officer nodded. "Paramedics are on their way. They can determine whether Ms. Marchand needs to see a doctor or not."

Eva allowed him to lead her to the front door. She slid into the pink and purple polka-dot flip-flops she had on the shoe rack and, like a robot, followed Scott down the path; her driveway, loaded with cop cars; and around the hedge to his house. Neighbors all down the block were lined up along the sidewalks and milling around in their front yards. A few daring ones had ventured down the road and were in groups, murmuring and speculating closer to Eva's home.

Everyone stopped and stared when she and Scott stepped out onto the sidewalk.

"Eva, darling, are you all right?" Mr. Gallagher from next door asked. "Saw that man sneak onto your deck, called the police because he seemed suspicious. You okay?"

"We'll update you later, Mr. Gallagher," Scott called back. "Need to get Eva checked out first."

Mr. Gallagher nodded, then conferred with the three people he was standing with on the sidewalk.

"Hope you're okay, honey," Mrs. Sandham from across the street said, hunched over her walker, with her little shih tzu, Yudi, sniffing the grass next to her.

Eva merely glanced back and nodded before turning her head forward again and following Scott and the police officer toward Scott's house.

They were just climbing the steps to the front door when an ambulance pulled into Scott's driveway and two paramedics jumped out.

"Come on, babe," Scott murmured into her ear, his grip on her elbow tightening. "Let's head inside. Get you checked out."

Eva sighed, turned to head inside, but was distracted once more by the cop car pulling out of her driveway and heading down the road. Todd was in the back seat, and the glower on his face as he stared out the car window at her was murderous.

Would she ever truly be free of the man?

"He can't hurt you anymore," Scott said, his hands moving to her waist, the heat of his palms a salve to soothe her damaged soul. "We'll make sure of it. Come inside where it's safe. Where I am."

Her eyes squeezed closed and she nodded, following him inside.

"I'VE BEEN on the phone with the district attorney," Liam said, pacing back and forth in front of the hearth of Scott's living room. "He's going for the maximum sentence. After he violated the restraining order, the breaking and entering into Eva's house, the attempted murder—which we got on tape— he figures we've got a pretty good case. Not to mention all the illegal stuff going on with Fletcher's business dealings. The DA is going to continue to work with McGregor and see how deep everything in Fletcher Holdings really goes. Sweep the leg and then geld him as Richelle likes to say. They've also arrested Officer Croy for tipping Todd off."

Scott exhaled a sigh of relief as he sat back down on his couch next to Eva and handed her the cup of tea he'd brewed her. The cops were gone, as were the paramedics. Eva's injuries, although terrible looking, were superficial. Her throat was already mottled with dark purple bruises, and there was a cut on her cheek from where he'd slapped her. Otherwise, she was deemed fine—at least physically.

He worried about her psychologically though. Emotionally.

She had been awfully quiet since the cops left. Even when the cops were there, she answered their questions but barely spoke otherwise.

They'd called Celeste to apprise her of the situation, and although her sister was obviously shaken up, she agreed that it was probably best if she kept the boys away from Eva until their mother was in a better mental state.

"I'm going to run," Liam said, checking his watch. "Let me know if you need anything, okay, Eva?"

She nodded and thanked him, but her gaze remained fixed on the shaggy faux fur rug at the foot of Scott's hearth.

Scott saw his brother out, then immediately returned to her side. His knuckle came up beneath her chin, and he lifted her head up gently until her gaze pivoted to his. "God, babe, I'm so sorry I didn't get here sooner."

She didn't say anything, but her eyes blinked several times, moisture gathering and causing the lashes to spike.

The look on her face gutted him.

Pressing his forehead to hers, he spoke soft and slow, as one might speak when dealing with a spooked horse. "Talk to me."

Her lashes fluttered closed and she shook her head, dislodging his knuckle from her chin. "I don't think I'll ever be rid of him," she croaked, her natural rasp even stronger. "Not really. Not unless he's dead."

Pulling his forehead away, he took her hands in his. He needed the physical connection probably as much as she did. Seeing her there on the floor with Todd's hands wrapped around her throat had been a nightmare come to life. The way her legs twitched as he slowly, determinedly squeezed the life out of her. That image would haunt him for a long time.

"The trial will be hard, yes," he said. "But hopefully, between all of us and the DA, we can put him away for as long as humanly possible. Until the boys are adults and able to think for themselves. I promise you, Eva, I will do everything I can to not let Todd Fletcher hurt you or your kids ever again. You have my word."

Green eyes glassy with unshed tears lifted to his face. "I'm scared."

He took the mug of tea from her and pulled her into his lap, holding her tight against his body to absorb her fear, absorb her anger—because there was probably a lot of that in there too—but most of all, to let her know that no matter what, he wasn't going anywhere.

Her body shook as the sobs came on. Hot, wet tears trickled down her cheeks and fell down his V-neck. Her fingers bunched, white-knuckled, in the fabric of his shirt. He rubbed her back and murmured shushing noises, the same sounds he made when Freddie was upset after falling off the jungle gym or waking up from a bad dream.

Slowly, he wasn't sure how long it took, the tears ebbed and the sobbing stopped. But he continued to hold her. It was a while that they sat there with nothing but understanding quiet between them and the faint *tick-tock* of the clock on his mantel.

She lifted her head from his shoulder, her eyes red-rimmed and unbelievably tired. "I think I love you, Scott Dixon."

He smiled. "I *know* I love you, Eva Marchand."

Her breath escaped her on a stuttered sigh, and she snuggled back into his body, her own body more relaxed now. She intertwined her fingers with his. "Where's Freddie?"

"With your sister and the boys at Aaron's. Figured it was the safest place."

She nodded in understanding. "You think Todd will get convicted and go to prison for a long time?"

"We can hope," he said, squeezing her tighter against him.

"I'm going to hope. Wish on every shooting star I see and maybe even pray," she breathed. "Not that I really do that. But I'll start if it will help."

"I'll start too." He pecked her on the temple.

"But you know what else I'm going to hope and wish and pray for?"

"Hmm? What's that?"

"That I never let you get away. I plan to keep you, Scott Dixon. You're one of the good ones, and I'm not letting you go."

His eyes met hers, and what stared back at him was not so much fear or anger anymore but resolve and determination. Hope and faith, and most definitely love. His lips hovered just above hers. "Didn't I tell you already, babe? We're inevitable." Then he sealed his mouth over hers and took away the last of her pain, replacing it with nothing but hope for the future. Their future, at the moment, looked fucking brilliant.

EPILOGUE

One year later ...

"LAST OF THE BOXES?" Scott asked as he met Eva in his driveway and took the final big box from her.

She dusted her hands off on her green yoga pants. "That's the last box. The boys and I are officially moved in with you and Freddie."

He wandered over to his porch and set the box down on the steps, unable to keep the mile-wide grin from his face. When he spun around, she was right behind him.

"I'll go into the house tomorrow and do a clean, then the carpet cleaners are scheduled to come Tuesday, electrician Wednesday."

"And the new tenants move in Saturday?"

"That's the plan." She beamed up at him, lifting up onto her tiptoes and wrapping her arms around his neck. They were about to kiss when three wild, whooping and hollering little boys came careening around the corner from the back-yard. "You're sure you don't mind giving up your home office so that each of my boys can have their own room?" The kids had now found sticks and were pretending they were magic wands, casting freeze spells and animal spells on each other.

"I don't mind at all," he said. "Besides, now that I'm running Dynamic Creative, I have an office five times the size of my home office, and I'm going to try to stop bringing my work home with me."

She nuzzled her nose against his. "I like that idea."

"And, if the house is feeling extra busy, we can always sneak next door to your salon for a *walk down memory lane*." They'd decided to rent out Eva's house but keep the basement as her salon and spa. The rental demand in Seattle was crazy, so it just made sense to invest in real estate. The boys had also been over-the-moon excited when he and Eva decided to take the plunge and move in together. The next morning, he found Kellen and Lucas on his front porch with packed backpacks and their pillows.

"Where's memory lane?" Freddie asked, holding still because Kellen had cast a freeze spell on him.

"Anywhere you have wonderful memories," Scott informed him.

Freddie nodded, then burst free from his spell and ran after Kellen yelling, *"Icicle Superificus."*

"That reminds me," Scott said, releasing Eva's waist and reaching into his front pocket. "We have *one* more box."

She wrinkled her nose. "No, we don't. I checked."

He shook his head, then dropped to one knee.

Her hands covered her mouth at the same time she gasped.

How had she not felt the enormous box at the front of his pants? It'd been driving him nuts all damn day.

"What's your dad doing?" Lucas asked, pausing his frog spell.

"No idea," Freddie replied.

All three boys joined them where they stood in Scott's

driveway. Which was perfect, because he wanted to do this when the kids were around. They were blending their families, after all, and the kids should be a part of it—even the proposal.

"Eva Danielle Marchand," he started.

"Is Mom in trouble?" Kellen whispered to Lucas. "Why's he saying her full name? Mom only says our full names when we're in trouble."

"Shhh," Lucas scolded.

Eva hiccuped a laugh as she smiled through the now streaming tears.

"Eva," Scott started again. "You are the best neighbor I could have ever asked for. Undoubtably the love of my life, and I would love nothing more than to be your husband and give you the happy, incredible life you so greatly deserve. Will you marry me?"

"Ohhhh," Freddie said with a nod. "Dad's asking your mom to marry him."

Lucas's eyes went wide. "Does that mean we'll get to be brothers?"

Both Freddie and Kellen each gave a cheer of approval, then all three boys began to chant, "Brothers! Brothers! Brothers!"

Chuckling, Scott focused back on the stunning redhead in front of him. "Well, what do you say? Do the *ayes* have it?"

She nodded like a broke-neck chicken, tears now racing down her cheeks. "The ayes have it." She was smiles now. All beautiful, bright white smiles. "Yes, I'll marry you. I'll marry you until the cows come home, and then I'll stay married to you even after that."

"That was really corny," he teased.

"Yeah, but you loved it anyway."

"I absolutely did. Finally, I get to be Mr. Green Yoga Pants. It really is all I've ever wanted."

She snorted and shook her head, smiling. She helped him to his feet, and his lips immediately captured hers in a kiss that spoke of years and decades of happiness to come.

"Why were they talking about cows?" Freddie asked. "Are we getting cows?"

"The yard doesn't seem big enough for cows," Kellen said. "Are we moving to a farm with cows?"

"Can we get chickens and pigs, too, if we're moving to a farm?" Freddie asked.

"We'll have to make a brothers blood pact," Lucas said, changing the subject.

This, unfortunately, caused Eva and Scott to break the seal of their lips and round on their boys.

"There will be no *blood* pact," Eva said sternly.

"What's a blood pact?" Freddie asked.

Lucas spoke out the side of his mouth. "I'll explain later in our tree fort."

Freddie and Kellen nodded solemnly, but the way their eyes slid sideways to each other said they had over a dozen schemes up their collective sleeves, and none of them were wise.

"Let's go!" Lucas declared, leading the charge back around the house to where their new tree fort stood high in the backyard.

Kellen and Freddie took off after him, their legs moving faster than the Road Runner's when he was escaping Wile E. Coyote.

They were alone once again.

"Do you want a big wedding?" he asked, his hands drawn to her waist.

She shook her head. "Something small and intimate. With our boys, family, a few friends. Just those who *really* matter."

"Sounds perfect to me." He pressed his lips against hers.

"We can celebrate properly tonight if you like. Break in our new king-size bed."

She hummed against his lips. "I couldn't imagine a better way to celebrate. Except maybe ... " Letting one hand drop from around his neck, she dug into the fancy pocket on the side of her yoga pants. "Here." She pressed a piece of paper into his chest.

Reluctantly, he released her, opened up the folded paper and read it. His heart rate sped up as his eyes scanned the page. He withdrew his gaze from the paper. She was smiling that smile he'd never get tired of waking up to.

"I owed you," she said. "I found out Allison DeWitt will be in San Diego next month for a signing, so I bought us plane tickets, booked the hotel and have bought tickets to the signing. We are going to meet and greet and take fanboy— and girl—pictures with Allison DeWitt."

Scott grabbed her by the waist and lifted her into the air, spinning her around as he cheered and hollered his excitement.

"Engaged *and* Allison DeWitt!" He shook his head in disbelief as he set her down on the pavement. "You are incredible."

He kissed her hard on the lips, his hands cupping her face, the piece of paper still in his grasp. When they broke the kiss, they were both panting.

"I can't believe you did this," he said, still shaking his head.

"I did it the day we found out about Todd," she said. "Knowing that he can't ever hurt any of us ever again has been a huge weight off my shoulders. Off all of our shoulders, and I figured we needed to celebrate."

"He had it coming to him," Scott said, determined to keep the arrogance from his tone. That motherfucker deserved to die in prison, and he had. Shanked in his cell, then thrown in solitary to keep him safe from his assailant, where he developed sepsis and died shortly afterward in the prison infirmary.

A pretty anticlimactic way to go, really. But beggars can't be choosers, and the fact of the matter was, he was gone.

For good.

The boys never asked about him, never wanted to go see him in prison. They even asked Scott if they could call him Dad. And now that he and Eva were engaged and living together, it was only a matter of time until he asked if he could adopt them.

"I can't wait to start this new chapter with you," she said, fresh tears forming in her eyes. "The boys are getting a father they deserve, and I am getting the husband I never thought I'd ever be lucky enough to have."

"And I'm getting a wife who considers me and doesn't take me for granted, and two incredible sons."

"We're going to have it all."

"And there isn't anybody I'd rather have it all with than you." Then he scooped her up and carried her inside *their* home, where they made lunch for their sons and started their new life as a family of five.

FLIRTING WITH THE SINGLE DAD - SNEAK PEEK

SINGLE DADS OF SEATTLE BOOK 9

Chapter 1

Thump!

"What the fuck?"

Atlas Stark rubbed his forehead and then his hip as he opened his eyes and found himself laying on his daughter's bedroom floor.

He must have fallen asleep again in Aria's tiny twin bed reading her a bedtime story. He'd been doing that a lot lately. Usually woke up with a horrible crick in his neck, one of his hands asleep and more exhausted than when he nodded off.

He wasn't a young man anymore either. He needed the comfort of his own bed, and his therapeutic cool gel pillow. But Aria—like most nights—had complained when he tucked her in, so he gave in to her demands, crawled in next to her and read her the twelfth book of the night. He wasn't sure who fell asleep first.

Rubbing the sleep from his eyes, he stood up to his full height, his back cracking, and knees grinding as he hinged over to kiss his daughter on the cheek.

Fuck, he hoped he hadn't slept the entire night away in her room—wouldn't be the first time. If luck was finally on his side, it'd be like ten or eleven and he could still pass out in his own bed. That was if Cecily down the hall didn't freak the fuck out and require him to hold her while she chugged back a bottle for an hour.

Yawning, he reached for his phone off the dresser. Oh thank God, it was only ten thirty. He brought up his messages as he wandered out of Aria's room, making sure to leave it open just a crack, otherwise his three and a half-year-old would give him shit in the morning.

There were only a handful of messages—most of them work related—and they could wait until tomorrow. But there was one that had been sent two minutes ago from a number he didn't recognize.

He scratched the back of his neck, wandered into the kitchen and poured himself two fingers of bourbon, a nightly ritual. The bottle nearly slipped through his fingers as he read the slew of messages from this strange number.

Did you know that Carlyle was engaged? Well, you do now. And if you DID know that he was engaged, shame on you for sleeping with an attached man.

Please tell Carlyle when you see him that he can find his belongings on the front lawn of MY apartment, though he might want to get there soon as the weather report is calling for thunder showers.

I'm keeping the ring. That motherfucker took five years of my life.

The text messages began rather polite, almost rational, and slowly meandered into more and more profanity, Capslock and exclamation marks.

And another thing! WHO THE FUCK NAMES THEIR KID CARLYLE? You can have him! WHO GOES BY CARLYLE and not CARL?! Pretentious fuckers, that's who!

Carlyle isn't returning my calls or messages. I'm assuming he's with you, so please relay these messages to my low-life fucking EX-fiance.

I want my dog back! Who the hell steals a dog? Forest is MY DOG! I had him before Carlyle and I even got together. I want him back or I WILL get a lawyer and sue his fucking ass.

The apartment is in MY NAME! So if he tries to get in, I'll call the cops! The two of you can go FUCK YOURSELVES. Have a nice life!

At this point Atlas was wide awake now, sitting on his black leather couch and sipping his bourbon.

Did you text back a wrong number? Particularly one this enraged?

But the person on the other end deserved to know that their message was not received by the intended recipient, right?

Did he want to engage with this person? They sounded kind of psycho.

But whoever they were, they deserved their dog back, didn't they? A dog was a family member, who the fuck kidnapped a family member?

Pinching the bridge of his nose, he finished his bourbon then tapped out a quick message to the furious texter.

You have the wrong number. I'm a man.

He squeezed his eyes shut and allowed the silence of the evening to wrap around him. He himself was a quiet person, preferring to have the television down low, the same for the music in the car. He liked things quiet. Or at least he used to.

It had been over a year and half since his wife, his best friend, the other half of his beating heart had died creating not only a void in his heart, but deafening silence in his home. Now, he hated the quiet.

IF YOU'VE ENJOYED THIS BOOK

If you've enjoyed this book, please consider leaving a review.
It really does make a difference.
Thank you again.
Xoxo
Whitley Cox

ACKNOWLEDGMENTS

There are so many people to thank who help along the way. Publishing a book is definitely not a solo mission, that's for sure. First and foremost, my friend and editor Chris Kridler, you are a blessing, a gem and an all-around terrific person. Thank you for your honesty and hard work.

Thank you, to my critique groups gals, Danielle and Jillian. I love our meetups where we give honest feedback and just bitch about life. You two are my bitch-sisters and I wouldn't give you up for anything.

Andi Babcock for her beta-read, I always appreciate your attention to detail and comments.

Author Jeanne St. James, my alpha reader and sister from another mister, what would I do without you?

Megan J. Parker-Squiers from EmCat Designs, your covers are awesome. Thank you.

Ana Rita Clemente, one of the first "fans" I've ever met, and now an amazing friend. Thank you for loving my books and beta-reading this one. You are a wonderful human.

My street team, Whitley Cox's Curiously Kinky Reviewers, you are all awesome and I feel so blessed to have found such wonderful fans.

The ladies of Vancouver Island Romance Authors, your support and insight have been incredibly helpful, and I'm so honored to be a part of a group of such talented writers.

Author Cora Seton for your help, tweaks and suggestions for my blurbs, as always, they come back from you so sparkly. I also love our walks, talks and heart-to-hearts, they mean so much to me.

Authors Kathleen Lawless, Nancy Warren and Jane Wallace, I love our writing meetups. Wine, good food and friendship always make the words flow.

Author Ember Leigh, my newest author bestie, I love our bitchfests—they keep me sane.

My parents, in-laws and brother, thank you for your unwavering support.

The Small Human and the Tiny Human, you are the beats and beasts of my heart, the reason I breathe and the reason I drink. I love you both to infinity and beyond.

And lastly, of course, the husband. You are my forever. I love you.

ALSO BY WHITLEY COX

Love, Passion and Power: Part 1

The Dark and Damaged Hearts Series Book 1

Love, Passion and Power: Part 2

The Dark and Damaged Hearts Series Book 2

Sex, Heat and Hunger: Part 1

The Dark and Damaged Hearts Book 3

Sex, Heat and Hunger: Part 2

The Dark and Damaged Hearts Book 4

Hot and Filthy: The Honeymoon

The Dark and Damaged Hearts Book 4.5

True, Deep and Forever: Part 1

The Dark and Damaged Hearts Book 5

True, Deep and Forever: Part 2

The Dark and Damaged Hearts Book 6

Hard, Fast and Madly: Part 1

The Dark and Damaged Hearts Series Book 7

Hard, Fast and Madly: Part 2

The Dark and Damaged Hearts Series Book 8

New Years with the Single Dad

The Single Dads of Seattle, Book 6

Valentine's with the Single Dad

The Single Dads of Seattle, Book 7

Neighbours with the Single Dad

The Single Dads of Seattle, Book 8

Upcoming

Flirting with the Single Dad

The Single Dads of Seattle, Book 9

Falling for the Single Dad

The Single Dads of Seattle, Book 10

Lost Hart

The Harty Boys Book 2

ABOUT THE AUTHOR

A Canadian West Coast baby born and raised, Whitley is married to her high school sweetheart, and together they have two beautiful daughters and a fluffy dog. She spends her days making food that gets thrown on the floor, vacuuming Cheerios out from under the couch and making sure that the dog food doesn't end up in the air conditioner. But when nap time comes, and it's not quite wine o'clock, Whitley sits down, avoids the pile of laundry on the couch, and writes.

A lover of all things decadent; wine, cheese, chocolate and spicy erotic romance, Whitley brings the humorous side of sex, the ridiculous side of relationships and the suspense of everyday life into her stories. With mommy wars, body issues, threesomes, bondage and role playing, these books have everything we need to satisfy the curious kink in all of us.

YOU CAN ALSO FIND ME HERE

Website: WhitleyCox.com
Twitter: @WhitleyCoxBooks
Instagram: @CoxWhitley
Facebook Page: https://www.facebook.com/CoxWhitley/
Blog: https://whitleycox.blogspot.ca/
Multi-Author Blog: https://romancewritersbehavingbadly.blogspot.com
Exclusive Facebook Reader Group: https://www.facebook.com/groups/234716323653592/
Booksprout: https://booksprout.co/author/994/whitley-cox
Bookbub: https://www.bookbub.com/authors/whitley-cox

JOIN MY STREET TEAM

WHITLEY COX'S CURIOUSLY KINKY REVIEWERS
Hear about giveaways, games, ARC opportunities, new releases, teasers, author news, character and plot development and more!

Facebook Street Team
Join NOW!

DON'T FORGET TO SUBSCRIBE TO MY NEWSLETTER

Be the first to hear about pre-orders, new releases, giveaways, 99 cent deals, and freebies!

Click here to Subscribe
http://eepurl.com/ckh5yT